I0733505

Guarding Home Ice

CANADIAN PLAYED
BOOK FOUR

CYNTHIA GUNDERSON

Copyright © 2024 by Button Press

All rights reserved.

No part of this book may be reproduced in any form or by any electronic or mechanical means, including information storage and retrieval systems, without written permission from the author, except for the use of brief quotations in a book review.

With Gratitude

Editing and Critique
Jordan Truex

Cover Design
Mitxeren

Author Note

Without becoming too heavy, this book discusses the repercussions of living in a toxic relationship and experiencing grief and loss. I adore romance stories because love is the only way we eventually find our way through.

xo Cindy

Find extended author notes in special edition copies at www.CindyGunderson.com

For the mama bears.

CHAPTER

One

6:00 a.m.

The numbers on the clock didn't make sense. Ryan blinked and pushed himself up, trying to clear the fog from his brain.

6:00 a.m.

Shit. He was supposed to be up at five thirty. No workout for him.

Ryan swung his legs out of bed, and his feet hit the cold floor. He rubbed a hand over his face, then reached for the elastic on his nightstand and tied his hair into a messy bun. He'd grown it out for Amaya. She loved to braid it, and he loved the way her eyes lit up every time he let her. And he looked like a hostel crawler if he did nothing with it in the morning.

Scrambling to his feet, Ryan grabbed his toothbrush and slathered on some toothpaste. He brushed frantically, then rinsed and splashed water on his face. He pulled on a T-shirt and black pants that looked like work slacks but felt like loungewear from his drawer, then shoved his phone into his pocket. Why did schools have to torture everyone? It was the end of the year. Couldn't they recognize that parents were barely limping over the finish line and take a break from early morning rehearsals?

Ryan padded down the hall to Amaya's room. He cracked the door and peeked in. "Amaya, it's time to get up, babe."

She mumbled something and rolled over, clutching her favourite stuffy. "Five more minutes."

Ryan chuckled. "How about five more seconds? We have to be at the school early for your choir practice, remember?"

Amaya sat up, her eyes still half-closed. "I'll get to sing my solo."

"Yep." Ryan stepped into her room and pulled out a pair of leggings and a shirt from her dresser. "Here, put these on. I'll make you some breakfast."

Amaya nodded, then yawned and stretched. "Thanks, Dad."

Ryan headed to the kitchen and grabbed the bread from the pantry. He slotted two pieces into the toaster, then opened the fridge and pulled out some orange juice. As the bread toasted, he checked his phone. There were a couple texts on the Snowballs chat he'd have to read later and an agenda from his boss, Marc, for the meeting that morning.

Ryan slipped the phone back in his pocket. They needed to be on time. It was a twenty minute drive from the school to his office, and he couldn't be late. His job as an engineer was demanding on a good day, but ever since he'd started playing with the Snowballs, it had become a juggling act. He was grateful Marc had let him take so much time off for the playoffs, but it was coming back to bite him in the ass.

The toast popped up, and Ryan spread butter and strawberry jam on each slice. He set the plate on the table just as Amaya walked into the kitchen, her hair still a mess. "Here you go, sweetheart. Eat up."

Amaya sat down and took a bite of toast. "Are you coming to the concert?"

Ryan nodded. "Of course. Wouldn't miss it for the world."

Amaya grinned and took another bite. "Good. I want you to hear my solo."

She'd mentioned it approximately five thousand times, and

he still wasn't sick of hearing it. He loved that she had something she was passionate about. Something she was good at. "I can't wait."

Amaya finished her toast, and Ryan handed her a glass of juice. She took a long drink, then wiped her mouth with the back of her hand. "I'm ready."

Ryan grabbed his keys from the counter and Amaya's backpack from the hook by the door. He grabbed the brush he kept on the counter and ran it through her hair. "Let's do this."

They stepped out into the cool morning air, and Ryan locked the door behind them. He and Amaya walked down the front steps and climbed into the car.

"I hope my voice doesn't sound tired." Amaya cleared her throat as she buckled her seatbelt.

"It'll be fine. Your teacher will do warm ups, right?" He knew nothing about choir, but he swore he'd heard her mention that before.

"Yeah. But my solo goes to a high F and even with warm-ups it's hard. It's kind of in my break."

"Uh-huh." Zero clue what that meant. His mind already raced with the day's to-do list.

It was never ending. He would never complain about having Amaya full-time, but after two years, he still hadn't gotten into a good, organized schedule. He was constantly missing the little things. Grocery shopping. Playdate planning. Homework checking. Let alone the books they were supposed to be reading and games they should be playing. It was all him all the time, and unlike hockey, the rules were always shifting.

Ryan pulled out of the driveway, and they set off down the street. The morning light filtered through the windshield, and he reached for his sunglasses. He glanced at Amaya in the rearview mirror. She tapped her fingers on her knee while humming one of her songs. She was nervous.

"You excited for French toast sticks for lunch?" he asked.

Amaya's eyes lit up. "I forgot!"

Ryan grinned as he turned onto the main road. Brake lights glared ahead in a never ending string. "You've got to be kidding me," he muttered under his breath.

Amaya looked up. "Good thing we left on time."

Ryan forced a smile. "Good thing." He tightened his grip on the steering wheel. It was fine. They had a few extra minutes to spare, and it wasn't the end of the world if he didn't get to grab coffee before heading to the conference room.

He was already well-versed on the project they'd be discussing. An energy-efficient design for a new office building downtown. It was innovative, cutting-edge, and exactly the kind of thing that could put their firm on the map. But it was also a logistical nightmare. Hopefully they'd be able to knock out some revisions that morning.

His eyes flicked to the clock on the dashboard. 6:35. "Shit." He glanced at Amaya, who was still blissfully unaware in the back seat. "That's a bad word. Don't say that."

Amaya giggled. "People at school say that all the time. And the F-word."

"Mmm. Fantastic."

"Don't you say that?" Amaya looked up.

He pursed his lips. "Sometimes."

"At hockey?"

He nodded as he finally made it to the turning lane.

"But you said those words make you sound unintelligent."

"Yeah. I should find a different word."

"What does it mean, anyway?"

"The F-word?"

Amaya nodded. "Toby says it's about sex."

Ryan frowned. "Who the hell is Toby?"

"That's another swear."

"Sorry."

Amaya pulled a pen from her backpack and started doodling on her arm.

"Don't draw on yourself."

"Why?"

"Because the ink seeps into your skin."

Amaya kept sketching. "Like your tattoo?"

Ryan glanced in the rearview and drew a deep breath. "So who's Toby?"

"He's in my class. He always wins tetherball."

And talked about sex with his ten-year-old daughter, apparently. "We can talk about the F-word later, okay?"

"We still have to talk about lingerie. You forgot to tell me what that meant."

Ryan stifled a laugh. She pronounced it "linger—ee," and he didn't want to correct her. He also didn't want to talk to her about lingerie. "Yep. We'll add it to the list."

Ryan's jaw clenched as the cars in front of him continued to crawl. He tapped his fingers on the steering wheel. They were less than a kilometre from the school, but at this rate, it might as well have been a hundred.

Amaya put the cap on her pen just as they pulled into the school parking lot. At least there were no cars blocking the drop-off lane this early.

He checked the clock. 6:55. Amaya's choir practice was supposed to start at seven. He shifted into Park and turned to Amaya. "It looks pretty dead around here. You sure you're supposed to be here this early?"

Amaya nodded. "Eli said his mom was dropping him off at six forty-five."

"Good for Eli's mom," Ryan muttered. He parked along the curb. "Can you run in and make sure it's all good?"

"It's all good, Dad." Amaya grabbed her bag.

"Yeah, but I want to make sure. Just come back out and wave or something."

Amaya nodded, then got out of the car and started up the sidewalk. Moseying.

Ryan rolled down the window. "Love you, Amaya. Also, if you could move faster than a turtle—"

"I love turtles!" She spun around, her eyes wide. Then she stuck out her tongue and broke into a jog toward the school.

He couldn't be late for his meeting. Going to Denver to watch Jack in the NHL playoffs had burned most of his available vacation days and possibly a bridge with his new boss.

Amaya disappeared into the brick alcove covering the choir and drama entrance. He expected to wait a minute before seeing her again, but she popped back out almost instantly. Not just her, another girl, as well.

Amaya cupped her hands around her mouth. "It's locked!"

Ryan frowned. He was about to get out of the car when a teacher passed from the parking lot.

"Are you girls here for the rehearsal?" the woman asked. Amaya nodded. "Mr. Owen cancelled that last night." She turned to Ryan. "I'm so sorry, didn't you get the email?"

Ryan's stomach sank as he pulled out his phone and swiped to his inbox. Nothing from the school. Though . . . He checked his other folders, and sure enough. A message from Mr. Owen in "Updates" instead of his general inbox.

Ryan forced a smile and nodded to the teacher, then swore under his breath. What the hell was he supposed to do now? He needed to get to work, but school didn't start for another forty-five minutes. He wasn't going to make Amaya wait outside the school.

"Dad? Is it really cancelled?" Amaya was close enough not to shout.

Ryan nodded. "Looks like it." He turned to the girl standing behind Amaya on the sidewalk. She looked to be Amaya's age. Her blonde hair was pulled back in a neat ponytail, and her backpack hung off one shoulder.

Amaya moved out of the way. "This is Bailey. She's in choir with me." Bailey gave a small wave.

"Are you okay?" he asked.

Bailey nodded. "My mom must not have gotten the email

either." She looked down at her hands. Ryan wasn't sure, but it looked like she may have been crying.

"She left you here?" Ryan asked, his protective instincts flaring. What kind of mother would drop off their kid and dash? Not checking whether they got in safely?

Ryan looked at his watch. He was going to be late. There was no way around it. He ran a hand over his face.

"I don't live far. Ten blocks that way." Bailey pointed down the street.

Was that little girl speak for, "Can you please take me home?" He doubted any mother would be thrilled with their daughter getting in the car with a stranger, but which was worse? Him giving her a ride or her sitting alone outside the school for forty-five minutes? She already looked chilled.

Ryan sighed. "Alright, hop in, girls. Let's get you home. Amaya, grab your backpack."

Amaya rolled her eyes and grabbed her bag off the grass. "I didn't know you lived so close to the school."

Bailey nodded as she waited for Amaya to get in the car, then slid onto the seat next to her. "My parents wanted to be close. So I could ride my bike. But now my dad won't let me."

Ironic. Overprotective dad and a mom who couldn't wait two seconds to make sure her daughter wasn't locked out. He blew out a breath. He shouldn't judge, but his current late-to-work status was colouring his compassion meter.

Amaya and Bailey started talking over each other. ". . . so lame we have different classes this year."

"Yeah, I'm in 4A."

Amaya sighed. "4B."

"I know."

"At least we had second grade together."

Bailey's eyes lit up. "Remember when Ms. Ellen brought in those baby chicks? They were so cute!"

Amaya giggled. "And then one escaped, and you tried to catch it and fell into the bin of construction paper!"

Ryan pulled out of the hug-and-go lane. At least the traffic was better going this direction. There wasn't any point in doing the mental math. By the time he dropped off Amaya, he'd have ten minutes to get downtown. That wasn't going to happen.

Had he known the practice was cancelled, he could've asked Emma or Tyler to pull him a solid and take Amaya to school, but since it showed up in the effing updates folder—

"Dad!"

Ryan slammed on the brakes. "What?"

Amaya pointed. "Bailey said to turn there."

Ryan caught his breath, his heart racing. "Maybe don't yell my name like that in the car. Unless we're about to hit someone."

"Well you were about to miss the turn." Amaya leaned back in her seat, her arms crossed.

"It's that house." Bailey pointed to a modern bungalow. There were potted plants on the steps leading up to the porch.

Ryan thought about letting her walk up to the door, but given the situation, he figured some explanation was required. *No, I didn't kidnap your child from the school, but while we're on the topic of kidnapping, you did leave her there alone.*

He parked and got out, walking Bailey up to the door. He stayed to the side on the porch, not wanting to get too close.

Bailey knocked. They waited. There weren't any sounds inside the house. After a few seconds, she reached up and rang the doorbell. It had a camera, and Ryan tried to look . . . not like a pedophile. It was difficult with the scruff on his jaw and the man bun. At least he was wearing a collared shirt.

"Do you want to call her?" Ryan held out his phone.

Bailey leaned closer to the door and shook her head. "She's coming. I think she was just upstairs in the washroom or something."

Ryan slipped his phone back in his pocket as the door flung wide.

"Bailey, what the—" The woman's eyes snapped up, then widened as she saw Ryan standing there.

Ryan had planned on an explanation. He'd mentally prepared to tell Bailey's mother that he'd found her at the school, practice was cancelled, and he was being a good Samaritan. But the words fizzled on his tongue.

Bailey's mother was a tall, lean, athletic looking woman with chestnut hair that was pulled up in a twist at the back of her head. There were water droplets on her shoulders and thighs.

Which he could clearly see.

Because she was standing in her doorway wearing only a towel.

CHAPTER

Two

AELIN CLUTCHED her towel tighter around her chest, cognizant of the dripping water pooling on the wood floor. A tendril of hair had broken free from her claw clip and now stuck to her shoulder, and her skin still prickled from the hot shower.

"Sorry, I was—" Her words caught in her throat, her brain short-circuiting. Why was a man standing on her porch? With her ten-year-old daughter? She set her phone on the edge of the pillar next to her so she could grip the towel with two hands.

"I can see that." The stranger shuffled on his feet, then awkwardly put out a hand. "Ryan." Aelin didn't take it since her hands were currently the only thing keeping her from starring in a neighbourhood soft porn.

Ryan glanced down, then pulled his hand back. He leaned on the railing, but his elbow slipped, and he nearly smashed into the porch column.

Aelin jumped and barely kept her feet from slipping off the threshold. "I'm Aelin." She pursed her lips as he straightened and smoothed his shirt.

Ryan gave that look that everyone gave her when they first learned her name. The one that said *"Are you Eastern European or do your parents speak Elvish?"*

"It's the second one," she said. Ryan blinked. "My parents were obsessed with Lord of the Rings, so they gave me a name that sounded like I was an elvish princess."

"Oh." He frowned, then scrubbed his hand over the back of his neck. "Are you the nanny, or—"

"I'm the mother. Her mother. That's—" She pointed at Bailey standing in front of them like a child zombie. "Bailey is my daughter."

"Did you leave her at school this morning?"

Aelin frowned, bristling, and yet it didn't keep her stomach from flipping. His dark eyes stared right at her, and with his dirty-blond hair tied up and his obvious musculature, she somehow felt even more naked than she was. She cleared her throat. "I *dropped my daughter off* at school this morning if that's what you meant."

"Choir was cancelled." Bailey huffed and slid past her into the house, making her towel split, revealing her entire upper left thigh.

"Cancelled?" Aelin turned. "How do you know it was—?"

"The door was locked. She was sitting outside," Ryan recited, his tone cool.

"Dad!" A little girl who looked to be the same age as Bailey leaned out the back window of the car. "Your work is calling!"

Ryan pulled his phone from his pocket. "I have to go."

Aelin's cheeks flushed. "She walked through the alcove, and I was in a rush."

"Yeah. Well, maybe next time, wait two seconds to make sure she actually got in." Ryan nodded once and headed for the steps.

"I did wait," she snapped. Why was she trying to defend herself to this asshole? Who showed up on someone's porch first thing in the morning when there's been an obvious miscommunication and accuses them of being a terrible parent? "What a treat, to meet the world's most perfect dad. Had I known you'd be on my doorstep, I would've dressed up for the occasion!"

Ryan stopped and glanced over his shoulder. His eyes

dropped to her towel as if that was enough of a rebuttal, then continued toward the car. Before he passed the last lilac bush, a voice boomed from the speakers.

"—meeting starts in less than thirty minutes, and I don't have those numbers in my inbox."

Ryan started to jog. "Amaya, did you answer?"

"I didn't mean to! It was ringing, and I tried to hit the red button—"

"Who the hell is that?" the voice snapped.

Ryan yanked on the passenger door handle, then swore under his breath when it wouldn't open. He lunged to the back, throwing his head through his daughter's open window. "Marc, I'm here. Sorry, the phone picked up through my car's Bluetooth."

"You're not in your car? You were supposed to be here—"

"Yeah, I know. Had a bit of a snafu this morning."

Aelin smiled to herself. She didn't usually enjoy witnessing another person's pain, but in this instance, it filled her with warm fuzzies. *What, Ryan? Are you caught in an unexpected circumstance and can't control every second of your life because you have children?*

She remembered that he'd been the one to pick up her daughter standing alone in front of the school and bring her home, and a bit of the self-righteousness drained out of her. But just a bit.

"I need those numbers. Now," the voice barked from the window, and Ryan smacked the top of his car, exhaling an inventive string of curse words that would've made her football coach of a father blink.

"Your daughter is right there," Aelin snarked, then realized she'd been standing on the porch in a towel for the past five minutes with her daughter very much not at school and an appointment of her own that she was supposed to get to.

What the hell was she going to do now? She had to leave for the lawyer's office at seven forty-five, the same time the doors opened at the school. The choir practice, as annoying as it was to wake up early, was why she'd scheduled this meeting today instead of last week.

She turned to go back in the house when the little girl in the back of Ryan's car suddenly came bolting up the front steps.

"'Scuse me, can I show Bailey something?" She grinned up at Aelin, and before she could answer, pushed into the house to her dad growling *"Amaya!"* after her.

Ryan jogged up the path holding a laptop in his hands, the door to his car flung out into the street. "Sorry, can I—"

"Be my guest." Aelin moved to the right so he could follow his daughter through the door, but Ryan went left, and before she could correct, his chest slammed into her. Ryan grunted, gripping her barely dry arm with one hand and saving his laptop with the other. His palm was warm and rough, and he smelled like . . . man. Like sea minerals and citron vibes, which she only had a name for because she'd purchased body spray for her nephew in May.

"You pass on the left!" Aelin clutched her towel and steadied herself.

"What?"

"You always go to your right, and then I go to my right, which means you pass people on their left side."

"Umm, okay. Didn't realize there were rules." He dropped his hand and stepped into the entryway. "Amaya!"

His daughter's voice floated down from the second floor. "Just a second, I'm—"

"No just a second, I'm already late!" he barked.

"You know, kids really respond better to calm, understanding voices."

Ryan shot her a look. "I hear they also respond well to not being abandoned before seven in the morning."

Aelin laughed out loud. "You're one of those guys, aren't you? The ones whose wife always does drop off but because there was a change in schedule you decided to be nice and take the hit, wake up early, and the second you get to the school, you decide you have all these opinions on things. Like 'why does the drop off lane run counterclockwise, and why did you tell me to park here because this spot is strategically better for getting back on the road and avoiding traffic.'"

"His wife can't do drop off." Amaya came running down the stairs holding a tiny stuffed keychain penguin. "My mom's in the hospital."

Aelin's eyes widened. "Oh, shit. I'm—"

"My daughter's right there." Ryan shot her a look. "C'mon." He put an arm around Amaya's shoulder and led her back onto the porch.

"Dad, you're not going to make it to work in time for your meeting. It takes more than thirty minutes to get downtown," she chattered.

"I'm aware."

Aelin watched them walk to the car. Ryan set his laptop on the hood, lifted the screen, and pulled out his phone. He was trying to hot spot so he could send whatever his boss had been asking for.

"That's not going to work." Aelin stepped out onto the mat.

Ryan huffed a breath. "Thanks."

"No, I meant—" She drew a deep breath. "There's not a great signal in this neighbourhood. You can use my WiFi if you want. If it would be helpful."

Ryan glanced up, considering. Finally he nodded and picked up his computer.

Amaya poked her head out the window. "Are you going to be a minute? Can I go see Bailey?"

Ryan started to shake his head, but Aelin said, "Sure. If it's okay with your dad."

Amaya's eyes lit up. His jaw worked, but he nodded. She jumped out of the car and ran back into the house with a hurried, "Thank you."

Ryan ascended the steps, his brow drawn into a scowl.

Aelin shifted on her feet and motioned to the porch swing. "Sorry. I don't have another chair out here." Ryan sat, and the bench creaked. "Um, the network is . . ." She paused, kicking herself for not changing it already. "DarylIsADouchebag."

Ryan glanced up.

"It's a long story."

He clicked on the WiFi network, then turned the screen toward her. Aelin started to drop into a crouch to type in the password, then realized her entire ass was dropping out of the bottom of the towel. She shot back up. "I—can you stand?"

"You can just tell it to me."

"I'd rather not."

His lip twitched. "It can't possibly be better than the network name."

Aelin pursed her lips. If he stood, she'd still have to either hen peck out the password with one hand or hope her armpit could hold up her towel while she typed. She debated for a moment, then accepted her fate. "The password is 'BJs!nmyPJs72.'"

Ryan's eyes widened. "Wow."

"Hm. Yep." Her face felt like the surface of the sun.

"Another long story?"

"Pretty short, actually," she quipped, then clamped her mouth shut. She shuffled back toward the door. "No apostrophes. The "I" is an exclamation point. The J's and the B and the P are capitalized."

He nodded. "So the BJ—"

"And the PJ. Mmhmm. Seventy-two." Aelin escaped inside and closed the door behind her. Sweat dripped down the inside of her arm. *Could that have been any more embarrassing?* Maybe if she'd had a penis drawn in Sharpie across her cheek like she had when she originally came up with that password *when she was a junior in college.*

There was something very wrong with her, and now, because of her sick sense of humour and her abject refusal to bring new passwords into her rotation, the angry hot dad on her porch knew far too much about her nightmare brain. And was definitely judging her for it. At least her twenty-year-old self hadn't gone with sixty-nine. There was that.

She glanced up at the clock. *Seven-ten?* Aelin's hands started to shake. She'd been dreading this morning for at least three weeks, and the stress of this situation was only making her anxiety worse.

She took the stairs two at a time and heard the girls giggling in Bailey's room. "Bailey, you have fifteen minutes!"

It would be fine to drop her off a little early, wouldn't it? There were other kids there, she wouldn't be outside of the school for long, and it wasn't like it was the middle of December.

When she reached the landing, she sprinted down the hall to her bedroom, dropping the towel the second she got into the washroom and closed the door. She hopped back into the shower, did a quick rinse to wash away her stress sweat, then dried off and applied moisturizer and deodorant. She ran a brush through her hair, hung up her towel, then rushed into the bedroom and grabbed underwear from her dresser.

She'd already laid out the outfit she planned to wear that morning. Something nondescript and comfortable so she had one less thing to think about while her ex, Clark, was coming after her for *everything else.*

Aelin fumbled with the clasp of her bra, her fingers slipping on the hook and loop, then finally got it on and pulled her blouse over her head. Aelin grabbed her jeans and pulled them on, zipping them up just as she turned to the mirror. Her hair hung in messy, damp tendrils around her face.

She ran back into the washroom, snatched her hairdryer from the drawer and plugged it in, the roar of the motor filling the room. As she worked the dryer through her hair, her eyes ran over the message she'd written to herself in dry-erase marker on the glass. *Bailey is #1. Let everything else go.*

Aelin drew a deep breath and switched the dryer to her other side. It killed her to think about walking into that office and allowing Clark to get away with only claiming a hundred grand in income the prior year. It felt like a succubus was draining her life force each time she imagined him driving home in his freaking Audi to his custom ranch in a brand-new gated community and then sitting there at mediation pretending he shouldn't have to increase his child support payments.

She felt the familiar spiral begin to take hold. She needed to find a job for the summer. A good one. That meant she wouldn't be around for Bailey, and since Bailey wasn't old enough to be home on her own, she was going to have to find childcare, which meant her job needed to be *even better*, and she was a terrible mother for missing the entire summer with her daughter, and—

Aelin shuddered. *Nope.* She wasn't going to think about that. She'd been working with her therapist on not catastrophizing, and she was getting better at it. But it was proving more difficult when her worst-case scenarios were staring her in the face.

Aelin turned off the hairdryer and swiped smoothing cream through her locks, tamping down the post-shower fluff.

She grabbed her makeup bag and pulled out her concealer, dabbing it under her eyes and over the spot next to her nose that always seemed redder than the rest of her face. She swept bronzer over her cheekbones, then reached for her mascara.

When she finished applying, she smoothed tinted lip balm over her lips and grabbed a hair clip just in case. Sometimes the feeling of her hair on her neck annoyed her. Especially when Clark was around. He hated when she wore her hair up.

Aelin took a deep breath, then exhaled slowly. Breathe in for four counts. Hold for four counts. Breathe out for four counts . . . It was supposed to ground her. Right then, it was only pissing her off.

Aelin rushed into the hall. "Bailey!"

"We're downstairs! I'm giving Amaya some Fruity Pebbles!"

Fantastic. Sugar cereal for breakfast. Yet another thing man-bun Ryan could judge her for. She glanced out the window when she reached the main floor and saw the back of Ryan's head. He was still on the porch swing. Still staring at the screen of his laptop.

Okay, looked like she was playing babysitter. She swept into the kitchen and found the girls sitting at the counter with their bowls of cereal. "Sorry to make you rush, babes, but we have to go now. I'm going to have to drop you off a little early. That's okay, right?" She cringed, realizing she wanted a ten-year-old to validate her life choices.

The girls whispered to each other, then Amaya slurped another mouthful of cereal and hopped off the stool.

"Bailey—"

"It's fine, mom. Just a sec. She's going to ask her dad something."

"Bailes, I don't have time for extras this morning." Aelin grabbed a protein shake from the fridge. The breakfast of champions slash soon-to-be-divorced moms who hoped to someday focus on getting back into shape but were still in the trenches of their emotional trauma.

"He said yes!" Amaya ran back into the kitchen, her eyes lit up like Christmas trees.

Bailey spun on her stool. "Amaya and I want to walk to school."

Aelin started to open her mouth, then froze as Ryan entered her field of view.

He cleared his throat. "Sorry. She left the door open."

Aelin turned back to Bailey. "I love this idea, but Bailes, you know your dad won't—"

"He's not even here anymore! Why does he get to say when I only go to his house after school?"

Aelin's cheeks flushed. Perfect. More of their dirty laundry just flung around for Ryan to inspect. She grabbed her keys from the bowl on the counter. "I can explain all of that later, but if we don't leave now—"

"He said I couldn't *bike* to school. He never said I couldn't walk. Plus I'll have a friend with me." She threw her arm around Amaya who was drinking from her bowl, and pink cereal milk sloshed onto the counter. "Then you wouldn't have to drop me off early, and you'd still be on time to the lawyer's office."

"Wow, Bailey. We're really just throwing it all out there," Aelin snapped, snatching the dishcloth from the sink and wiping up the mess.

"I can take them." Ryan leaned against the wall, and when Aelin looked up, she felt a little like a bird who'd just run head-first into a sparkling glass window. There was a man in her kitchen. A man with grey eyes and an impressive jawline wearing a collared shirt and pants that looked like they had to be Lululemon athletic fit.

"Dad, you have a meeting," Amaya whined.

"They sent me a Zoom link. I can turn it on in the car."

Aelin exhaled, grabbing her purse from the counter on the other side of the fridge. "No service, remember?"

Ryan opened his mouth, then closed it.

Aelin put her hands on her hips. "You're okay with them walking together?"

He shrugged. "It's what, a ten-minute walk?"

"Something like that." Aelin ignored the girls squeezing their arms around each other and crossing their fingers.

"I could take the meeting here. Amaya has a watch. If something happens, I'll be just a few seconds away," he said.

Amaya held up her wrist, showing off her device. Aelin had thought about getting one of those for Bailey for Christmas, but it required an extra data plan.

Aelin nodded. "Fine. But stick together and look both ways across the street."

She couldn't even hear herself over the sound of their elated cheers. They cleared their bowls and ran to the front entryway to slip on their shoes and grab their backpacks.

Aelin followed, then stopped when she noticed Ryan hadn't moved.

"You left this. On the porch." He held up her phone, and Aelin exhaled. She hadn't realized she didn't have it.

"Thank you." She took it from him and glanced at the screen. Three new messages. Her heart punched through her chest at the preview glaring at her from Clark Moses.

This would all be a lot simpler if you weren't so difficult and exhausting to love

Aelin blinked, her eyes suddenly swimming. She needed to say something, to act normal, but her throat felt like it was clamped with a chip clip.

"I'll be right here on the porch." Ryan's voice floated down the hall. Thank heavens he wasn't still standing in front of her. Aelin grabbed a tissue and pressed it to the corner of her eyes.

A second later, Bailey rounded the corner and threw her arms around Aelin's waist. "Love you, mom."

"Love you." Her words were more of a breath than a whisper as she clutched her daughter to her chest. "Have a great day at school."

Bailey ran back to the front door, and Aelin didn't say a word about her running through the house with her shoes on. She strode directly to the back door and opened the garage.

She did not pass GO.

She did not collect two hundred dollars.

CHAPTER
Three

THIS WOULD ALL BE *a lot simpler if you weren't so difficult and exhausting to love.*

Ryan chewed on the text message he'd seen pop up on Aelin's phone. He hadn't meant to look, but it was hard not to with a message like that.

With Bailey mentioning going to her dad's house and Aelin on her way to the lawyer's, it didn't take a genius to figure out Aelin had to be going through a divorce. Still. What an asshole.

Aelin had disappeared through the garage before he had a chance to ask her about locking up. He left the door open for the time being, just so he could use the washroom if he needed. He wasn't going to go tromping through a stranger's house, though he had to admit, this stranger had piqued his curiosity.

The WiFi password alone. And the towel.

He felt like an idiot for spouting off about her parenting and asking if she was the damn nanny. Clearly, the universe had decided he was worthy of falling into one of his teenage fantasies, and it had taken him all of five seconds to screw it up.

Ryan sat back down on the porch swing and clicked the Zoom link. His screen populated with a message telling him to wait for the host to start the meeting. Tom Beech. He worked out of the head office in Vancouver. This parking garage was a massive project, made more difficult with the ribbons of clay that ran through Calgary soil. Not a surprise that he wanted to be updated.

He leaned back and checked the time on his watch. Five more minutes. He picked up his phone and swiped to his messages. There were seventeen notifications from his brother, his mother-in-law, and Tyler's girlfriend's sister who he'd been invited to double date with the week before. He ignored them and started with the team chat, scrolling to the last message he sent.

> I need to get back to the rink on start times. Thoughts?

BRETT:

> I'm not dragging my ass out of bed at five in the morning to make it to the rink at six.

SEAN:

> School's out in a week and a half, dumbass. We don't need to start that early

Ryan laughed. He typed out a message.

> Just let me know what you want for the
> younger group. 8-12yo will be from 3:30-6

TYLER:

> That works. Starting July 2?

> That's the plan. We're already full that first week

He set his phone down. They'd been trying to start up a hockey camp for kids for the past two years, but getting ice time between peewee practices, figure skating, and general skates was like trying to get a parking spot at Lake Louise.

Now things were finally lining up. Brett and Sean were taking the younger group since their work was more flexible. He and Tyler were taking the older kids. All the other guys on the team were filling in where they could.

He'd already arranged with work to come in early for the three weeks they were offering the camp. Then the last week of July he'd booked off to spend with Amaya. It had been over a year since they'd last gone on a trip that wasn't visiting family.

Ryan's laptop dinged, and two faces popped into view on the screen. At least he wasn't the only one.

He adjusted his laptop and pressed mute as Tom welcomed them. The rest of his team was in-person, and the camera showed them sitting around the conference table. His boss Marc who'd been asking the entire neighborhood for numbers through his bluetooth earlier gave a nod to the camera. Chris immediately sent him a private chat.

On location?

Ryan sent him a middle finger emoji, then tried not to grin and give himself away as a smile crept onto Chris's face on camera. They'd both worked for Apex for the past two years, and he played hockey. It hadn't taken more than that for them to become buds. And start giving each other shit during meetings.

Tom started, "We need to make sure the load distribution is balanced. We can't afford any more delays, especially with the subcontractors ready to roll."

Ryan nodded along. Load distribution. Structural integrity. Cost overruns. He unmuted his mic. "I'll be running a few more simulations to see if there's a way to optimize the beam placement."

Marc nodded. Ryan had sent him the cost analysis and initial load calculations. It was already on his list to dial in.

Ryan muted himself again as the others chimed in with their updates. He noted the tasks for his team and tried to knock off a few graphs Chris needed for a different project.

His phone buzzed on the bench, and his heart jumped, thinking it may have been Amaya. Ryan glanced down. It was a message from Brett outside of their group chat, and he realized school had started over fifteen minutes ago. He didn't make a habit of checking messages during meetings, but his curiosity got the better of him.

BRETT:

Have you gotten a final invoice from
Carpenter's?

Ryan frowned. *Had he gotten an invoice?* He opened up his inbox on his laptop, only to realize the call had gone quiet. Marc stared into the camera expectantly. *Shit.*

"Sorry, it stalled out there for a second. Could you repeat the question?"

Marc nodded. "I was asking if you thought the revised calculations would change our timeline."

Ryan nodded. "I don't think so, but I'll let you know if anything comes up. I should have them done by the end of the day."

The conversation moved on to material costs and supply chain issues. When the meeting ended, Ryan felt oddly . . . not annoyed. Sitting outside in the shade and listening to birds chirp probably had something to do with it.

He hadn't found an invoice from Carpenter's Ice Centre, which wasn't overly concerning. He did have written confirmation that they were booked, and the camps weren't starting for another couple of weeks. He could give them a call and make sure the bill hadn't gotten lost in the ether of the internet.

He closed his laptop and opened the message from his mother-in-law.

It's a good day today. Could you bring Amaya
by for a visit?

Ryan read the message three times, his thumbs hovering over the keyboard. He should say yes. It had been two weeks since they'd gone over after school. But he knew what that would mean for Amaya, and he wasn't sure if he was ready to deal with the fallout. He slipped the phone back in his pocket.

It felt wrong walking back into Aelin's house, but she had technically given him permission to be there. Ryan set his laptop on the bench in the entryway, took off his shoes, and found his way to the washroom. He relieved himself and washed his hands, then padded across the hardwood floor to the kitchen and slowly opened the cupboard next to the sink. The doors were a sleek, polished wood with a hint of rustic charm, fitting perfectly with the rest of the house's clean lines and natural materials.

He paid attention to things like that.

He tried not to snoop, but liked that her dishes were neatly arranged. Nothing fancy, just simple white bowls and plates. He pulled out a glass and filled it at the fridge dispenser. He took a long drink and noticed a pad of sticky notes on the counter on his left.

He could leave a note. Thank her for the water and the WiFi. Ryan set his glass in the sink, then found a pen in a jar next to the paper. He took off the lid and paused, his heart suddenly picking up speed.

It was a thank-you note, it didn't need to be impressive. But then he remembered what he'd said to her on the porch, and a flush crept up his neck. He'd been an ass. She'd been a bit of a brat, too, but he'd definitely started it.

His mouth went dry as he wondered whether that scene could've gone differently had he not been stuck in his head about the meeting.

A pang of guilt hit his stomach.

He was still married. He shouldn't be having thoughts like that, and yet they seemed to be entering his head with increased frequency.

Ryan ignored the pressure in his chest and started to write.

Thanks for the WiFi. I hear RyansADouchebag is a contender for the current network settings.

R

. . .

Ryan walked to the front door, slipped on his shoes, retrieved his laptop, then opened the door. He paused with his hand on the handle. Aelin had been flustered when she'd left. He assumed she wouldn't want to leave her house unsecured, but he had no way to contact her and find out which lock she preferred. Since he didn't know the garage code, he flicked the lock on the handle and exited to the porch.

He drove to work and missed morning traffic, had a working lunch with his favourite Cobb salad from Sam's in the basement of his building, and finished up in time to pick up Amaya from her after school program at five. Considering how the day started, he'd ended with a significant upgrade.

Ryan waited in the pick up line as Amaya finished chatting with her friends and ran to the car. She jumped into the passenger seat, her face flushed.

"Playing soccer again?"

Amaya nodded, buckling her seat belt. "I scored on Kenny twice."

Ryan made his best "mew" face that Amaya had made him practice for hours over spring break and put all his energy into the word, "Slay!"

Amaya scoffed. "Please don't ever say that again, Dad."

She tried to hide it, but she was grinning. He pulled to the edge of the parking lot already thinking ahead to what options he had for dinner. There was leftover pizza from Saturday night, but Amaya thought the sauce was too spicy. He needed to sit down and make a menu for the week. "Anything else happen today?"

Amaya shrugged. "I got a hundred percent on my math quiz."

"Fantastic. Those practice problems must've helped."

She nodded, then put her hands on the dash as her eyes lit up. "Ooh! Guess what? Bailey's mom got locked out of their house! Can you believe that? We were just there!"

CHAPTER

Four

"OKAY, YOUR TURN." Aelin shifted on the grass, staring at her cards laid out on the paving stone. If they had to be locked out, today wasn't the worst day for it to happen. They didn't have any plans that night, and being outside forced Bailey to hang out with her instead of instantly jumping on her tablet and talking with her friends after school.

They had food and drink, courtesy of Wendy's, and she wasn't staring at Clark Moses's smug grin. That was a win.

Bailey bit her lip as she deliberated over her next move. She reached out a tentative hand, her fingers hovering before seizing a card, then groaning when she saw the picture. "It has a bent corner! I thought it was the Queen of Hearts!"

Aelin laughed. "I saw you scoping that out."

"Did you bend the corner on the Cookie Queen?" Bailey looked scandalized.

"It was too obvious otherwise."

"Mom!"

Aelin played a four, a two, and a six, then picked up three new cards. Her phone buzzed, and she glanced at the screen, hoping it was an update on the spare key.

When she saw Megan Moses's face on the screen, she asked Bailey to pause and answered.

"Hey! Any luck?"

Megan paused. "Yep. Key's on the way." Her voice was a little too chipper.

"Megan—"

"Ugh, Aelin, I tried. I told him I was going to pop by after work, and he did that thing he does where he makes you feel like an idiot. He was like, "That makes no sense. We're all adults here, and I'm already home, plus I need to pick up my camping mats—"

"He does NOT need to pick up his camping mats. I told him he's not getting those until he brings back my mother's table runner." Aelin's jaw ticked.

Megan sighed. "Yeah. Well. He's on his way."

Aelin turned to face the side yard and squeezed her eyes shut. What was wrong with him? Why couldn't he just leave her alone? Why did he insist on digging in his claws at every damn opportunity? And why didn't she leave a spare key under the mat like a normal person?

"Mooom, it's your turn."

Aelin sniffed. "Yeah, I know, baby."

"I'm sorry, A." Megan groaned.

She nodded. "No, it's not your fault. Thank you."

"Drinks next weekend?"

"Yeah. I'll be there."

Megan exhaled. "'Kay. Stay strong. Call me after if you need to vent."

"Thanks, Megs."

Aelin dropped the phone from her ear. So much for not seeing Clark's smug face.

She turned just in time to see a grey sedan turning onto the block. *Speak of the devil.*

"Hey, Bail's, good news. Your dad—" Aelin froze. That wasn't Clark's car.

Bailey turned to the street and jumped up from the grass, grinning from ear to ear when she saw Amaya in the passenger seat window. "Did you call them, Mom?"

"No, I didn't call them. I don't have her dad's number." She didn't know why that felt important to explain, but it did. Possibly because Ryan's face—*okay, and body*—had popped into her head multiple times during mediation.

It had just been such a shock. Seeing him there in her kitchen. Her house had been man-free, besides the guy checking their internet connection, for the past fourteen months.

That was why the image of him leaning against the wall had branded itself in her brain and her stomach did a little flip when he stepped out of the car. It was a good thing. A gift, really. Since Clark had moved out, she wondered if she'd ever find another man attractive again.

With Clark, the option had been to wear her emotions on her sleeve and get burned or shove them all down deep. No expectations meant no disappointment. Burying was better than hurting.

But after all this time, it was kind of comforting to know she was still capable of feeling . . . something.

Ryan closed the door and rounded the hood. He wore the same clothes he had on that morning, but they looked different in the afternoon. The top button of his shirt was undone, and he'd rolled up his sleeves. Not to mention that his bun was decidedly messier.

Bailey abandoned the card game and ran with Amaya into the backyard.

Aelin shoved her hands in the back pockets of her jeans. "Let me have it. How did I fail as a parent this time?"

Ryan stopped partway up the paving stone path and glanced down at the card game. "Amaya told me you were locked out."

Aelin drew a breath. "It wasn't your fault. If that's why you're here."

He glanced up at the front door. "It wasn't because I locked the door handle when I left this morning?"

"Well, yeah, but I didn't give you any instructions. It was a little chaotic." She rocked on her feet. "I don't blame you. I took the wrong set of keys and the garage pad thingy is busted."

Ryan frowned and turned to scan the side of the house. "What's wrong with it?"

She shrugged, following him as he walked over to inspect it. "I don't know. It hasn't worked for the last six months, which hasn't been an issue because the opener in my car works." Ryan glanced at her car in the driveway. "Bailey took it out of my car yesterday because she went to a friend's house three doors down and didn't want to knock when she came home. It's sitting inside on the counter."

Ryan gave a soft "Hmm" then lifted the cover on the pad. He pressed the buttons and when they didn't light up, dropped the cover. "Does the other electrical work out here?" He pointed to the two covered outlets on the porch.

"Not sure. I didn't put Christmas lights up last season, so they haven't been used in over a year."

He nodded once. "Do you have a bobby pin?"

Aelin blinked. "If you're going to shove a piece of metal in the outlets, I can think of easier ways to pay penance."

"I thought it wasn't my fault?"

She shot him a look. "Why do you need a bobby pin?"

"To unlock your door."

Aelin blinked. "Ryan, I appreciate you coming back, but you really don't owe me anything. Our spare key should be here any second, and . . ." She trailed off, remembering *who* was bringing said spare key. Clark was going to be pulling up in front of her house and witness her talking with another man. An attractive, athletic man who possibly knew how to break into houses.

"You know what? I'm intrigued." Aelin turned back to her purse still sitting in the grass. "How many bobby pins do you need?"

"Just one."

She dug in the zipper compartment, moving aside the lip balm, Neosporin, Band Aids, and the Bluetooth headphones for her phone. "Got it." She dug a bobby pin out of the crease at the bottom of the pocket and straightened, then crossed the yard and handed it to him.

Ryan took it and started to straighten it out.

"This isn't going to ruin the lock?"

He shook his head and climbed the porch steps, then dropped to one knee in front of the door. He moved closer to the handle, slipping the pin into the key slot.

Aelin leaned against the porch railing, glancing back at the street. If Clark could show up right about now . . .

She turned back, noticing how Ryan's shirt stretched against his shoulders as he manipulated the pin in the lock. "Should I be concerned that you know how to do this?"

"Depends."

"You know where I live. You could break in whenever you wanted to."

Ryan pulled the pin out a few millimetres and reinserted it. "I guess I could." There was a soft click, and he slipped the pin free, then lowered the handle and the door swung open.

"Seriously. Where did you learn to do that?"

Ryan turned and handed the splayed out bobby pin back to her. His thumb brushed hers, and she shivered. "My parents used to lock the door at midnight. If I got home late, I had the option of staying with a friend, sleeping in the garage, or—" He pointed at the lock.

"What was the ratio?"

"What?" He frowned.

"Like, a third staying with friends, a third sleeping in the garage, and a third breaking and entering?"

Ryan's lip twitched. "Two-thirds with friends. One-third breaking and entering."

"No garage sleeping."

"Correct." Ryan didn't drop his eyes, and Aelin's cheeks started to heat. She was fumbling for something to say when she heard a car coming up the street.

She turned, and her heart jumped into her throat. Holy hell. This was happening. Clark was going to get out of his perfectly detailed car to find her standing on the porch with another man. Aelin felt like she was standing on a bridge about to bungee jump.

"Okay, listen. I'm a bit of a dick for not telling you to leave right away." She flashed an apologetic smile, then walked to the stairs.

Clark got out of the car. He looked at Aelin crossing the lawn, then flicked his eyes to the porch. "Megs said you needed the spare key."

"Mm. Yeah, I called her earlier. I thought she'd probably get off work before Ryan did." She nodded casually over her shoulder. "That was nice of you to bring it over."

Clark's jaw tensed, and Aelin forced herself to keep a straight face. Man on the porch. Door already open. She wanted to point a finger in his face and announce, *"See? You're useless to me."*

Earlier that morning, Clark had sat across the table from her and calmly described how her refusal to budge on his parent time was causing him emotional trauma. After he'd missed two of his last daddy-daughter dates—circumstances outside his control—and cancelled the trip he'd planned with Amaya for spring break. Like an asshole.

"Hey, you must be Clark?" Ryan stepped up next to her, and her pulse fluttered at her throat. What was he doing, and how did he know her ex's name?

Clark's eyes locked onto Ryan like a pit bull hearing a dog whistle. He flashed a smile and rounded the hood. "And you must be . . . the handyman?"

Ryan chuckled, but Aelin could've sworn his stance widened. He put out a hand. "Not exactly."

Clark shook it, his expression cagey. "Is Bailey here?" He dropped Ryan's hand and turned his attention to Aelin.

"She's with a friend." Aelin crossed her arms over her chest and took a step back on the grass.

Clark nodded. "Hmm. You know, Aelin, I wondered if I could get those camping mats. I think I left them in your garage."

Aelin's nostrils flared. He'd flipped her off last week when she'd told him he couldn't have them, and now he was pretending like this was the first she'd heard of it? "I have them ready for you, actually. As soon as you're able to bring by my mom's table runner, I'd be happy to exchange."

He chuckled, his smile never faltering. "Do you see this, Ryan? A guy can ask nicely." He shook his head. "I haven't had any luck finding it, but I'll look again."

"Sounds great." Aelin's nails bit into the skin on the backs of her arms.

Clark glanced at the open gate to the backyard. "Let Bailey know I stopped by."

"Sure, and can I have my key please?" Aelin swallowed hard. The last person in the world she wanted to have the key to her house was Clark Moses.

He cocked his head. "Your key? Last I checked, the title for this house was still in both our names."

Aelin pursed her lips. They'd agreed in their last mediation that the house would stay with her and Bailey, and they'd divided all their other assets. The only thing they had left to figure out was custody and child support. "Clark—"

"Have a good night, A. Ryan." He waved and stalked back to the car, getting into the driver's seat and peeling away from the curb without a second glance.

Aelin deflated like a balloon.

"Are you okay?" Ryan's voice was low.

"How did you know his name?" She rubbed her hands over her arms to stop them from shaking.

Ryan's jaw worked. "I saw a message on your phone. When you left it on the porch."

"Ah." She turned and walked toward the backyard, her ribs tightening around her lungs, wringing her out. She knew exactly the message he was talking about. *This would all be a lot simpler if you weren't so difficult and exhausting to love.* "Thanks for opening the door, Ryan. I'll get Amaya."

She worked to draw a full breath as her shoes crunched over the gravel in the side yard. He was gone. It didn't matter if he had a spare key, he wasn't allowed to enter the premises without her permission per their mediation. If he did, she'd have grounds for a restraining order, and Clark was far too proud to be a partner at Nelson and Sons to risk getting arrested.

He wouldn't do it. She was safe here.

"Hey girls!" she called out. Amaya and Bailey were up in the tree house. "Amaya, your dad is waiting for you out front. Bailey, time to get dinner ready."

"Is the house open?" Bailey popped her head out the open window.

Aelin smiled. "Yep. You can pee in a real toilet!"

Bailey rolled her eyes. "Gross, mom. I don't even have to go that bad."

Aelin waited for the girls to climb down the ladder, then walked with them back to the front. Ryan leaned against his car looking at his phone. Amaya gave Bailey a hug, then jogged across the grass. Ryan looked up.

"Can we get food before we go see Mom?" Amaya asked, and Aelin's stomach twisted. Ryan had come here to pick her lock when he was supposed to be visiting his wife in the hospital?

Ryan nodded. "Sure." He opened the door for her, then closed it and turned back to Aelin. Before he could say anything, Amaya was pushing her door open again.

"Can Bailey play on Saturday?" She poked her head out, kneeling on the seat.

Bailey ran up next to Aelin, pulling on her arm. "Please?"

"Since when are you two best friends?" Aelin asked. She could count the number of times Bailey asked for a playdate on one hand since the holidays.

Bailey gave her a look that said, *Do not embarrass me, Mom.*

"Sorry, okay. Umm, your dad is picking you up at noon for his date, so I don't know if that works great."

"I don't sleep in on Saturdays. We always make pancakes, but we don't have to make those so I could come early." Amaya said.

Aelin was about to say that Bailey never woke up before ten when her daughter blurted, "Me, too. Mom, can Amaya come over at nine?" Her pupils dilated until she resembled an anime cat.

Aelin looked up at Ryan. "I—I don't even know what to do with this."

Ryan shoved his phone back into his pocket. "I can bring Amaya over Saturday at nine. I can pick her up at eleven thirty. Or right at noon if that's helpful." He raised an eyebrow, and Aelin's mouth suddenly felt like it had been swabbed with gauze.

She straightened. "Eleven thirty would be great."

Ryan nodded. "Okay, then. Saturday."

Bailey jumped up and down, pulling on Aelin's arm and dragging her into the house.

"We have to clean up the cards." Aelin laughed, pulling her hand free and crouching to pick up their game. Bailey helped, and by the time they walked inside, Ryan's car was gone from the street. "This only happens Saturday if you do your chores."

"I know!" Bailey ran up the stairs, her hair flying behind her.

"I'm talking washroom, bedroom, everything."

"I *know*, Mom!"

Aelin shook her head and retrieved Bailey's backpack from the porch. She set it on the bench in the entryway, then tidied their shoes and walked into the kitchen. It wasn't until she pulled out the shredded chicken and cilantro from the fridge that she noticed the sticky note on the counter.

CHAPTER
Five

RYAN SAT on the couch with his mother-in-law, Laura, the fabric soft against his palms. The facility his wife, Kara, lived in now was a clash of worlds—one side of the building sterile and clinical, her personal space a shrine to a life that felt increasingly distant.

They'd tried to soften the edges with family photos and Kara's favourite books, but the hospital smell seemed to be rubbed into the carpet. At least there were a couple of Amaya's drawings taped to the side of the dresser, and a comforter and throw pillows that had come straight from their bedroom.

The sound of a nurse's footsteps echoed down the hall, and he gripped the armrest. He shouldn't hate coming here. He should be glad to see his wife, to see Kara interacting with Amaya. But ever since his mother-in-law Laura texted, his stomach had been churning.

He was a husband. A father. This should be him caring for her, not a rotation of strangers in scrubs. Kara needed professional care, round-the-clock attention, and they'd all agreed it wasn't possible for him to provide that. Not with work. Not with Amaya.

All of that was true, and yet every time he saw her here, it felt like abandonment.

Kara and Amaya sat at a small table, a checkers board between them. Kara's brow furrowed as she concentrated on the game, her fingers hovering over a piece. Amaya grinned and made her move, hopping one of Kara's pieces to the side of the board.

Kara's eyes flicked over the board, and Ryan tensed. He knew the signs by heart. How her face would go blank. How she'd blink too many times. He moved to the edge of his seat.

Kara's movements became more agitated, her fingers twitching as she tried to figure out her next move. "That's not fair," she muttered.

Amaya looked up, her eyes flicking to Ryan's. "What's not fair?"

Ryan felt like a belt was being cinched around his ribs. "Hey, why don't we—"

"You skipped over my checker. You can't do that." Kara's hand hovered over one of her pieces.

Amaya frowned. "I didn't skip it, I jumped it. That's how you play the game."

Ryan stood, and Laura moved to put her hands on Kara's shoulders.

"No, it's not!" Kara pushed her mother's hands away as her voice went up an octave. "You're cheating!"

Ryan pulled Amaya to his side. "It's okay, babe," he whispered. "Just an episode."

Amaya nodded. "Did I do something wrong?"

Ryan shook his head as Laura moved to stand between them. "Kara, sweetheart, it's just a game. Take a deep breath."

Laura was there with Kara more often than he could be. She was a retired teacher, and she'd done all the training to be able to de-escalate situations like these. Ryan had learned just by watching her, but Kara always seemed to respond better to her mother than to him.

Kara's hands balled into fists. "It's not fair, Mom. She can't cheat and then act like she didn't."

Laura reached out and put a hand on Kara's back. "I know, love. It's frustrating, isn't it?"

Validate. Don't try to correct.

"But remember what we talked about? Breathing in and out when we're feeling overwhelmed." Laura rubbed slow circles over Kara's back.

Just watching it made his throat constrict. After Kara got out of the hospital, he'd tried having her live at home. Thought he could handle it. It had been an unmitigated disaster.

It only took two hours of her being back for them to experience an episode. The doctors had encouraged him to keep it simple, so he'd picked up pizza, and they were sitting on the couch, watching a movie.

Kara asked for a blanket, and Ryan got her one, but she wanted a specific throw he hadn't seen in months. He looked in the chest, then went down to the basement, but when he came back empty-handed, that was it. The spark that lit the powder keg.

"Where the hell is it?" Kara's voice had been a whip crack, slicing through the air.

"I don't know, babe. Maybe it's in the laundry?"

"It should be right here!" She stood, her eyes wild as she started tearing apart the cushions. "We always keep it here, Ryan!"

He'd tried to calm her just like Laura was doing then, consoling her. Reminding her to use her skills. But she was already in motion, knocking over a vase on the end table.

She swore at him in front of Amaya, then bolted past him to the front door.

• • •

"Kara, it's freezing outside. You can't go without a coat."

She turned on him, her breath coming in ragged gasps. "Don't tell me what I can and can't do!"

He had to drive behind her on the street until the police arrived. Amaya had cried herself to sleep when he'd arrived back home.

That was just one night.

There had been countless others. Nights where she couldn't find her book, or where the remote wasn't where it was supposed to be. Little things that would set her off, and he never knew when it was coming.

It wasn't safe. Not for her, and definitely not for Amaya. He couldn't risk her waking up to one of Kara's outbursts. He couldn't risk her being in the line of fire when Kara threw something or tried to storm out of the house.

Ryan rubbed his hands over his face, the memory of that night playing on repeat. That was why he'd brought her here. Why he'd made the hardest decision of his life.

"There we go." Laura kept rubbing Kara's back, her voice a gentle murmur. "It's just a game, Kara. Just a game."

Kara closed her eyes, her shoulders relaxing minutely. "I don't like it when people cheat."

"I know, love." Laura's voice was barely a whisper.

Kara's breathing started to steady. She opened her eyes and looked at the board, her expression a mix of frustration and resignation. "I just wanted to win for once."

Laura leaned in and kissed her on the temple. "I know, sweetheart. Next time, okay?"

———

They stopped by the restaurant on the way out to the parking lot. Amaya loved the chocolate cake there, and the kitchen staff always seemed to have a piece on hand when they visited, even when it was off hours. Ryan was positive Laura had something to do with that.

Laura brought a fork and gave Amaya a big hug before sitting down next to them. "So, how's that hockey camp of yours going?"

Ryan turned, trying to muster a smile as Amaya dug into the cake. "It's good. Really good, actually. We've got a solid group of kids coming in this summer."

Laura clasped her hands on the table. "That's wonderful. You must be thrilled to share your love for the sport with the next generation."

"I get to go," Amaya said with her mouthful.

Laura's jaw dropped. "No way! You're dad's letting you get on the ice?"

"About damn time." Ryan grinned, and Amaya beamed at him.

He chuckled, scrubbing a hand over his jaw. "Tell her about the poetry contest."

Amaya didn't need much prompting. She dove into the story of her submitting a poem to the teacher and it getting lost and not being entered, so they had to do the judging all over again.

"I came in second place. In the whole school." Amaya licked frosting off her fork.

Laura clapped her hands. "Well, of course, you did. You know English was my favourite subject to teach, right?"

Amaya nodded and took one last bite before pushing her plate away from her. Ryan raised an eyebrow, then stole her fork and finished the last strip of barely any cake with mostly frosting. Not the worst.

When he finished, Amaya took the plate and fork to the trash and walked to the water dispenser.

Laura shifted, her eyes flicking to his. "And what are you doing for yourself these days?"

Ryan shrugged. "Prepping for the camp keeps me pretty busy."

Laura shook her head. "You know that's not what I'm asking."

Ryan opened his mouth to respond, but the words caught in his throat. His days were a blur of work, taking care of Amaya, running the house, and trying to be there for Kara as much as he could. "I'm still playing hockey." He'd thought about quitting the Snowballs, but sometimes getting out on the ice was the one thing keeping him going. Summers were the hardest with no games and only one practice a week.

"You remember we're taking Amaya next Saturday night?"

Ryan nodded. He loved that they wanted time with her even if he suspected they specifically planned sleepovers for Saturdays so they could take her to church in the morning.

Laura's eyes softened, and she reached out a hand. "Ryan, it's been two years. I know you're dedicated to Amaya and Kara, but . . ." She hesitated, choosing her words carefully. "You're still a young man. You can't be expected to live your whole life—"

"I'm not looking for anyone else, Laura."

Laura sighed. "I know, and I'm not suggesting that you should. But, Ryan, we love you. When you married Kara, you became like a son to us. I would never—" Her voice caught, her throat working. "You're allowed to want more for yourself. You're allowed to have a life, too."

Ryan's jaw clenched. He stared out the window, watching an ambulance pull into the parking lot below. "In sickness and health. I'm not going to abandon her."

Laura pulled out a manila folder from her purse. "I expected as much, and I love you so much for loving her." She set it on the table between them, her eyes glassy. "I prepared everything. You've lived apart for over a year. The lawyer says it should only take two to four months to be approved—"

"Laura—"

"Don't decide right now." She caught his hand, placing it on the envelope. "I want you to seriously consider this, Ryan." She glanced up at Amaya walking their way with a cup of water. "Kara is only one out of three."

CHAPTER

Six

SATURDAY MORNING RYAN sat at the kitchen table in his sweats and T-shirt, his hair still wet from the shower. He stared at the paperwork in front of him. Even though they were entering the last week and a half of school, Amaya's school counsellor had recommended an assessment for ADHD and dyslexia.

He'd already entered in her personal history, and now the cursor hovered over the first box of the questionnaire. Provokes others: frequently, somewhat often, sometimes, never or not at all. How was he supposed to know the difference between "sometimes" and "somewhat often?" *Fails to follow instructions. Excessive use of video games or TV.* He probably should've chosen a day to fill it out when he hadn't heard her making music videos in her room until one a.m. the night before.

"Dad! Are you ready?" Amaya bounded into the kitchen, her ponytail bouncing. She was already dressed in a pair of bright pink shorts and a tank top, her sandals set by the front door.

If he wasn't with her twenty-four seven, he could've been convinced that his ten-year-old daughter was doing cocaine. "It's barely seven, babe. Bailey's not even awake yet."

Amaya put a hand on her hip. "You don't know that. I texted her last night and told her I'd be over first thing."

Ryan raised an eyebrow. "We agreed on nine."

Amaya shrugged. "Bailey said I should just come when I woke up."

Ryan grinned "Well, if Bailey said it, then . . ."

"Dad." Amaya rolled her eyes.

Ryan pushed back from the table, setting the forms by his computer. "You're awake. But you still have to eat breakfast and brush your teeth."

"I'm not even hungry."

"Uh-huh." He poked her ribs as she walked past. "And what if I told you we still had time to make pancakes?"

———

Ryan led Amaya through the sliding doors of Canadian Tire, the oddly comforting scent of rubber hitting them like a wave. The store was a maze of aisles, each one lined with tools, equipment, and gadgets. He pulled out his phone and checked his list, then headed straight for the hardware section.

Amaya trailed behind him, her eyes wide as she took in the shelves of shiny objects. "You said we were going to Bailey's."

"We are." Ryan searched the signs for the aisle he was looking for.

"Then why are we at the store?"

Ryan didn't have a great answer for that. Nor could he explain why he'd spent an hour searching up common issues with garage code pads the night before while listening to Amaya cry out the lyrics to *Down, Bad*.

He opted to ignore the question and stalked toward the back of the store. When they got to the electrical section, Amaya loitered at the end of the aisle. "Dad, look at this!" She pointed to a display of LED flashlights. "Can we get one? For camping?"

"Like, as a gift for a family that camps?" Ryan reached for a keypad, then a spool of wiring, and dropped them into their basket.

"Dad." She shot him a look. It was so much more fun being a parent when she was old enough to understand how witty he was.

Ryan chuckled. "Put it on your birthday list."

"Camping? Or the flashlight?"

His grin widened. "Damn, girl. Don't do me like that."

Amaya's eyes sparkled as she walked up next to him. "What's that for?" She pointed to the spool of wire in his hands.

Ryan straightened. "Uh . . . for fixing the garage keypad at Bailey's house. Remember? I told you it was broken."

Amaya nodded. "Why can't they just get a new one?"

Ryan smiled. "Because sometimes it's more cost-effective to fix things than to buy new ones. Plus, it's satisfying to solve the problem yourself."

Amaya pursed her lips. "But they aren't solving the problem themselves. You're solving it."

Okay. So it was possible he'd ruined her.

They left the store and drove toward Brentwood. Ryan pulled up to the curb in front of Aelin's house and did everything he could to explain away the flutter of excitement in his chest.

It was nerves. He shouldn't have bought the supplies without asking first. Amaya didn't make friends easily, and he didn't want this playdate to end in a flaming pile of dog crap.

It definitely wasn't that he was still thinking about Aelin standing on the front porch in a towel or replaying the way her cheeks had stained pink as she recited the WiFi password.

Amaya was already halfway to the door by the time Ryan retrieved his supplies from the back seat. He hurried up the path and was climbing the porch steps when Aelin opened the door.

Her hair was swept back into a clip, and she wore soft cotton pants that were cropped at the ankles with an oversized sweater. She looked like she'd just uncurled herself from the couch where she still had a good book and a cup of coffee waiting for her. *Relaxed. Well-rested.* It was possibly hotter than the towel.

"Thanks for bringing her over." Aelin frowned and peered into the bag. "You brought me . . . electrical wire?" She grinned at her joke, then glanced past him and saw his tool kit sitting on the edge of the porch. "Ummm . . ."

"I thought I could take a look at the garage pad. If you don't already have someone coming to fix it."

Aelin blinked, and she shifted her weight. "You're more than absolved of your unintended crime. If that's what—"

"No, I don't mind." He glanced down at the bag, suddenly feeling like an idiot.

She worried her teeth over her lower lip. "You don't have anything better to do on a Saturday morning?"

Definitely an idiot. "I'll just . . ." He pointed to the car and turned to go, but Aelin rushed onto the porch.

Her hand brushed his before she snapped it back to her side. "I don't have anyone coming to look at it." She curled her toes on the deck boards. "I just—that's really nice of you to offer. I'm not used to people doing nice things without . . . you know."

A slow heat crept up his neck. "I'm not—I wasn't trying to—"

"No, I know." She put up a hand. "This is a me problem. It turns out, when you're married to a selfish prick for twelve years, you tend to wear narcissist-coloured glasses."

Ryan nodded, not sure what to say to that. Aelin continued in a rush. "You aren't one. I don't think. I'm pretty good at spotting the signs."

"Good to know."

Her cheeks flushed, and she pulled the sleeves of her sweater into her palms. "So. Do you need me to open the garage?"

Ryan drew a breath and turned to the side of the house. "Not yet. I'll take a look." He took the bag and set it down on the steps next to his toolbox, then flipped the latches to open the lid.

Aelin hovered for a moment. "Do you need anything? Water? Coffee?"

Ryan looked up. "I'm good, thanks. This shouldn't take too long."

"Right. I'll . . . be inside if you need anything." Aelin walked back into the house.

Ryan glanced back over his shoulder just in time to catch her through the side window. She leaned up against the inside of the door and planted her palm to her forehead.

He snorted and dropped his eyes back to the toolbox. At least he wasn't the only one.

———

At ten forty-five, Ryan snapped the casing open and turned while Aelin punched in her garage code. He wasn't sure if it would work or if she'd have to reset it, but as soon as she hit enter, the pulley ground to life.

Her eyes lit up. "It works! What was wrong with it?"

Ryan picked up one of the sections of wire he'd replaced. "The wires were corroded. Did you have gutter issues on this side of the house?"

Aelin considered the question, then stepped back to look at the roof. "You know what, we did. There was a leak in the garage on this side. Hail damage. But that all got replaced last year."

Ryan threw the wire back in the bag with the rest of his trash. He'd already checked the other outlets, and they all seemed to be working fine.

"I can take that." Aelin reached for the bag, and he let her take it. She passed him on the porch, and he caught the scent of her coconut shampoo.

Aelin pulled the door open. "The girls made lemonade, and I promised I'd bring you in to try some."

Ryan wiped the sweat from his forehead with the back of his arm. "Sure, that sounds great." He followed her inside, set his shoes on the mat, and walked to the kitchen.

"Dad!" Amaya looked up from the table, her hands kneading something that looked like jello. "Bailey had all the stuff to make cloud slime. Her mom is making us grilled cheese for lunch."

Aelin took the pitcher of lemonade from the fridge. "I do make a mean grilled cheese."

"They're the best. She uses cheddar, not that gross cheese," Bailey said, launching the girls into chatter about their favourite lunch foods.

Aelin poured him a glass and handed it to him.

"Thanks."

Aelin smiled as she retreated to the business side of the kitchen. "Thank *you*." The counter extended past the cabinets to make a desk, and she had a computer sitting there with an organizer and office supplies.

Ryan immediately noticed the note he'd left her. It was stuck to the counter next to the notepads. *She hadn't thrown it away.*

Ryan's thumb slipped on the glass as he took a drink.

"Is it good?" Amaya watched him for a reaction.

He nodded as the sweet and sour liquid flooded over his tongue. "Excellent." It was too sweet for his taste. He preferred his lemonade to be puckering, but he wasn't going to tell Amaya that.

"Mom, can you get us the activator?" Bailey asked.

Aelin looked over her shoulder, her hands pausing on the keyboard. "I thought it was on the table."

"It is, but my hands are sticky."

Ryan strode to the table. "I can get it."

Bailey pointed at a clear squeeze bottle, and he passed it to her.

"Sorry, I'm almost done." Aelin's fingers tapped over the keys.

Bailey poured liquid over her and Amaya's individual balls of slime. "She's applying for jobs."

"Oh, yeah?" Ryan took another drink of lemonade. "What kind of jobs?"

Aelin straightened and turned toward the table. "I'm looking at night jobs. With summer coming, I figured I could find something that allowed me to stay home."

"See?" Amaya slapped her hand down on the ball of goo. "You could do that, Dad. Then I wouldn't have to be with a stupid nanny."

"Amaya." Ryan gave her a warning look that said, *Just because you're trying to impress your friend doesn't mean you can be a sass.*

She shot one back that said, *I'm only telling the truth,* and his lip twitched.

"You have a nanny lined up for summer?" Aelin asked.

Ryan nodded. "Not a nanny. Childcare. We've been using her for the past couple of years."

Aelin catalogued this. "Do they have openings?"

"Not sure." He motioned for her to pass him a notepad and pen, then wrote the name down for her.

Bailey set down her slime and went to the kitchen sink to wash her hands. Aelin watched her as she slid the notepad to the edge of the counter.

"I'm looking for jobs, Bailes."

Bailey nodded. "I know."

Aelin pursed her lips, then set the pen back in the jar on her desk. "Okay, how about some grilled cheese?"

Ryan suddenly felt like he was intruding. He set his glass in the sink, then glanced at the clock on the stove. 11:05. "I'll go get things back in the car."

Aelin nodded. "I'll make you a sandwich."

"You don't have to—"

She shooed him out of the kitchen and opened the fridge door. He walked back down the hall to the entryway. He liked the open floor plan of the house. Light poured in through the windows in the sitting room, filling the space up to the second floor.

He took his toolbox to the car, then got in the driver's seat and pulled out his phone. He hadn't missed much, just a couple of messages on the team chat.

ANDRÉ:

Dusty Rose tonight!

COUNTRY:

Jenna and I are out. She's not feeling great.

BRETT:

So Jenna's pregnant?

COUNTRY:

Still practicing

Sᴇᴀɴ:

> Kelty says I have to go

Ryan laughed, then typed out a text.

> I have Amaya this weekend. Next Saturday?

He didn't want to go out, but when Laura and Russ had Amaya, he didn't have a choice. The one time he admitted he'd stayed home and cleaned, Laura had clipped him in the ear. Going out with his team was the least terrible option.

Ryan looked up as Amaya ran out onto the porch, waving his grilled cheese sandwich like a surrender flag.

He set his phone on the console and got out. "Have fun?"

Amaya nodded. Aelin stepped out the front door and cupped her hand around her mouth. "Thank you!"

He waved, got in the car, and took the grilled cheese from Amaya. It was steaming hot, wrapped in a paper towel.

"Dad, can we go to that new trampoline place tomorrow?" She contorted in the seat to press in her seatbelt.

"The one over by Grandma's church?"

Amaya nodded.

"Yeah. I didn't realize you were into that." He pulled up to the stop sign, then turned left and drove past the school.

"I want to go at eleven o'clock."

He glanced over at her, but she was staring straight out the front windshield. "Any reason for that?"

"Eleven is the perfect time. I can sleep in and then have plenty of time to get ready."

He nodded. "Alright then. Eleven it is."

CHAPTER
Seven

SATURDAY NIGHT, Aelin sat at the kitchen table, staring at the empty fields of the childcare application for the place Ryan had recommended on her computer screen. She ran a finger along the rim of her coffee mug.

Just do it.

She'd received two interview requests after submitting a slough of applications, but neither of them was for a night shift. It was like bait fishing in the middle of the afternoon. She was getting no bites.

Her gaze flicked to the photo on the fridge. Bailey, beaming in her bright red swimsuit at the lake last summer. She was so small, her hair soaking wet, her eyes filled with the kind of unabashed joy that only kids seemed to know how to access. She clicked back through the four open tabs with job listings, scrolling for any new options that had posted during the night.

The idea of telling Bailey that they were not going to be having an adventure summer like last year made her want to jab a hot poker into her eye. But she didn't see another option. Getting a night job would suck balls, but at least she could sleep for a few hours, go out and do something fun, and then nap in the afternoon. Movie time or play dates. She could make it work.

It was moments like these she desperately missed being in California. Her parents and sister were there . She could easily ask Mariah to adopt Bailey during work hours and it would be the best of both worlds. She could have normal hours, and Bailey would be surrounded by cousins and plenty of sand and sun. She'd brought up the idea of spending time there, but Clark had shut it down with zero consideration. He didn't even give a shit about his time with her, but he sure as hell wouldn't give up a daddy-daughter night on paper so his daughter could have a good summer break.

I hope you can find a good work situation. That might not look great in court.

Aelin wanted to light his house on fire. Which also wouldn't look great in court.

Laughter echoed from upstairs, and Aelin straightened. It wasn't often that Bailey was in a good mood after coming home from Clark's. He always talked a big game, but when it came down to it, he often chose to sit at his computer and work while Bailey played with some new game or device he'd purchased to make up for it.

Aelin pushed her chair back and walked upstairs, pausing in the doorway of Bailey's room. She was on her bed, her head propped up on her hands as she stared at her tablet. Amaya's face filled the screen, the camera so close, Aelin could only see two eyes and two nostrils.

"You guys exchanged numbers?" Aelin picked up the dirty socks on the floor and threw them in Bailey's laundry bin. Her heart did a little happy dance that Bailey was giggling with a friend in her bedroom. She'd spent hours on the phone with her friends growing up, and it felt like a lost art.

Aelin walked over and sat on the edge of the bed, and Bailey looked up, barely able to speak through her giddy laughter.

"Mom, look at this meme Amaya just sent me." She turned the screen, and Aelin squinted to make out the words.

How do you find a cat? Look behind the couch.

She raised an eyebrow. "That's it?"

Bailey giggled. "No, Mom, you have to see the picture." She clicked the meme, and it expanded, showing a picture of a cat and the caption. *Look, it's the same cat!*

Aelin had never felt more like a thirty-eight-year-old than in that moment. She smiled, even though she zero percent understood what the hell it was saying or why the girls thought it was funny. A perfect metaphor for her parenting at the moment.

"It's almost time for bed." Aelin stood and walked back to the door. "Are you staying on while we do your nighttime routine?"

Bailey nodded. "Is that okay?"

"Yes, but you have to say goodnight once your teeth are brushed."

"Got it."

Bailey and Amaya talked about a YouTube video they'd both watched about a family who did a twenty-four-hour challenge in their trampoline room—*what the actual?*—and Aelin pretended she wasn't eavesdropping on every single word.

"I think Dariel likes you. He was staring at you in choir yesterday." Bailey washed her face with a microfiber cloth she'd purchased with her allowance money.

"Girl! He just doesn't know the words!" Amaya laughed.

The whole interaction suddenly made Aelin feel like she was breathing through a drinking straw. *Skincare routine? Boys?* How were these girls not talking about friendship bracelets and Polly Pockets or something? "Alright, tablet away. Time to brush teeth."

Bailey nodded and ran the tablet into Aelin's room, then padded back to the washroom to brush. She changed into pajamas, and that only made Aelin think of standing on the front porch giving Ryan her WiFi password. A zing flashed through her at the image of him sitting on her porch swing, his eyebrow raised as he clarified whether BJ was capitalized.

She should change it. But Clark had hated that password. Since she'd come up with it before they'd gotten together, he was immediately jealous of whoever had inspired the phrase. Now that she was finally free of him, she kind of wanted to keep it even if it was awkward. A spite password sounded delightful. She would change the network name to ClarkIsADouchebag if she thought he'd ever see it instead of his phone automatically connecting.

Bailey picked up *Island of the Blue Dolphins*, and they continued where they'd left off. After a few chapters, Bailey's eyes drooped. Aelin pulled the comforter up over her shoulders, then stood and flipped off the light.

Aelin slipped out of Bailey's room and left a small crack in the door, just how she liked it. She went downstairs and finished loading the dishwasher, then locked up and climbed the stairs to her bedroom. When she walked in, she saw Bailey's tablet propped up on her nightstand, the screen still bright.

Aelin walked over to turn it off, and frowned. There was something on the—

Her eyes widened, and she nearly dropped the tablet on the floor. Amaya's screen was pointed directly at the couch where Ryan relaxed with a book. Shirtless. *He was a reader?* She could count on one hand the number of men she knew who read actual paperbacks and didn't listen to podcasts or audiobooks.

His hair was down. It came just past his shoulders. Her eyes traced the lines of his bare chest and the dark trail of hair that started at his navel and disappeared into the waistband of his fitted sweatpants.

Aelin's mouth went dry, which was when she realized she was *spying on him in his own house*. What the hell was wrong with her? She hit the red button to end the video call, and then the blood rushed from her face when she thought about what that had sounded like on his end. Was the tablet silenced or had it made a weird "this call has ended" noise?

She fell back on the bed, dropping the tablet onto the mattress. He was going to know. He would be able to look and see when the call had ended.

She groaned and forced herself back up to sitting. Maybe he would think it had timed out. Ended on its own. He didn't know that she'd been looking. *But she sure as hell did.*

———

The next morning, Aelin stood in the kitchen watching as Bailey cracked eggs into a pan. "You sure you don't want me to do that?"

Bailey shook her head, chewing on her bottom lip as she focused on the hot burner. "I've got it, Mom."

Aelin smiled. She leaned against the counter and sipped her coffee. It was Sunday, and they had big plans. *Two more weeks.* "What do you want to do after the trampoline place?"

Bailey gave her a sly grin. "I don't know. Maybe . . . brunch?"

Aelin laughed. "Are you going to pay for that?" Bailey dropped her eyes, and Aelin drew a deep breath. "Kidding. Of course we can do brunch. Then maybe the park?"

Bailey's eyes lit up, and she nodded. When the eggs were finished, they ate breakfast together and talked about the only two things that seemed to be on Bailey's mind at the moment. The end of the year choir concert on Tuesday night and the sky-high list of things she wanted to do over the summer. Bailey talked about the books she wanted to read and the craft projects she wanted to try. Parks. Playgrounds. Friends. Movies.

Aelin took a large gulp of her coffee.

After they finished eating, Bailey ran to her room to grab her things. Aelin packed a bag with snacks and then they were out the door. The drive was quick, and as they walked in, Bailey's eyes lit up at the rows of trampolines and massive slides stretching out before them.

"Mom, look at that one! It has a basketball hoop!" Bailey

pointed, but Aelin didn't hear her since her eyes had snagged on the guy filling out waivers at the counter. He was tall, with broad shoulders and a strong build. His hair was tied up in a bun.

She pulled Bailey close. "Did you tell Amaya we were coming here today?"

Bailey grinned and scanned the room, then launched forward when she caught sight of her friend at the counter. Aelin didn't know what to do with her hands as Ryan put the pen down and turned. Their eyes locked, and Aelin gave a half wave, immediately imagining him lounging on a couch half-dressed.

Damn him and his broad shoulders for fixing her garage code pad. Her antiquated ovaries were not equipped to handle that.

"Hey." Ryan's voice was low and smooth as he walked past the stanchion and ropes that along with the neon colours and the smell of foam pits decidedly gave the place a wax museum vibe. Aelin's stomach flipped. *Married.* She could not give in to having dirty thoughts about the married dad of her daughter's friend, and what kind of person was she to do so when his wife was in the hospital?

She was a very broken person. That's what she was. Which meant she should not be spending one-on-one time with a very not single man who knew how to fix things at her house.

"Hey." She tried to keep her tone casual, but when her hands turned into finger guns and pointed at him, she knew she'd swung too far in the other direction. She shoved her hands in her pockets.

Ryan glanced at Amaya. "So. Eleven o'clock."

Amaya shot him a cheesy grin as she twisted her wrist band. Bailey stood at the counter waving Aelin over.

"I'm going to go pay." She walked past them and pulled out her wallet. Was he going to expect her to sit and talk the whole time the girls played? She'd worn athletic clothes and brought her grip socks so she could jump with Bailey, but with Amaya there, she doubted she'd make the cut for number one friend. But Aelin didn't know what was worse. Sitting and talking to Ryan for two hours or jumping in front of Ryan for two hours. She was probably going to pee a little.

As they walked to the cubbies to store their shoes, Bailey turned to her. "You're going to jump, right?"

Her heart swelled. "Yeah, baby. Of course."

They put on their grip socks and walked out to the trampoline area. Ryan wore brand new grip socks, and Amaya was already asking him to bring her the zip-line rope. He jogged over to it and stretched his arms above his head to grab it, and his shirt rode up, revealing a strip of what she already knew existed under there.

Aelin turned and pretended to be very interested in the mechanics of the obstacle course.

"Mom! Show Amaya your double backflip!"

Aelin turned and found Bailey on the trampoline next to the zip line. Ryan was waiting to retrieve the rope again if needed. He was staring at her.

She waved her daughter off. "Maybe later."

Bailey scoffed. "Do it now! I told her you could teach her how to do a single."

Aelin gritted her teeth, then padded over to the tramp. She never thought twice about doing her old gymnastics tricks, but she didn't usually have an audience. She jumped on and double-bounced Bailey, sending her into a fit of giggles. Bailey rolled to the edge and motioned for Amaya to come watch. Aelin kept her back turned to where she knew Ryan was still standing, and pushed off. That familiar swoop of exhilaration hit her gut. She bounced twice, then flipped, landing easily on her feet and slowing her momentum.

Amaya gaped at her, then she nudged Bailey's shoulder. "I thought you were lying."

Bailey beamed. "She can do way more tricks than that. She was a gymnast when she was a teenager."

"A long time ago," Aelin pointed out.

"My dad only knows how to do a front flip." Amaya bounced over to her.

"Not true." Ryan's voice sounded behind her, and she shivered.

Amaya gave him a look. "You never land your backflips. That doesn't count."

"You don't have to land them in the pool." He walked up to make a triangle between Aelin and the girls.

Amaya reached out and grabbed his hand. "Maybe you should learn, too!"

Aelin's cheeks heated. "I'm not sure I'm the best teacher."

Amaya pulled Ryan onto the tramp, and Aelin didn't bother with any more protestations. She started with backdrops, over-the-shoulder rolls, and tuck jumps. After a few minutes of practice, she turned to Ryan. "Is it okay if I spot her?"

He nodded, and Aelin motioned for Amaya to come closer. "Okay, you're going to jump and tuck like we practiced. When you throw your legs up, I'm going to help you get around, okay?"

Amaya nodded. The first attempt, she ended up nearly kicking Aelin in the face. The second wasn't much better, but by the third and fourth, she made a full rotation. Bailey gave her a high five.

"Okay, your turn!" Amaya moved to the mats, watching her dad. Aelin turned to follow, but Amaya shook her head. "He needs a spotter!"

Aelin pursed her lips. She slowly turned to face Ryan. "I'm sure you'll be fine, right?"

Ryan opened his mouth, but Amaya looked indignant. He drew a deep breath. "I weigh a lot more than her, A."

"Which means you could hurt your neck if you land on it." Amaya crossed her arms over her chest.

Aelin gave in and walked back onto the trampoline. "She should be a lawyer when she grows up."

He exhaled a puff of air. "You have no idea."

Aelin stood next to him, her arms ready to catch his legs and give a little push. He jumped and tucked, throwing his momentum up and back. Aelin caught his calves and gave a bump. Ryan landed on his feet first try.

Amaya's jaw fell open. "Not fair!"

He nodded, then gave Aelin a tight smile. "Thanks for the help."

He might as well have been thanking her for picking up a quarter she'd found in the parking lot with his lack of enthusiasm. "No problem."

They spent the next hour jumping, playing dodgeball, and trying out the various obstacle courses. Aelin escaped to the couch along the side, checking her phone and avoiding all eye contact with Ryan or the girls. It worked for about twenty minutes before Bailey insisted she go down the mat slide.

Finally, at around one o'clock, they collapsed on the sidelines, sweaty and out of breath. Aelin leaned back against the wall, her legs like jelly. She was *not* in gym shape.

It was then that she noticed Ryan hadn't joined them. He was still over by the slide, pacing with his phone to his ear.

"That doesn't look good," she murmured.

"Probably work. Or Grandma." Amaya peeled off a damp sock.

Aelin watched him rub his temple. She couldn't help herself, she was curious about him. Ryan was quiet. His expressions rarely gave a hint at what he was thinking, but without realizing it, she'd already started to catalogue tidbits about him. There was a strained relationship at work. He'd do anything if Amaya asked him to. *He didn't talk about his wife.*

Aelin cleared her throat. "He's close with his mom?"

Amaya shrugged. "Not really. But he talks with my mom's mom all the time."

Aelin's heart tugged. Adorable. She took the girls to the café and got them water cups, then pulled out the snacks she and Bailey had packed that morning. "Now I see why you wanted to bring two Fruit by the Foots." She raised an eyebrow, and Bailey had the decency to look at least a bit chagrined.

Ryan walked up a few moments later, his expression grim.

"Everything okay?" Aelin asked, busying herself with cleaning up the trails of contact paper trash.

He nodded once. "It'll be fine." Aelin dropped the wrappers into the bin next to their table. "If you haven't already, don't apply to the childcare place I gave you."

She put her hand on her hip. "I was planning to do that tonight."

"Yeah. Well, they just decided to shut down."

Amaya looked up, her eyes wide. "Ms. Christy isn't doing it? Why?"

He shook his head. "She didn't give details, just said she has some personal issues she needs to deal with."

Aelin blinked. "A week and a half before school's out."

Ryan's jaw ticked. "Looks like it."

He kind of looks like Tarzan, Aelin thought. With his hair pulled back and that brooding expression on his face. She cleared her throat. "I can send you some of the other places I was looking at if that's helpful."

"NO!" Amaya shouted, and both of them jumped. "No, no, no." She hopped up from the table, and nearly tripped on the bench as she ran over to them. She put out her hands like two stop signs, grinning at them. "You need a job, right?"

Aelin frowned, not sure whether she should play along.

Amaya turned to her dad. "You need a place to ditch me for the summer."

"Okay, ouch," Ryan's brows pulled closer together.

Amaya looked between the two of them, miming first to Aelin then to Ryan. "Dad! Why don't you hire her to be my nanny for the summer!"

CHAPTER
Eight

AELIN THREW the pile of old magazines into the recycling bin, then swept her hair up into a high ponytail. Two days of dejunking was exactly what her cold dead heart needed after mediation that weekend, and since she'd woken up feeling like a seventy-year-old woman after her trampoline shenanigans, puttering around at home was the correct life choice.

She couldn't get the idea of nannying Amaya for the summer out of her head.

Except for the fact that she'd have to see Ryan every morning and night, the whole thing was perfect. She'd chew off her own arm to spend the summer with Bailey, so forcing her lady parts into compliance seemed like a small price to pay.

But Ryan hadn't immediately jumped on the suggestion yesterday. He didn't have her number, and she didn't have his, and they hadn't crossed paths at drop-off that morning.

When she finished cleaning the main floor toilet, a thought hit her like a brick.

The choir concert. It was at six that evening, and Ryan would definitely be there.

But what was she going to say to him? If he hadn't already asked, was there a reason? Every parenting moment she'd had over the past week replayed in her head, and she cringed. The first time he'd met her, she'd just left her daughter at the school unattended. Not a great first impression.

But she had let the girls make slime and made grilled cheese. She'd shown she could be responsible, hadn't she?

Ugh. She pulled open the junk drawer and started throwing everything into a box. When it was empty, she grabbed the nozzle to the vacuum cleaner and sucked out the dust and old pieces of plastic and pencil lead. She was a good mom. She wasn't perfect, but she went above and beyond to make things fun for Bailey. Clark hated that about her. He would've been thrilled if Bailey loved him and only him. His strategies had worked when she was smaller, but now she was smart enough to see through the smoke and mirrors. *She hoped.*

Aelin dug through the items in the box and sorted out everything that was worth keeping. She put them back in the drawer knowing full-well it was going to be chaos again in a week or two, then emptied the remnants from the box into the trash. She washed her hands and put away the vacuum, then grabbed a water bottle and went downstairs to the workout room in the basement. They had a walkout, so it didn't feel dark and sad down there. That had been important to her when she'd bought the house.

She put on her runners and stepped onto the treadmill. Once her water bottle and earbuds were in place, she started the fourth episode of Better Call Saul and pressed the start button. The belt started moving. She walked for a bit, then adjusted the speed until she found her rhythm.

As she ran, Aelin's mind began to blur. The world outside of her workout room faded, and her focus narrowed to the hum in her legs and Saul scamming some sociopath in an alley.

After twenty minutes, she slowed the treadmill to a walk, then stepped off and moved to the free weights. She lifted, stretched, and did a core workout on her yoga mat, then put her shoes back in place next to the treadmill and headed back upstairs for a shower.

Her mind slowly drifted back to reality as she stepped into her ensuite and turned on the shower. She peeled off her sweaty clothes and draped them over the laundry basket. The washroom filled with steam as she twisted her hair into a bun and secured it with a clip, then she stepped under the hot stream. She closed her eyes and let the water cascade over her shoulders.

Okay. She needed a plan. She'd set up interviews for Thursday, but she could easily cancel them if Ryan was, in fact, open to the idea of her watching Amaya for the summer. But how much would he be willing to pay? The place Ryan had planned to use wasn't traditional. It was a small program that seemed to be a blend between an arts and crafts summer camp and paid field trips. The price had been five hundred and fifty a week.

She assumed that was lower because there were twelve spots available, which meant the woman running it was making a fantastic weekly rate. But if Ryan only wanted to pay five hundred and fifty . . . there was no way she could survive making that little. She had credit card debt she was trying to pay off thanks to Clark deciding it would be best to buy their flights to Europe in 2023 on her card since it had a better percentage back. Three weeks before the trip, she found out he was sleeping with his personal assistant. Which betrayal was just two years after he'd cheated on her the first time. She'd believed him when he pleaded for her to forgive him. She wouldn't ever make that mistake again.

She had lawyer fees, the mortgage—it all added up to an insurmountable burden without full-time work.

All in all, it wasn't a compelling sell. *Hey, do you want to pay twice as much as you were planning on for childcare this summer so I can spend time with my daughter and keep my house?*

Aelin grabbed a bottle of body wash and poured a dollop into her palm. She lathered it over her skin, inhaling the scent of eucalyptus and mint as she worked through a potential approach. She would be with the girls full-time. It was one adult to two kids, so the level of care and attention would be astronomically higher. She could show him the list Bailey had made for all the things she wanted to do over the summer and throw in . . .? She scrambled. Some overnights? Time for him to go and be with his wife while she was recovering?

She rinsed off and turned off the water, then stepped out and wrapped herself in a towel. As she dried off, her mind flitted through Ryan's potential responses. Would he tell her he'd already found something else? Or that he couldn't commit to a higher rate? Or—*or*. There was a chance he could say yes. Wasn't there?

Her phone dinged, and she picked it up from the washroom counter.

MEGAN:

Any thoughts on that double date?

Aelin exhaled. She'd looked at Megan's original text, but hadn't thought twice about it.

The 27th, right?

The 27th or 28th. Whichever is best.

I think the 27th is best for me.

So . . . is that a yes?

Aelin chewed her lip. Was it a yes? It was just dinner. Megan had a guy, Colin, she knew through a mutual friend who she swore would be a perfect fit for her.

I don't want him to think this is more than it is

I promise. He knows it's just dinner.

Aelin's heart pounded so fast, she thought she was going to pass out. She was still married. It didn't mean anything to Clark. Hell, it hadn't meant anything to them even when he swore he wanted to make things work. But it meant something to her. He could be a cheater, but she would never be. As if reading her mind, Megan sent another text.

This marriage is over, Aelin

You would've been done with this by now if Clark didn't keep trying to stab you in the back to get custody of Bailey. This is on him, not you

You deserve to have some fun and to feel like a woman again

I'm Clark's sister, so if anyone should be biased in this matter, it's me. And I'm on your side, babe. You deserve so much better.

Tears pricked her eyes.

That's a hell of a speech

Did it work?

Tell Colin it's JUST DINNER

Megan sent a GIF of a cat doing a happy dance, and Aelin laughed as she threw the phone on the bed and walked into her closet, scanning the rows of hanging clothes. She pulled out a stretchy pale blue shirt and a pair of dark jeans, then slipped them on. The fabric was soft against her skin, and the blouse's colour somehow made her eyes look deeper brown.

She put a pin in the dinner she'd just agreed to since it was making her slightly nauseous and returned to her more pressing conundrum. How could she convince Ryan that she was the best fit for summer childcare? Aelin pondered this as she towel-dried her hair and brushed it until it fell in sleek waves over her shoulders, suddenly wishing she had time to blow dry and curl it. It took her two minutes to apply a touch of makeup—mascara, a hint of blush, and a swipe of lip gloss—then grabbed her phone and swept out of the bedroom.

Aelin walked into the kitchen, opened the fridge, and pulled out the container of leftover pasta from last night. She dumped it onto a plate, and stuck it in the microwave. She knew what would be most important to her as a parent, so maybe she only needed to make it clear what she could offer. When the microwave dinged, she retrieved her plate, grabbed a fork, and leaned over the counter. The noodles were still a bit cold in the centre, but she didn't care. She needed fuel, not a Michelin-star experience.

When she was finished, she rinsed her plate, then put it in the dishwasher and strode to her desk. She didn't have his email or phone number, so she'd have to do this old-school.

Aelin thought of the old babysitter flyers she'd made in middle school and snorted. This would have to be better than that.

———

Aelin arrived at the school and took the bouquets of flowers she'd picked up on the way past the main office and into the main hallway. She was only going to get one, but then wondered if Ryan had thought to get something for Amaya and opted for two. It couldn't hurt to do something nice even if he didn't consider her summer proposition.

Reminders of school rules and kids' artwork hung from the brick walls. She passed the "Artist of the Month" display and smiled to herself. Bailey had been over the moon when she was chosen back in April.

She joined the stream of parents and children making their way to the auditorium and found a seat in the fourth row of the raised seats, close to the aisle. The kids were still in rehearsal, and she tried not to look too desperate as she scanned the rows of other parents.

Aelin spotted Ryan immediately. His hair was tied up in his usual messy bun, and he was dressed similarly to the first time she'd seen him. Collared shirt. Nice slacks. She thought about standing up and walking to him then, but paused when a smile split his face.

The sight of it made something squeeze inside her. Had she seen him smile like that before? He was always so serious. She dropped her eyes to her phone, then glanced back to figure out who he was talking to. There were two men on either side of him, both athletic looking, one with a worn ball cap turned around backward and the other in a T-shirt and jeans. Did Ryan only hang out with other men who looked like they could be in a firemen's calendar?

Married, married, married, she reminded herself.

His eyes flicked up and caught hers. Aelin turned her head to stare at the empty stage. *Shit.* He'd absolutely just caught her looking at him. If she would've waved or something it would've looked more accidental and not like she was trying to figure out why his eyes always looked a little sad.

The last thing she wanted to seem was desperate, even if it was the truth.

Her phone buzzed, and she glanced down to see Clark's name on the screen. Her stomach tightened.

CLARK:

> I was thinking I'd take Bailey to Edmonton next month

Aelin's stomach dropped. Clark only went to Edmonton for work, and that last word required air quotes.

> Won't you be in meetings?

Taking Bailey somewhere fun on his weekend was not the norm. Clark taking her anywhere that required effort or advanced planning sent off all the alarm bells.

CLARK:

Going to take her to the mall

I was thinking I'd take Bailey to Edmonton next month. She tried to parse out the meaning because with Clark, she could never take anything at face value. He didn't say "a work thing" which meant he was either trying to make her think it was personal or it actually *was* personal.

Clark only went out of his way for two things. Money or sex. She was guessing it was the latter.

If you're meeting someone, I don't think that's the best situation for our ten-year-old daughter. And you'd be violating our separation agreement

The three dots appeared, then retreated. The doors to the stage opened and a couple of teachers filed in, leading the kids to their row on the risers.

CLARK:

Classic. I try to do something nice and it's still not good enough for you

Aelin bit down hard and flinched when she caught the inside of her cheek. She flipped her phone over and set it in her lap. It was his weekend. He had Bailey from Friday after school until

Sunday night, and taking her to Edmonton didn't break any of their mediation rules. There was nothing she could do about this.

Aelin tried to draw a full breath as she found Bailey in the second row. The kids were dressed in white shirts and black pants or skirts, each sporting a colourful sash or tie. Bailey had been insistent that she needed red, and she'd gone to Walmart late the night before to pick up a scarf.

The kids fidgeted, whispering to each other and adjusting their outfits. One boy with a cowlick was trying to smooth down his hair, while a girl next to him giggled and pointed at her little sister in the crowd.

There were two people between Bailey and Amaya, but they leaned forward, talking to each other anyway. Aelin couldn't help but grin at that. All she wanted in the world was for people to love Bailey as much as she did.

A few minutes later, the music started, a blend of classic choir pieces and a few contemporary songs. The children's voices filled the room. Not entirely on key or rhythm, but all she could see was the joy on their faces as their mouths rounded into tall O's.

Between songs, she glanced over at Ryan. His attention was fixed on Amaya, a contented smile still hanging on his lips. He looked *nice* sitting like that. Like a nice man. A nice dad. Someone who wouldn't take his daughter to a hotel so he could hook up with some woman he met on Hinge.

Aelin sighed and settled in for the final number. She perked up when she saw Amaya step down from her riser and walk across the stage to the microphone. She waited for her choir teacher to adjust it, then stood straight, her hands at her sides.

The music swelled, and she sang the opening stanzas, her voice clear and strong. When she finished her part, she retreated back to stand with the rest of the choir, grinning from ear to ear at her dad in the crowd.

Aelin didn't know whether she wanted to rage text Clark or

start crying. Would Bailey ever have an experience like that? If Clark had deigned to show up for this, he sure as hell wouldn't have been looking at his daughter like that. Unless he knew someone was watching.

When the applause died down, and the lights went up, Aelin wound her way through the crowd and into the hall. She spotted Bailey and Amaya lined up a few feet ahead, hugging their friends and glowing with post-performance adrenaline.

She stepped up to them, flowers in hand, realizing she hadn't paid attention to whether Ryan had flowers already.

Bailey's eyes lit up. She took one of the bouquets and handed it to Amaya, somehow understanding exactly why she'd brought them.

"You girls sounded amazing up there," she said. Bailey beamed at her. "And Amaya, your solo? Perfect."

Amaya's cheeks turned pink, and she clutched the bouquet to her chest. "Thanks." The girls turned to chat and take pictures with other friends. Aelin glanced around at the other parents. It was always moments like this where she felt the most alone.

When Bailey was little, she'd met other moms at park groups and found a couple friends in the neighbourhood. Once she and Clark split, all those poker night and wine-tasting invitations dried up. She spent more time with her married sister-in-law than she did her friends of the past six years. Ironic.

"Thanks for the flowers." Ryan's voice sounded next to her, and she turned, her pulse kicking into second gear.

"Oh. No problem. I was stopping anyway, and I knew Bailey would love that I got Amaya some too." Aelin straightened and tucked a strand of hair behind her ear. Ryan's friends were still back in the auditorium. She spotted the baseball cap.

"Uncles?" Aelin nodded to them.

Ryan shook his head. "Friends from my hockey team."

Aelin's eyes widened. "They came to your daughter's grade four concert?"

He shrugged. "We're a family."

A large group passed through the middle of the hallway, and Ryan moved in closer to avoid getting caught in the tide. His hand pressed against the wall next to her, and suddenly all she could feel was the heat of his body, the scent of that sea breeze body wash.

He moved back when the coast was clear, and Aelin prayed her face wasn't beet red. Because her thighs were. Her body didn't care, apparently, that this man had a very nice, very practical wedding band on his left hand.

She straightened her shirt. "Hey, so I wondered if we could talk about that thing." *That thing?* The sentence she'd just blurted was nowhere close to the verbiage she'd rehearsed in the shower earlier.

His brow pinched.

"About summer childcare. What Amaya said at the trampoline place."

Ryan exhaled. "Right. Sorry about that. She has no filter between her head and her mouth."

Aelin stilled, her mind scrambling. So, he hadn't considered it. Or wasn't considering it. Or thought it was a mistake Amaya had said it in the first place? He'd seemed a little embarrassed, but she'd thought that was only because his daughter had practically made the suggestion over a loud speaker in a public space.

"Oh, right. No, I understand." She turned her head, searching for Bailey, but before she could make her escape, Ryan stopped her with a hand on her elbow.

Her arm lit up like she'd been sitting with her cord dangling and he'd suddenly plugged her into an outlet.

"Were you interested?"

Aelin turned back and nearly sighed as his hand dropped from her skin. Something about his sad grey eyes broke down the wall of professionalism she'd intended to keep up during this conversation. He'd already been witness to her worst moment that didn't involve Clark Moses over the past ten years. So. She was going to cut the bullshit.

"Yes, I was interested. I've been searching for jobs that would allow me to stay home with Bailey this summer and haven't found anything. I was so sure I'd be able to find something that worked that I didn't hedge my bets. Now every available camp or au paire or nanny is going to cost me an internal organ, and since my ex-husband is currently committing tax fraud so he doesn't have to pay more child support, I'm debating between a kidney or a lung. So yes. I was definitely interested."

Aelin glanced at the people still milling through the hall, hoping they hadn't heard a syllable of that depressing monologue.

"Oh." Ryan crossed his arms in front of him. "What would you charge?"

Aelin opened her mouth, then closed it. Then tried again. "Eight hundred a week." She'd done the mental math on the way over. If she got a full-time job and had to put Bailey in a summer camp, that was about what it would even out to. She didn't want to ream him, and that amount was completely manageable.

She continued, "I would be giving undivided attention to the girls. We'll do at least three field trips a week and on the two days we're home, we'll do baking and crafts and projects in the backyard. I grew up an athlete, so physical activity is important to me. I'll make sure they eat healthy, but not so healthy that they hate me. I can offer one overnight a week so you can have time off and be with your wife."

Her throat felt like it was going to swell closed, and Bailey's choir director was going to have to trach her with a ball-point pen. When Ryan didn't respond immediately, she somehow defied biology and kept talking. "I can do a background check if you want. I'll work as an independent contractor, so you don't have to worry about taxes, and—"

"You don't need to do a background check." Ryan watched her, his eyes steady.

Why could she never figure out what was going on in his head? "Okay."

He dropped his arms, putting his hands in his pockets. "Okay."

"So . . . did you want to think about it and—"

"I don't need to think about it. That sounds great."

The voices in the hallway faded into an amorphous buzz. She nodded, then clenched her fists to try and get feeling back into her fingers. "So it's a yes?"

He nodded. "Send me a contract."

"Right. Yes. I'll ask Chat GPT to make me one tonight."

The corner of Ryan's mouth lifted. "Do you need my email address?"

"Mmhmm." She pulled her phone from her purse and opened a new contact, quickly realizing the only thing she knew about him was his first name. "Here." She handed it to him. Let him fill out whatever information he felt comfortable giving her.

She waited for him to finish tapping his fingers on her phone screen, pretending to be interested in anything other than the fact that his hand was wrapped around her cell. When he handed it back, she scanned the contact page. *Ryan Vargo*. He left his phone, email, and address along with a note, "Amaya's dad." She had a feeling she'd never need to search for his daughter's name to remember where to find him.

"I'll be in touch."

Ryan nodded once, then walked back toward his friends. Aelin pressed her palms against the cool, painted cinder block wall. She got a job. She got a job that wasn't a night shift and didn't require her to leave Bailey.

She pulled out her phone and hesitated a second too long on Ryan's contact before pulling up her texts and typing a message out to her lawyer.

CHAPTER

Nine

RYAN PULLED up to the house and killed the engine. Amaya was already unbuckled and halfway out the door before he had a chance to say anything. He stepped out and grabbed her overnight bag from the back seat, then walked it up to the front porch of his in-laws' home.

Laura opened the door, her face lighting up the way it always did when she saw Amaya. "There's my girl!" She pushed the screen door to the side, and Amaya bolted into her arms.

Ryan waited for them to move past the threshold, then set the bag on the tile floor just inside the entry. "Thanks for watching her, Laura."

"Of course. We love having her here. I just finished up some banana bread and Russ is home from the garden centre, so we have plenty of time to devote to this precious one." She pressed a kiss to Amaya's head.

Russ joined them from the back porch, wiping his hands on a cloth. "Ryan, good to see you."

"You too, Russ." Ryan extended a hand, and Russ gave it a firm shake.

Laura smiled. "Do you want some bread?"

Ryan shook his head. "I appreciate it, but I should get going."

Laura's eyes brightened. "Any fun plans?"

He shoved a hand in his pocket. "I'm picking up some friends from the team. Going out for a bit."

Russ gave him a pat on the back. "Don't get home before midnight." He turned to Amaya. "Ready to help me with the garden? The tomatoes are getting big."

Amaya's eyes lit up. "Can we pick some?"

Russ chuckled. "Not quite yet, but I'll show you how to prune the vines."

Ryan gave Amaya a hug, then went back out to the car and drove down the winding country road with the window down. The air smelled of fresh hay.

He turned off onto a gravel road, and Country's ranch came into view. He turned into the driveway of the first house on the road with Country's truck out in front of the garage. He walked up the steps and found Jenna already opening the door for him.

"Glad you could make it," Country called out from the kitchen. He leaned out and waved. In a flannel shirt and jeans, he looked every bit the cowboy he was, complete with a ten-gallon hat. Jenna, on the other hand, looked like she'd stepped out of a magazine, her blond hair pulled back in a loose bun and a strappy dress flowing around her legs.

Ryan gave Jenna a quick hug.

She grinned. "You ready to get your dance on?"

"Yeah, I'm not dancing."

She rolled her eyes. "Country, he says he's not dancing!"

"He's dancing!" Country yelled back, then walked into the front room. "You know she only agreed to come because you and Polk were going to be there, right?"

Ryan smirked. "And here I thought it was because she loved you sloppy drunk."

Jenna snorted. "Mmm. Yes. Give me more groping please."

Country scoffed. "Maybe I'm playing hard to get tonight."

"You'll definitely be playing hard." Jenna gave him a look, then seemed to remember Ryan was still standing there.

Ryan chuckled, but the sight of them together hit him in the gut. He'd accepted that his marriage and the relationship he'd had with Kara died the night she collapsed on the living room floor, but sometimes a kernel of grief popped out of nowhere. He cleared his throat. "Wedding plans coming along?"

Jenna twisted the ring on her finger. "Not much to plan since Polk has taken over."

Ryan raised an eyebrow. "He's planning things?"

Country slung an arm over Jenna's shoulder. "I asked him to take over building a dance floor, and that's extended into patio lighting, a new arbour, seating, and menu planning. He says they all contribute to the ambiance, and the floor won't work unless they're right."

Ryan laughed. "He realizes he only has a month, right?"

"August twentieth. The shotgun wedding we always dreamed about." Country grabbed his keys off the coffee table, and Jenna snatched them from his hand.

"If I'm the DD, I get to drive both ways. So you have to endure me driving your truck sober." She grinned.

Country ground his teeth, and Jenna's smile grew wider.

Ryan followed them down the steps, his mind drifting back to his wedding. Or lack thereof. He'd been the one pushing to elope, and Kara had been only too happy to go along with it. Would he have done it differently if he'd known they'd only get eleven years?

Polk appeared through the back gate just as Jenna opened the truck doors.

"Ryan." Polk tipped his hat, and Ryan saluted him. They all piled into the truck, Ryan and Polk taking the backseat.

"Careful back there. Polk's in a dry spell." Country waggled an eyebrow.

Polk leaned back. "That's all changing tonight."

Jenna rolled her eyes. "You know we're going to Dusty Rose, right?"

The conversation shifted to replacing the shingles on the barn and the accidental double booking in the VRBO in the back. Ryan learned they were almost done with retrofitting the second silo, and they already had a month-long stay booked in September.

He was happy to sit back and listen since the only thing interesting to talk about in his life left him feeling unsettled. In just under two weeks, he'd locked a woman out of her house, done voluntary electrical work at her house, and hired her to be his nanny for the summer. He'd seen Aelin Tomlison more than anyone else in his life and had an email from her in his inbox.

The offer at the choir concert earlier that week had been unexpected but a massive relief. Aelin had looked like she might be sick at Amaya's bold declaration at the trampoline place, so it hadn't occurred to him that she'd been considering it. He couldn't decide if she was hard to read or if he was rusty after living as a bachelor for the past three years. If Polk was having a dry spell, he was living in a desert.

Jenna parked the truck, and they walked into the Dusty Rose, the scent of stale beer and wood smoke hitting him like a pressure wave. The place was already packed. Country music pulsed through the air, and the bass reached through his chest and buzzed along his spine.

"There they are." Country nodded toward a set of round tables near the edge of the dance floor where André, Boyd, Sean, and Kelty already settled in.

"About damn time." Boyd grinned, his hockey mullet swaying as he leaned back in his chair.

"It's seven thirty, bud." Country clapped him on the shoulder. "Has your bedtime moved up to ten o'clock?"

"Only if she's setting it." Boyd pointed to a pretty blond in Daisy Dukes.

"Show her your flipper. That'll seal the deal." Kelty winked, and Boyd flipped out his front right tooth, giving a goofy smile.

Rhonda and Anne walked over from the bar, setting their

beers next to Jenna. "Boys, you better be on your best behaviour tonight." Rhonda gave a meaningful look at Boyd and André.

"Always." André narrowed his eyes and ran a hand through his hair. "Who am I working to impress?"

"Nobody. My friend Megan is bringing her sister-in-law tonight, and she hasn't been out in a hot minute, so don't scare her off."

"Single?"

Rhonda scoffed. "She wishes." Then took a long drink from her glass.

Country nudged Ryan, and they went to the bar. Dusty Rose wasn't high-class by any stretch of the imagination, but they had a hell of a selection of craft brews. They both ordered a Village Blonde and walked back to the tables.

". . . and it's such bullshit. She's trying to do the right thing, and he's using women like napkins." Rhonda adjusted the strap of her tank top. "I saw him at this random charity event, and he had his hand literally up his date's dress under the table while he was flirting with the girl across from him. *That* was while they were still together."

Anne looked disgusted.

Jenna shook her head. "Good for her for staying friends with her. Does her brother know?"

Rhonda shrugged. "I don't think she talks with him much."

Ryan turned toward Country, Polk, and Sean, pretending he wasn't eavesdropping and wishing he could punch whatever guy they were talking about in the balls.

"Catch the news about Brodie's suspension?" André leaned over the table. "Third one this year. He's got a loyalty card for the penalty box."

Ryan shook his head. "That cross-check was filthy." He tilted his head as another piece of the women's conversation hit his ears.

". . . I told her Colin's a good guy," Rhonda was saying. "She says she wants to wait until the divorce is final, but Megan's wearing her down."

He didn't know why he was so distracted. Possibly because dating again sounded like his own personal hell.

Sean tapped his glass on the table. "Hastings is what, 220? Shouldn't have chirped him."

"Still. He dialed the gooney up to eleven," Polk added.

"Did you see the CCHL got Richards?" Country asked.

Boyd nursed his beer. "That kid is one to watch. Speaking of, how's the camp looking? Starts in July?"

Ryan nodded. "We're all set over at Carpenter's. We—" He paused when Sean's face went stoney and turned to the door of the bar.

Jordan, the captain of Pucks Deep, strolled into the Dusty Rose.

Sean muttered something under his breath just as Kelty sidled up next to him.

"We're not going to have a problem tonight, are we?" She fluttered her eyelids.

Sean's jaw worked. "As long as he doesn't start something."

Rhonda's voice raised in pitch behind them. "We should dance, right? Why are we still standing here."

"Let me get you another beer." Ryan took Sean's empty glass and wound his way to the bar.

"Get in line, bud." Tyler moved in front of him, and Ryan put his hand up, threatening to mess up his perfectly styled hair.

"Ooh, he'll chop off your hand for that." Emma slid in next to him.

Ryan laughed and set Sean's glass on the bar. "I didn't see you two come in."

"We've been waiting for a bit." Tyler nodded to the slammed bartender, then noticed Jordan leaning in to talk to someone across the bar. "Where's Sean?"

"Being corralled by Kelty."

Emma grinned. "I call next." She leaned in and patted his

messy bun. "How long is your hair these days? That bun is looking thick."

Ryan pulled out the elastic. "Amaya won't let me cut it. She says I have to be her hair model."

Emma's eyes lit up. "Please tell me she tries TikTok trends on you."

"YouTube shorts."

She laughed, and he tied his hair back up just as the bartender set Tyler and Emma's drinks in front of them.

Ryan ordered another beer for Sean. "You two go ahead, I'll wait."

Tyler and Emma made their way to the table, and Ryan surveyed the room, mentally calculating how late they were likely to be there. He liked driving with Country and Polk because they usually had something at the ranch to wake up for the next morning.

He was making a strategy for passing the time when the door to the bar swung open again, and Ryan's nervous system slammed on the emergency break. It was so out of context, for a moment, he couldn't compute what he was seeing.

Aelin walked in with another woman. She wore a black, strapless shirt tucked into light jeans that sat perfectly at her waist, accentuating her curves. The image of her towel splitting over her thigh sent a jolt straight to his crotch, and he turned back to the bar only to see her walking toward their table in his peripheral vision.

The two of them cut through the crowd like a hot knife through butter. Men turned their heads, their eyes dropping low as they passed. Ryan had the urge to throat-punch every last one of them.

His shoulders tensed as Rhonda's comments from earlier locked into place. Clark Moses. Text message guy. Camping mats guy. *That* was who she'd been talking about?

The bartender set Sean's beer on the counter, and Ryan momentarily froze. He shouldn't care that Aelin was at the

Dusty Rose. She was an acquaintance. A hired employee. A member of the community who happened to play a role in Amaya's life, like her teacher or librarian.

Not the best analogy since he was then imagining Aelin wearing that outfit with glasses and a pencil between her lips.

Take the beer back to Sean. Say hello. That was the normal thing to do.

He felt like a robot following lines of code as he found his way back to the table. Aelin looked up from the girls' table behind them the second he set the beer down. Her lips parted, and she blinked three times before closing them.

He gave a small nod, then became very invested in André's retelling of the World Junior's draft even though the only thing he could hear was the ringing in his ears.

Before he'd driven to Laura and Russ's house, he'd looked over the contract she sent to his email. It was exactly what he'd expected. He'd sent an email to his boss to switch his vacation week since Aelin listed the third week in July as the only time she would be gone during the summer. It was an easy enough change. He'd signed it and spent an embarrassingly long time trying to decide what to say when he sent it back. In the end, he'd settled on, "Thanks. Ryan."

He'd felt like an idiot the second he pressed send. Something about her made him second-guess everything, and right then, standing in the Dusty Rose, he knew what it was. He was attracted to her, and he wasn't supposed to be. He had a wife that he'd promised his life to, and he was imagining another woman's thighs.

As much as he pretended it didn't exist, his body knew otherwise. He was like a forward trying so hard to fake out the defence that he overskated and bungled the play. He couldn't be himself around her. He was trying so damn hard not to look at that puck.

The girls' table erupted in laughter, and Rhonda dragged Aelin and her friend—sister-in-law?—to the dance floor.

"Sounds like she's got more baggage than Patrick Roy in '95." Boyd nudged his shoulder. "Don't blame you for wanting to try, though."

Ryan dropped his eyes. "I was—" He cleared his throat. "Just thinking."

Boyd laughed. "Bud, this isn't the inquisition." His expression sobered when he saw Ryan wasn't laughing. He changed the subject to their summer practice schedule.

It didn't last long. In less than two minutes, Rhonda, Aelin, and her friend were approaching their table.

CHAPTER

Ten

RYAN LOOKED up as the three women stopped in front of him, and Boyd stepped back to make room, his eyebrows raised.

"You know Aelin," Rhonda stated.

Sean and Country's conversation fizzled faster than wet Pop Rocks.

Ryan straightened, his hand still on his glass. "I do. Hello." He needed to just look at the puck. It wasn't a crime to notice, and if he was going to survive the summer, he needed to stop acting like a deer in headlights every time she entered his field of view.

Aelin nodded. "Hello." Her cheeks were rosy, but she'd just been on the dance floor.

Ryan stopped letting his eyes slide past her. When she lifted her chin, he met her gaze head-on. A soft puff of air left her lips.

"Your kids go to school together?" Rhonda prodded.

Ryan cleared his throat. Might as well get it out in the open. "Right. They're both in grade four at Meadowbrook. My plan for childcare this summer fell through. She's nannying Amaya this summer."

Boyd coughed as if he'd just choked on his beer. When he

finally composed himself, he shot a look across the table that Ryan ignored.

"That's in my spank bank." André took a long swig and finished his glass.

"Your what?" The woman next to Aelin frowned.

André leaned over the table, but Kelty cut him off. "He's saying it's his secret fantasy. To sleep with his nanny. Which he doesn't have because he's not in a relationship and doesn't have kids."

André looked wounded. "I have a dog. They have dog nannies."

Boyd laughed. "Not as hot. She has to be at your house late at night, like, "Oh, I just put the kids to bed, I didn't know you were back from that meeting—""

Rhonda smacked his shoulder. "This is their real life. You realize that, right?"

Boyd scoffed. "I was kidding!"

André leaned into Aelin. "Serious question. Did you have a third party conduct the background checks, or did you check each other's backgrounds—"

Rhonda let out an exasperated sigh. "This is your best behaviour? So disappointing." She motioned for Aelin and her friend to go back to the dance floor.

As soon as they were gone, Country grinned like a Cheshire cat. "Not sure how you forgot to mention that on the entire drive over."

Ryan shrugged. "Didn't seem notable."

Country shook his head, seeing right through his bullshit. "Okay. Not notable. Got it."

Ryan tapped his fingers on the table. "We only finalized things earlier this morning."

"In person?" André asked matter-of-factly.

"Over email."

André nodded. "So are you going to sit here the rest of the

night and pretend your new nanny isn't a total smoke show? That it never once occurred to you—"

"I'm not blind." Ryan tipped his glass and sipped the dregs.

André let out a relieved sigh, putting a hand on his heart. "You worried me for a second. I thought we weren't going to be able to talk about it."

Ryan held out his hands. "There's nothing to talk about."

Polk snickered. "Right. You, the guy who hasn't gone on a date in three years, is spending the entire summer with a Jennifer Aniston doppelganger and there's nothing to talk about."

Ryan shot him a look. "Can you not?"

Polk held up his hands. "Hey, I'm just saying. If I had a nanny like that, I'd be working from home a hell of a lot more often."

Country laughed. "You already do work from home."

"It's a euphemism." André grinned. "He has to bale hay and chill."

Ryan raised a hand to the server making rounds and ordered another beer. "How long do you think 'til this is out of your systems?"

Sean grunted. "This one's going to have a long half-life. Settle in."

Ryan fingers tightened around his empty glass, the condensation slicking his palm. He glanced over to the dance floor to see Jenna and Kelty had joined the others. They laughed and danced, carefully staying in their group so there wasn't room for the men who circled them like piranhas to cut in.

The Dusty Rose was packed, and yet he had zero problem finding Aelin in the crowd. She spun, her hair fanning out around her, and Ryan swallowed hard.

André forced him out to the floor to line dance. He normally would've put up more of a fuss. Kara always wanted to go dancing, and he'd never made the time. It felt wrong to do it now without her. But this was a matter of survival. The momentary guilt was easier to handle than the looks he got anytime Aelin raised her arms over her head and shook her hips.

When he got back to the tables, the girls were doing a second round of shots. He tried to notice anything other than the way Aelin's lips glistened in the lights or how her skin was dewy from dancing.

He successfully avoided her until an hour later when he walked out of the washroom.

"Ryan!"

He turned and found Aelin resting against the rail next to the bar. She waved, and the alcohol in his system convinced him he didn't want to be rude. He walked over to her. "Having a good night?"

She nodded, her smile loose and relaxed as she leaned in to make her voice heard over the music. "Just waiting for Rhonda and Megan."

"In the washroom?"

"Yep. Wardrobe malfunction."

He wasn't totally sure what that meant, but he smiled. "I'm surprised you haven't been accosted yet."

She gave an amused grin. "By who?"

"Every guy in here. They've been staring at you all night."

Aelin rolled her eyes. "Not true." Her shoulders curled, making shadows shift over her collarbone and a gap form along the top line of her shirt. Ryan tried to keep his eyes up and failed.

Aelin sighed. "I don't care about guys anyway."

"No?" He wet his lips.

"This isn't really my scene." She swayed and put a hand on his chest to steady herself.

Ryan was like a light that had just been clapped on.

Aelin's eyes widened, and she snapped her hand back so fast, she almost slapped the railing behind her. "I shouldn't have touched you."

"It's fine—"

"No, it's not fine. Now I'm going to think about it." She scrunched up her face.

Ryan's heart beat like a bass drum. *She was going to think about it?* His brain laser-focused like he'd just slammed a Red Bull. How was she going to think about it? *What* was she going to think about it?

Aelin exhaled. "I already think about you with that toolbox and the time I saw you on the couch."

Ryan's brow furrowed. The couch? He'd never been on the couch at her place. "When was that?" he asked, hoping it wouldn't stem the flow of deeply intriguing information.

Aelin rolled her eyes. "I was spying on you. Not on purpose, I would never do that on purpose."

"Right."

"The tablet was still on after Bailey went to bed, and you were sitting on the couch with your—" she motioned to his chest. "*All of that out,* and now I see it all the time. Especially when I open my garage."

She was a talkative drunk, and he was going to lose his damn mind. She'd been watching him over video chat? He was about to drag her off into a corner and ask her what she thought about the first time they met or when they talked at the choir concert. He was hanging on to his last thread of self-control when Rhonda and Megan appeared next to them.

"Hey, there." Rhonda's eyes narrowed. She put a hand on Aelin's shoulder. "You good?"

Aelin beamed up at her. "So good. Ryan's here. He's still not smiling though. Did you know he only smiles when he's watching Amaya?" She lifted a hand and pressed it against his cheek. "He's so serious all the time. Maybe sad?"

"Ooookay, I think it's time to go." Megan shot Ryan an apologetic look. "This is my fault. I wanted her to have a good time and forgot she's a lightweight."

"It's fine." Ryan's cheek burned where she'd touched it.

Megan and Rhonda led Aelin to the door, and his head was a rock tumbler, spinning her words until they shone.

He's so serious all the time. Maybe sad?

"Hey," Polk stalked toward him. "Jenna's ready to head out."

Ryan nodded and walked back to the table to pay his tab.

Now I see it all the time. Especially when I open my garage.

Each sentence was like an oasis. A hit of pure euphoria. How long had it been since he'd heard a woman was thinking about him? Of course he noticed women looking in his direction or the small flirtations at the pub after games or on nights out, but he'd perfected the art of looking not interested. Women didn't make advances when he refused to make eye contact or didn't smile when they made a bid. It was second nature for him to shut things down before they even started.

He'd done all of that with Aelin, and somehow she'd still noticed him. Thought about him. The sheer desperation it brought out in him sent adrenaline surging through him.

The ride home was uneventful. Polk and Country were half asleep, and Jenna was listening to a sports commentator. By the time they got to the house, Ryan only needed another twenty minutes to fully sober up.

He used the washroom and rested on the couch until his alarm went off, then got in the car and drove home.

———

His head felt thick when he answered the door to Laura, Russ, and Amaya on the doorstep at eleven.

"Morning, Dad!" Amaya threw her arms around him. Was she always this loud?

"Morning, babe."

Amaya dropped her bag on the floor, slipped off her shoes,

and ran into the house. Probably straight for her tablet. He ignored the thought that he should check if Aelin was somewhere behind the camera.

"How did it go?" he asked.

Laura beamed at him. "We all had a lovely time. She's such an amazing girl. You're doing a great job, Ryan."

The compliment settled into him in layers, and he read the subtext. *We see you're doing this by yourself. We were afraid not having Kara would ruin her. We lost our daughter, but at least we have her.*

Laura glanced over at the manila envelope sitting on the counter. Ryan pulled the door a little closer to his shoulder.

"Did you have a good time last night?" Russ asked, noting his sweatpants and T-shirt.

Ryan nodded. "Yep. Great."

He gave an approving smile. "Two weeks?" He stepped closer and put out a hand.

Ryan shook it, then gave Laura a hug. "See you soon. Love you."

"Love you." Laura waved, and the two of them walked back to the car.

Ryan had barely closed the door when Amaya burst into the hall. "Dad! Can Bailey and I have a sleepover tonight?"

He blinked. "You're going to her house first thing in the morning. Tomorrow's the first day of summer break."

Now I see it all the time. Especially when I open my garage. Ryan dragged a hand through his hair.

Amaya's shoulders slumped. "I know, but if I went over there, you wouldn't have to get up so early, and then the start of summer would be reeeally special." Her eyes grew to the size of an anime kitten.

"I thought we were going to watch a movie?" His phone buzzed on the kitchen table, and he reached for it.

"Bailey's mom says it's okay with her if it's okay with you." She bounced on her toes.

Ryan read Marc's message on his screen.

Emergency. Look at the soil contamination
report ASAP

Ryan swore under his breath and opened his email. Soil contamination? What were the chances?

"Dad . . ." Amaya whined.

He scanned the beginning of the report.

Incident Summary

On June 22nd, 2024, during the early excavation phase of the Downtown Parking Garage project, the construction crew encountered unexpected environmental contamination in the form of chemically contaminated soil. The soil appeared discoloured, emitted a strong chemical odour, and preliminary on-site tests revealed elevated levels of hydrocarbons and heavy metals, indicating potential contamination from previous industrial activity on the site.

Details of Discovery

Time of Discovery: 10:45 AM, June 22, 2024

Excavation Depth: 6 feet below ground surface

Area Affected: Approx. 50 square meters in the northeast quadrant of the project site

Initial testing was conducted using a portable gas analyzer, and soil samples were sent to a laboratory for further testing. Results confirmed that the contamination consists of the following:

Hydrocarbons (e.g., benzene, toluene, ethylbenzene)

Heavy Metals (e.g., lead, arsenic)

Volatile Organic Compounds (VOCs) at levels exceeding threshold limits.

Well, shit.

That was going to set back their timeline.

"Okay." He nodded at Amaya, and she jumped up and down. Ryan flipped to his phone contacts. He found Aelin's number and dialled.

He opted not to explain the entire situation and instead just let the girls do the work. Bailey was working on her mom just as hard, and it didn't take much convincing. Unfortunately, hearing Aelin's voice brought back every minute of their time at the Dusty Rose.

Was she thinking about him with his shirt off right then?

Without the alcohol clouding his head and rerouting his blood south, the idea of her looking at him—wanting him even a little bit—made him feel like he'd just been hit with a taser. He couldn't allow his head to take off in that direction. It wasn't fair to Kara or Amaya, and he was going to be seeing Aelin all summer.

He needed to backpedal whatever had happened that weekend to the safety of a professional relationship. She was his employee.

"Dad, I'm getting in the car!" The door slammed as Amaya disappeared into the garage.

Countdown to trial run: fourteen minutes.

AELIN FIDGETED with her shirt as Ryan walked up the path with Amaya. She moved back from the window framing the door so she wouldn't look like she'd been watching for them. She was hoping to go for an *Oh, you're here already?* look instead of *I changed my shirt and pulled my hair up five minutes ago.*

She'd been thinking about the Dusty Rose nonstop. What exactly had she said to him outside of the washroom? The whole interaction was fuzzy, but he'd smiled at her. She'd told him about seeing him over video chat, and the moment she'd remembered that tidbit, she'd wanted to crawl into a hole and die. Hopefully he'd been too far gone to remember?

It was stupid how nervous he made her, especially since there was no way she was going to do anything about it. He was married. Full stop. But she couldn't kick the compulsion to want to impress him anyway.

Ryan knocked, and she waited a few seconds before swinging the door wide. He wore joggers and a T-shirt, and his hair was deliciously mussed.

Aelin smiled stiffly. "Hey."

Ryan fidgeted with his keys. "Hey."

Amaya ducked under her arm, dropped her bag and pillow,

and called for Bailey. When Ryan didn't move to come in, Aelin stepped out onto the porch.

Ryan took a step back. "Thanks for doing this. I wasn't going to ask, but something came up at work."

"Oh? Not good?"

Ryan rubbed the back of his neck, and the flush on his skin made her hands start to sweat. "Not great, no."

"Sorry to hear that." Aelin crossed her arms in front of her. He wasn't meeting her eyes. *He normally looked at her, didn't he? What had she said at the bar?*

He exhaled, his lips pressing into a thin line. "Amaya will be safe here, right?"

Aelin frowned. What kind of question was that? "My top priority is always safety."

Ryan glanced up at her tone. "I didn't mean it like that."

"How did you mean it, then?" Their first encounter on the porch came swinging back into focus. Was she not allowed to ever be human? She got drunk at the bar, and now he was judging her parenting? "If this is about the other night—"

"It's about your ex." He looked up, finally meeting her gaze. "I didn't think to ask about it, but then I was driving her over here and . . . I got nervous."

Aelin's hands started to tingle. "Right. Yeah. That makes sense."

"Does he come over here?"

"No. Hell, no." She stepped forward to the railing and leaned against the porch rail. "He only came the other day because his sister told him I was locked out."

Ryan nodded. "He has a key to the house."

"Mmhmm. The house is technically in his name, but our contract states he's not allowed to come here without asking me first. The other day was an anomaly. He took advantage of it."

Ryan exhaled, turning and dropping his hands onto the rail. "What's to stop him from taking advantage again?"

Aelin's thoughts splintered just like they did every night

when she was crawling into bed. What if Clark had a bad night? What if he got a crazy idea in his head and drove over in the middle of the night? He'd never been violent, but he'd come close. Two weeks before he moved out, he'd cussed her out and turned so red in the face, she shook for an hour after he left.

But he hadn't broken the terms of their agreement, and there was only one reason why. "I don't think he will. His strategy is to make my home life look unstable so he can upend the custody arrangement. He only had every other weekend through the school year, but now it's summer, and next year will be Bailey's last year at this school." She blew out a breath and turned toward him. "I don't think he'll do anything that could look terrible for him in court."

Ryan clicked his tongue. "At least he has one priority straight."

She scoffed. "Not even close. He doesn't give a shit about custody. He only wants me to lose." Aelin thought back to Clark sitting across the table from her at the last mediation.

"Wouldn't it be best for us to share the same home? It would give her more stability." Clark was fighting for her to move out every other week, and live . . . where? With what money?

Aelin rubbed her arms, the cool night air making her shiver. "He's a narcissist. It's not about Bailey. It's never been about Bailey. It's about him looking good and me looking bad. He wants control. But at least for now, that's working in my favour."

She'd been doing nothing but gathering evidence about Clark's lack of involvement in their daughter's life and his manipulative and abusive behaviour. She had records showing when and where he'd cheated, and she was working on getting his tax records.

Ryan nodded, his expression unreadable. "Right. Well, I hope it all works out."

"Thanks." She forced a smile. "I'm sorry my personal situation isn't ideal."

Ryan huffed a laugh. "Whose is?"

Something flickered behind his eyes, and Aelin had so many questions she wanted to ask him. Besides hearing his wife was in the hospital, she knew nothing about his life. Just as she was mustering the courage to open the topic, Ryan gave a polite smile and stepped back.

"Thanks again. I'll get here around five thirty tomorrow. She should have everything she needs." He paused at the steps.

"Right. Sounds good. We're going to a park tomorrow."

Ryan nodded once, then turned and walked to his car.

———

The girls stayed up too late that night watching a movie and painting their nails, and Aelin didn't regret the mess for a second. She'd always felt a bit guilty for not giving Bailey a sibling, especially since her own siblings were her best friends. She'd always held out hope that Clark would change. That it was just a stage. He'd been so sorry. Now she was beyond grateful she hadn't gotten pregnant when they briefly tried five years ago.

Monday morning, they grabbed muffins at a café in the Beltline and went to a brand-new playground with a splash pad. Since it was only the end of June, it wasn't hot enough to get soaking wet, but the girls loved the misters and tempting fate by daring each other to stand over the intermittent fountains.

For a moment, Aelin let herself forget about the mediation, forget about Clark, and just enjoy a few hours together. She timed them on the monkey bars, walked down to the pond to admire the gaggle of baby ducklings, and pushed the girls on the swings.

Not one moment passed without her remembering that she was so damn lucky to be doing this. To not be working a night shift so she could bring energy to her time with Bailey. It was a gift.

They made sandwiches at home for lunch, and the girls spent hours making a stop-motion animation movie with Bailey's dolls. Aelin cleaned the basement and prepped vegetables in the fridge for the week. It was so close to the perfect day it physically ached.

By the time Ryan showed up at five thirty to pick up Amaya, Aelin's heart felt like it was going to burst at the seams.

Ryan gave her a look as she opened the door, her face splitting into a smile.

"Can I just say thank you?" she gushed. Ryan blinked, and she knew she was probably coming off like a crazy person, which was the last thing she wanted, considering she was in charge of his only child, but she couldn't help herself. "Today was incredible. My dream, really, and you made that possible, and I'm just so grateful—" Holy hell, she was crying. Was she crying? Aelin sniffed and clenched her jaw, trying to will the tears back into her ducts.

"Today was good?" Ryan looked alarmed.

"So good," Aelin squeaked.

Amaya ran down the stairs behind her. "Dad!"

Aelin moved to the side so Amaya could get through the door. Amaya threw her arms around her dad's waist, and he grunted.

"Hey, baby," he murmured, cupping a hand around her head and hugging her close.

There it was again. The softening of his face. The sadness in his eyes dissolving into warmth, like he'd just dropped onto the couch after a long day of work. *She was his safe place.* Something inside of Aelin twinged.

"Do you have your things?" he asked.

Amaya pulled back. "Just a second." She ran back inside the house.

Aelin felt like she'd just stumbled into a chapel in street clothes. She sniffed. "Good day at work?"

"Decent."

With every one-word answer, the screw labelled "Dusty Rose" twisted tighter. "Ryan, did I—?"

Amaya burst back out onto the porch with her overnight bag and pillow.

Ryan's eyes flicked from Amaya to Aelin. "Thank you again."

She nodded, placing her hands on her hips, still propping the screen door open with her shoulder. "No problem."

"See you tomorrow!" Amaya called, and the two of them walked to the car.

The next two days were much the same. Ryan barely said two words to her when he dropped Amaya off in the morning, and Aelin's worry about the weekend took a U-turn as she drove the girls to the pool. They were grown-ass adults, and he couldn't even have a conversation with her about what she'd done to make him so uncomfortable?

The only thing she could think of was that she'd alluded to being attracted to him. That wasn't a secret nearly deep and dark enough to elicit the silent treatment, especially not for someone like Ryan. He had to have women noticing him constantly, with or without his wedding ring.

Aelin hadn't flirted with him. She'd spent the whole night with Megan and her friends. She'd danced with other people, she'd barely seen Ryan besides saying hi at the beginning of the night and then talking to him that *one time.*

His behaviour was juvenile.

Aelin imagined all the ways she could tell him so as they went down the water slides and played keep away in the pool. Eventually, the anger burned down to a low simmer, replaced only with the anxiety of her double date that night with Megan, her husband Tag, and their friend Colin.

They were meeting at a restaurant twelve minutes from her house, and Amy, their fourteen-year-old neighbour, was going to hang out and play games with Bailey until she got home. Two hours. That's all she was committing to, though Amy had given her permission to stay out longer and pay her more money.

The girls showered when they got home from the pool, then settled down to keep working on their movie. Aelin put the towels and swimsuits in the wash, then retreated to her room to start getting ready. She took her shower, curled her hair, and put on light makeup, then tried on three different outfits, finally deciding on a black tank top, wide-leg khakis, and hoop earrings. Simple. Comfortable. It was the best she could do at the moment.

She changed her bed sheets and switched the laundry, then paid a few bills and called to reschedule Bailey's well-child visit since she'd booked it six months prior and it now landed on the week they were going to be at Flathead with her family. At four o'clock, she made the girls spaghetti and meatballs. She sat with them and listened to them relay the *most hilarious thing that happened* while they were filming a scene involving a cardboard piece of pizza and a Barbie toilet.

At five thirty, the dishes were done, the floor was swept, and there was a stack of board games at the kitchen table for Amy and Bailey to play together. Aelin stood at the kitchen island, tapping her nails on the granite. She should've saved a chore or two. Amy was getting there in ten minutes, and all she had to do was wait for Ryan to get there.

She picked up her phone and started scrolling. During the middle of a stand-up comedy clip, a text from Megan came through.

Leaving now! Colin's meeting us there

She tapped out a quick response.

. . .

Just waiting on the babysitter. See you soon

It was nearly five forty, and Ryan wasn't there yet. Aelin walked to the front door and peered out the windows. Nothing. He'd never been late before, but this was the first week. It wasn't like she had a long history to draw from.

Inconsiderate. The coals that had been smouldering all day flared to life with new fuel. Was this how the whole summer was going to be? No communication, even when it was something she needed to know for her job?

Amy walked up the sidewalk, and Aelin opened the front door. She was about to open the screen when another text message popped up on her phone.

RYAN:

Emergency. I'm going to be late

CHAPTER
Twelve

RYAN PULLED up to Aelin's house just as the clock in his dashboard clicked to seven. He sat there for a moment, his hands glued to the steering wheel. He couldn't get the image of Kara writhing on the floor out of his head. He'd been exiting the elevator to the main floor of the building when the call had come through. Kara's caregivers had already tried Laura, but it was Thursday night. She was with Russ at a charity event in Canmore, so they'd called him next.

It wasn't optional. He had to drive there immediately. Every seizure she experienced had the potential to be life-ending, or at least to require medical power of attorney. He and Laura were both listed on all Kara's medical forms. Laura was listed on his, too. Thankfully they'd had the foresight to complete their wills after Amaya was born. It hadn't made navigating the endless string of advice from doctors and specialists easy, but it had made the legal side easier.

Tonight, they'd been able to stabilize her. By the time he'd arrived, she was already halfway gone from the sedation they'd resorted to after she'd nearly bit the face of one of the nurses.

Ryan dropped his head on the wheel and gasped for air. It felt like his insides were being sucked through his midsection, and in minutes he'd be an empty carcass. Like the moulted cicada skins he found glued to the cinder blocks of his front garden bed.

When he was finally able to draw a full breath, he forced himself out of the car and walked up the path to Aelin's. The idea of seeing her and needing to explain why he was an hour-and-a-half late picking up Amaya felt like a Swiss Army knife to the ribs, but he gritted his teeth and stopped in front of the door.

The muffled sound of a movie filtered through the door, and a warm glow seeped through the curtains. He raised his fist to knock, but the door opened before he could make contact.

Aelin stood there, her arms crossed over her chest.

Ryan's stomach dropped. "Hey." He paused, noting the glint in her eyes and considering his next words carefully. "I'm sorry I'm late."

Aelin's eyes flicked back down the hall before she stepped out onto the porch. "I tried to call you. I left a message."

Ryan nodded, his pulse quickening. "I know, I saw it. I'm sorry I didn't call you back—"

"I know it probably doesn't seem like it, but I do have a life."

His mouth went dry. "I didn't think—"

"I had a date tonight, Ryan. A first date. I had to cancel when my friends were already at the restaurant and send a babysitter home who was counting on earning money tonight."

Guilt and annoyance flashed hot through his chest. "Got it. Next time I'll ask my wife to put off her seizure by a couple of hours." Aelin reeled back like he'd slapped her, and he wanted to reach out and grab his words and cram them back down his throat. He wanted to apologize, but he couldn't do that either. If he opened his mouth, the dam he'd barely managed to build around the chaos swirling inside him was going to crumble, and he had no idea what would flood out first.

"I—" She swallowed hard. "I don't know what to say."

He turned, running a hand over his face. "You don't have to say anything." He stared at the sprinklers turning on one yard over. The hiss of water overpowered the sound of voices up the street, the misting droplets glittering in the softening sunlight. "I'm sorry I ruined your date."

Aelin stepped up to stand next to him. "I don't understand what the situation is. It might be good for me to know. Since Amaya's going to be here all summer."

Ryan's jaw worked. It was a fair statement. He'd told the story a hundred times at that point, but the words didn't seem to want to roll off his tongue. "My wife Kara is in assisted living. Amaya calls it a hospital, and they do offer medical care there, but it's a long-term solution. She had an aneurysm a few years ago and has permanent brain damage."

Aelin didn't turn to look at him. "How bad is it?"

He sucked in a breath. "It's not definable. She doesn't regulate emotions well. That's why we couldn't keep her home with us or with her parents. She gets violent. She knows who we are but doesn't have the ability to build or understand relationships."

Aelin leaned on the porch rail, blowing out a breath. "Ryan, I'm so sorry."

He let out a soft "hmm" then shoved his hands in his pockets. His head felt thick. "My mother-in-law, Laura, is there every day. She's the first emergency contact. They're at an event out of town tonight, so I don't anticipate this happening again."

"Ryan—"

"I can't make up for missing tonight, but I'd like to take the girls tomorrow night so you can go out then. And I'll pay your babysitter."

Aelin shook her head. "That's not—"

"Let me do this. Please." His voice was low, teetering on the point of breaking.

He'd spent the entire day sending information back and forth with his team and the contractors mitigating the soil contamination, and nothing had been solved or decided. Then he'd gone straight to Kara where there weren't any answers.

Everything in his life was like a car engine that he'd torn apart, the pieces spread across his garage floor. But this part he could do something about.

Aelin worried her lower lip. "I don't know if tomorrow will work. But I can ask."

Relief washed over him, and he nodded, then pulled his wallet from his pocket. "Where does your babysitter live?"

Aelin looked as if she was going to protest, then closed her mouth and pointed up the street. "The blue house with the roses out front. But—"

"I'll drop this off on my way home."

CHAPTER
Thirteen

RYAN PULLED into Aelin's driveway at six o'clock on the dot. *Compensating for something?* She would've laughed at her own joke had his tortured expression from the night before not been branded into her retinas.

His wife had permanent brain damage. The reality of it had kept her up the night before, her thoughts spinning behind her closed eyelids until she had to flick on the light and read to be able to fall asleep.

She thought knowing her situation would satisfy her curiosity, but instead it had only ramped it up. What was he going to do? Was he planning to stay married to her forever? Was she expected to live long? Did Amaya like seeing her, or did it only make everything worse?

That was what did her in. The idea of a ten-year-old girl having to accept that her mom was gone but still alive? In some terrible reality where she couldn't think or act like an adult? He said it happened a few years ago, which meant Amaya had been young the last time her mother had been herself.

All of it was heartbreaking. Add in the guilt she felt over snapping at him for being late for her stupid date, and the first time Aelin teared up was before ten a.m.

The girls scrambled away from the front window where they'd been watching on their knees so they wouldn't get their shoes on the carpet. Aelin hadn't even nagged them to get ready. The second she'd mentioned to Bailey that she got to go to Amaya's house that night, the two of them had become an impromptu mosh pit.

"Hurry! We only have until eight thirty." Amaya leaped to her feet when she hit the hardwood, and Bailey ran to the door after her.

Aelin felt a little bad taking Ryan up on his offer to watch Bailey after the missed date the night before. It wasn't like he'd been gallivanting. Colin, Megan, and Tag had been more than happy to reschedule. When she'd texted, she'd assumed the answer would've been a kind "No thanks," but Megan instead responded with:

We don't have to prep dinner two nights in a
row? Yes, please

She'd sent the address of a different restaurant, a Thai fusion place. Aelin opted for the same outfit since she'd already changed into loungewear by the time Ryan showed up to pick up Amaya.

Aelin followed the girls to the front yard.

Ryan stood in front of the car. "What, no hug?"

Amaya was already sliding into the back seat with Bailey. "At home, Dad."

Aelin stood on the steps, her hands in her back pockets. "Thanks for doing this."

Ryan glanced up, and it felt as if she suddenly existed in a vacuum. Her skin pricked as his eyes travelled over her.

He cleared his throat. "You look nice."

"Thank you." She fought against the urge to adjust her shirt or hair or . . . dodge behind the pillar on the porch. "I'll be back as soon as I can."

"You have my address."

She nodded, thinking about that moment in the elementary school hallway when he'd been so close she could hear his breath.

He opened the car door. "Don't stress about timing. I don't have plans tonight. Just . . . have a good time." Ryan paused as if he was going to say something else, then patted the door and dropped to his seat.

———

Aelin pulled up to the restaurant Megan had sent her the address for. She parked in the back and walked around to the front entrance. As soon as she stepped through the doors, she was greeted by wooden furnishings, colourful upholstery, and flickering lanterns. Soft, live music floated from a small stage at the back of the room to her right.

"Aelin!" Megan stood and waved from a table near the back. She grinned at the hostess and walked over, her heels clicking on the polished hardwood floors.

If it wouldn't have been for the small cleft in her chin, Megan Moses would've looked nothing like her brother. Aelin wondered if that had anything to do with their ability to remain friends through everything. Her dirty-blond hair fell in waves just past her shoulders, and she wore a blouse that hung off her right shoulder, eighties style.

Megan pulled her into a hug, then moved over for Aelin to sit next to her on the bench. She looked up to find Megan's husband, Tag, and her date for the night, Colin.

Colin watched her with an easy smile that created smile lines at the corners of his eyes. He was clean cut with a close-cropped beard, just a hint of grey in his sideburns. She quickly glanced at Tag, who was sporting a rugged professor look with Harry Potter style spectacles.

"Those are new." Aelin pointed at his glasses, and Tag chuckled.

"Megan bought them for me."

Aelin grinned. "I like them."

"See!" Megan reached across the table and patted his hand, then turned back to Aelin. "Okay, Aelin, this is Colin. Colin, this is Aelin."

Colin put out a hand, and Aelin shook it. "Nice to meet you." He had a nice handshake. Warm. Firm, but not abrasive.

"You, too. I'm so sorry about last night."

Colin waved her off as he pulled his hand back. "Please. I know how it goes."

"You have kids?" Aelin picked up her glass of water and took a sip.

"Uh, no, not yet. But I have a niece and two nephews. My brother and I missed a Blizzard game at the Saddledome because of a lost blanket."

Aelin laughed. "Sounds about right."

"Yeah, and yours was a medical emergency. So please, don't apologize." Megan patted her hip. Aelin hadn't told her the details of what happened with Ryan's wife, but she was glad that it sounded more substantial than Colin's example.

"So you're a dentist?" Aelin searched her memory for anything Megan had told her when she'd been trying to convince her to say yes to a date.

"Yep, I own a practice in the Northeast."

Aelin pointed between Colin and Megan. "And how do you know each other again?"

Megan took a sip from a glass that looked like it held something fruity. "Colin and I go way back. We went to the same church growing up, and our moms were in the same book club."

Colin nodded. "She was the annoying little sister I never had."

Megan gasped. "Hey, I was not annoying."

Colin raised an eyebrow. "You chased me around the church parking lot with a dead squirrel."

Aelin's mouth dropped open. "You picked up a dead squirrel?"

Megan rolled her eyes. "I was nine. It was a phase."

Tag picked up his menu. "Was it, though? You hid in the basement until I came down to get a Dr. Pepper yesterday. I almost shit my pants."

Megan's shoulders shook. "You're just so easy to scare." She turned to Aelin. "He did this thing with his hands, like he was going to karate chop me or something."

Aelin laughed, then scanned the appetizers. "Have you been here before?"

Megan shook her head. "No, but we found out last night that Colin spent three weeks in Thailand on a humanitarian trip last November."

Aelin raised an eyebrow. "Impressive."

Colin shrugged. "A friend of mine found the opportunity, I just tagged along."

"You were doing dental care?" she asked.

"Mmhmm, as much as we could. They retrofitted rooms in an abandoned school so we could set up equipment."

Aelin nodded. "Wow. Was it totally free or discounted?"

"Free. It was almost all extractions. Pretty humbling to see how many people live with the pain of teeth and gum tissue that are rotting out of their heads. Maybe not the best dinner conversation." He huffed a small laugh.

She wasn't pretending to read the menu anymore. "Must have been rewarding."

"Absolutely."

Megan slapped her menu on the tabletop. "Tell her about the cliff jumping."

Colin launched into his story, his eyes sparkling, his hands gesticulating. He was funny. Charming, but not in an in your face way. He seemed practical, smart, and kind. Put together.

Aelin should have been interested. Attracted, for sure. But as she sat there listening to him talk about climbing a rope ladder up the side of a waterfall, she found herself more concerned with what he was thinking of her than anything else.

Did he look at her and see a mom? She shuddered at the thought, but it was the same one she'd had at the Dusty Rose. She'd been existing in such a small microcosm of the world for so long, she didn't know where she fit outside the walls of her own house. Was she attractive? Was she fun?

That idea was laughable. She didn't know the first thing about being fun if it didn't include playgrounds or craft supplies. Here Colin was talking about his world travels and humanitarian service, and all she had to contribute was her work on a PTA fundraiser and the compost she'd worked into the front garden beds.

Clark's words echoed in her head. *Vanilla. Boring. Insecure.* She thought of the countless times he'd tried to push her to come out and party, or to have sex on the balcony of their hotel, or to sign up for a meditation retreat that sounded mostly like an acid trip.

All of it disgusted her. *He* disgusted her. She didn't know what she liked or what she wanted because the last twelve years of her life had been swaddled in *him*. Did she like spicy food? Did she want to travel around the world? Would she have climbed up the waterfall and jumped? Who the hell knew.

Colin helped them make choices from the menu, and Aelin went with his recommendation, Khao Soi, a Thai coconut curry noodle soup. She ordered it at the same spice level as he did, wondering if she was going to regret it.

Probably. Most likely. But it felt like the right thing to do, because she was on a date for the first time in over fourteen months, damn it. On a date with someone that wasn't Clark for the first time in twelve years, and she wanted to know something about herself for once.

Megan paused in the middle of telling them about a doctor who, after a lunch meeting about a new drug to treat diabetes, asked her if she wanted to come back to his place for an edible and put a hand on her shoulder. "You okay?"

Aelin nodded and forced a smile. "Yeah. Just . . . yeah." She took another sip of her water. She wasn't drinking, not during dinner, and possibly not ever again after the other night at Dusty Rose. She hated that she couldn't remember exactly what she'd said to Ryan, and worse, that she had no witnesses to pump for information. Considering where her brain was at, she wasn't going to chance a lack of filter tonight.

Once dinner arrived and she started eating her soup, crunching the noodles into it like she watched Colin do, she didn't have space in her head to worry about Ryan or Clark or anything else because her lips, tongue, and gum tissue were on fire. She tried to be a good sport, but Colin eventually noticed her nose turning red and her eyes watering so bad, she had to wipe them with her napkin.

He laughed and offered to order a new soup without spice, but she declined. Maybe it was some sick desire to self-destruct, but the plasma in her mouth felt oddly good. When she finished her soup, every part of her seemed to buzz, her insides humming with warmth and her brain less foggy.

"Is this what microdosing feels like?" Aelin wiped her tingling lips with her napkin. Maybe she would've liked that retreat after all.

Colin's grin widened. "I can't believe you ate the whole thing."

"She's a masochist." Megan twirled her Pad Thai noodles on her fork.

It wasn't too far from the truth. Why else would she have taken Clark back after he'd cheated the first time?

Aelin laughed, her head feeling lighter than it had in months. "C'mon, you know I'm only into spanking."

Megan nearly choked on her water, then eyed her bowl suspiciously. "What the hell was in the soup? Comments like that usually only come out of you after ten o'clock."

"Yeah, watch out. After ten o'clock Aelin is feisty." Tag nudged Colin.

Colin leaned back in his chair. "Well, we're definitely not ending the night here, then."

Aelin's pulse quickened as his eyes tracked over her face, dropping just below her jaw, then lifting to her eyes. He *was* handsome. She placed her napkin in her lap. "Ten o'clock Aelin doesn't come out much anymore, I'm afraid. She has an early bedtime now."

Megan scoffed. "You have a babysitter, right? And it's not like you have to get up super early."

Aelin opened her mouth to give a rebuttal, then stopped. She did have a babysitter. Ryan had even said she shouldn't worry about timing. The idea of showing up later than expected at Ryan's sent a wave rippling under her skin.

She was having a good time, wasn't she? If she showed up late, Ryan would also know she'd been having a good time.

Aelin exhaled. "What are you suggesting?"

"There's a folk music festival at Prince's Island. Goes 'til eleven I think." Colin raised an eyebrow.

Aelin pulled out her phone and typed a quick message to Ryan.

> Hey, dinner's over, but we're thinking about stopping by the music festival. Okay to be out a bit longer?

. . .

She watched her screen, and her heart flipped when she saw the "Read at 7:59" notification appear beneath her message. The three dots appeared, then evaporated. They started again, and that time a message came through.

Sounds good. Girls are doing great.

The top on whatever had been building inside her twisted off, and her shoulders dropped. "I'm all set."

Colin nodded approvingly. "Mango and sticky rice first, though."

———

The night air was crisp, a perfect beginning of summer evening. They walked the short distance to the park, following the sounds of live music and laughter. Strings of fairy lights hung from the trees, and for a split second, Aelin fell in love with the vision of a different version of herself.

Someone who fit perfectly there. Who knew about folk music and had festivals on her calendar and who said things like, *"There's nothing like hearing it live."* She would have a nose ring and a tattoo of some deep quote by Aristotle scrawled on her ribs in cursive, and she'd hold hands with men she barely knew because human connection was that imperative for maintaining her feminine energy.

The idea was so intoxicating she didn't even flinch when

Colin slipped his palm against hers and asked her to dance. They wove past people sitting on the grass and joined the couples swaying in the makeshift aisles.

Colin slid his arms around her waist, and she looped hers around his neck. "I'm glad we got a do-over."

Aelin nodded, her voice breathy. "Me, too."

He laughed low in her ear. "Megan told me a lot about you, but I think she undersold you."

Aelin's cheeks warmed, the sentiment so flattering she didn't quite know what to do with it. And then, for the first time all night, Bailey settled back at the forefront of her mind, and the fun-loving, fictional woman she'd been constructing disappeared in a poof of smoke.

Colin sighed. "I love this band. They're from Okotoks. I saw them at a bar downtown a few months ago and got hooked."

Aelin smiled. *Of course he did.*

They danced and chatted for a few more songs, and she held his hand as they walked along the booths next to the river. At ten o'clock, they all walked back to their cars and said their good-byes. Megan and Tag did their best to escape and give her privacy with Colin, but they passed Aelin's car first. She gave him a hug, and he pecked her cheek. He asked for her number, and she gave it to him, then hopped in her car and punched in Ryan's address.

At every stoplight, the music festival vibes seemed to be digested a little more by the realization that she'd left Ryan watching her daughter until after ten o'clock. What had she been thinking? He'd signed up for a couple of hours, not four.

Her stomach flipped as she parked and jogged to the front door of Ryan's place. She appreciated that his car was in the driveway, so she didn't have to obsessively check whether she had the right house.

She knocked, and after a few long seconds, the door swung open. Ryan stood on the other side of the storm door, his hair tied back, wearing joggers and a T-shirt that made his grey eyes look more blue than usual.

He pushed the door open and motioned for her to come in. "Hey."

"Hey." Aelin kept her voice low, matching his volume. "I'm so sorry. I didn't even realize how late it was."

Ryan shrugged, but his stance was tense. "I told you to take your time." Aelin nodded, scanning the living room. "The girls are asleep in Amaya's room. They were reading in there. Didn't last long."

Aelin's throat tightened. "Oh. Okay."

Ryan turned and walked past the couch into the kitchen. His house had an open ranch floor plan. She loved the minimalist lighting and muted colours on the walls. It felt very . . . him. Though she couldn't put her finger on why.

"Do you want a cup of tea?" he asked. "I just heated up some water."

Aelin nodded, not sure why she was accepting the offer when it was already so late. But Bailey was already sleeping. It wasn't going to make a difference whether she left right then or in ten minutes.

She took off her heels, set her purse next to them, then walked into the kitchen that was illuminated only by a glow from the under-counter lighting and took a seat on one of the stools at the island.

Ryan pulled another mug from the cupboard and filled it with boiling water from the kettle. "I've got peppermint or apple spice."

"Mm. Peppermint."

He nodded and opened a tea bag, then reached across the counter and set the mug in front of her. He repeated the same process with his own tea, then stood across from her, playing with the string as it steeped. "So. Good date?"

A flush crept up her neck. She nodded. "Great."

Ryan's jaw ticked. "Great."

Aelin blew on her tea. "You say that like you're surprised."

"No." He kept his eyes trained on his mug.

She tightened her grip on the ceramic handle. "'No' as in you're not surprised or 'no' as in you didn't say it that way?"

"Does it matter?" He looked up, his eyes stormy.

Aelin's hackles rose. Yeah. It mattered. She just couldn't figure out why. Why should she care if he saw her as someone who could have a good time on a date?

She took a sip of her tea, the mint cooling against her irritated lips. "Probably not."

They sat in silence for a moment. Ryan was the one to break the silence. "I don't remember the last time I went on a date."

She blew out a breath. "Over a year for me."

"Last one with your ex?"

She nodded. "Unfortunately."

His lips curved at the corners. "Were there any good moments?"

Aelin pulled on the tab for her tea bag. "When I was growing up, my mom always used those plastic grocery bags in our washroom trash cans. She had a bag full of them under the sink. Then when I was sixteen, my sister and I went and stayed with our uncle for a month over the summer to work at his vet clinic. A little summer job. My aunt bought these bags that fit the cans perfectly, and they had some kind of deodorizer in them. I stared at them every time I went in the washroom, amazed at how they didn't get pulled or wadded up on the edge of the can." She laid the string back along the side of the mug. "I don't know if that makes sense, but my marriage was kind of like that."

Ryan pressed his hands into the countertop. "Nobody talks about it."

Aelin nodded and took a sip. "My parents divorced when I was little. I didn't have any idea what the options were."

"Maybe you should've looked in more trash cans," Ryan murmured, and Aelin snorted, nearly sloshing her tea over the side of her mug. *Maybe she should get that scrawled on her ribs.*

"What about you?" she asked.

Ryan drew a deep breath. "Lots of good moments. I think we were happy." He tapped his finger. "Sometimes I think it would've been easier if Kara would've died." Aelin dropped her eyes, and Ryan hissed air through his teeth. "Shit. Sorry, I shouldn't have said that."

She frowned. "Why not? I wish my ex was dead all the time."

Ryan dragged a hand over his hair, tugging at his bun. "Yeah. Well."

Aelin understood what he was getting at. He was still married, and his wife hadn't chosen to blow their marriage apart. Her heart picked up speed. "I took him back the first time because I'd done a shit-ton of research on narcissism. How it's a disease, you know? I told myself he was sick, and I'd promised to stick by him in sickness and in health."

Ryan stilled, his mug halfway to his lips.

Aelin continued, "Then, one day when I had a panic attack in the shower, I realized that staying in the marriage would make it impossible for me to support anyone in sickness or health. I couldn't take care of myself, let alone get Bailey chicken noodle soup when she stayed home from school with the flu."

Ryan watched her, unblinking.

"Anyway. You didn't sign up for the after-ten-o'clock version of me." She took a long drink from her mug and set it on the counter. "I should grab Bailey and get going."

He gave a tight nod, then left his tea and led her down the hall. A nightlight on the dresser gave off a soft, pink glow, making the girls look like cherubs. Aelin knelt down next to Bailey, trying to figure out the best way to hoist her into her arms.

"Here. I can do it," Ryan whispered.

Aelin stood and moved to the side as Ryan dropped into a crouch and pulled Bailey into his arms like she was a ragdoll, cradling her head against his chest. He kept the blanket wrapped over her as he stood and turned toward her.

Holy hell. The sleeves of his T-shirt stretched across his biceps as he smoothed Bailey's hair from her cheek with his thumb.

She didn't realize she was staring until Ryan glanced between her and the door. *Right.* She spun and exited, nearly smashing her shin against the door frame. She worked to swallow the lump that was suddenly clogging her throat as she strode to the front and slipped her shoes back on. She opened the door, walked straight to her car, and didn't look back.

CHAPTER

Fourteen

AELIN AND BAILEY stood on the crowded sidewalk, the morning sun already beating down on their shoulders. Bailey tugged on her shirt, eyes wide as the band marched down the street at the start of the Canada Day parade. Floats adorned in red and white crept down the street, people waved Canadian flags, and children darted past the curb to collect the candy that was most certainly cracked and crumbled inside the wrappers.

Aelin leaned down to Bailey. "Remember when we went to the Rose Parade with Grandma and Grandpa?"

Bailey nodded. "Yeah, there weren't any bagpipes."

Aelin laughed. "True, definitely lacking in bagpipes." She looked back at the procession of men in kilts.

"I want to be in a parade." Bailey grabbed a sucker that landed next to her shoe.

Aelin smiled, ruffling her daughter's hair. "Ooh, you guys should do it as a choir next year!"

Bailey beamed at her. "Do you think they'd let us?"

Aelin shrugged. "Wouldn't hurt to ask."

After they were hot and sweaty from walking through the Indigenous Artisans Market and watching a few performances on the main stage, they made their way to Megan's house.

The backyard was a welcome haven from the crowds at the Confluence and the parking lot on all the streets leading from the East Village. Tag stood in front of the grill manning the burgers, and Aelin took her dill pickle salad to join the rest of the sides on the picnic table.

"Glad you made it!" Megan greeted them with a bright smile and a wave. Her hair was pulled back into a ponytail, and she wore a sleeveless blouse and denim shorts that showed off her somehow already-tan legs.

Aelin gave her a hug, and Tag waved from the grill. "Hope you're hungry. I put on extra burgers."

Aelin nodded. "Starving. Thanks for having us." She followed Megan into the kitchen and helped transport paper products outside as neighbours and friends began arriving, then set up camping chairs and jumped into small talk with some of the people she'd met last year.

Bailey disappeared after only eating half her burger and some chips and spent the rest of the afternoon playing dodgeball on the neighbour's trampoline. After dinner was put away and a few wine coolers later, Aelin and Bailey walked with the others along the sidewalk toward the park.

It was only seven thirty. They still had three-plus hours to wait until fireworks but there were horseshoe pits, a playground, and a disc golf course to keep them busy. They played and chatted until it started to get dark, then staked out their spot on the hill.

Megan was talking with some women from her neighbour-hood, so Aelin pulled out her phone and scrolled to her sister's contact. After a couple of rings, Mariah's voice came through.

"Happy Canada Day!"

Aelin laughed. "I know you don't think it's a real holiday. You don't have to pretend."

"They still have the queen on their money. That's all I'm saying."

Aelin stood and walked up the hill a ways. "Ugh. I miss you. Why is it still two weeks until we get to hang out?"

"Okay . . . speaking of which. I have some bad news."

Aelin's stomach dropped. "If you tell me you're not coming—"

"No! No, we're coming for sure, but Blake dropped out."

Aelin groaned. "Seriously? He's known about this for over six months." Blake, their youngest brother, wasn't flaky, and he loved Flathead more than both of them combined. "What happened?"

Mariah sighed. "He got some opportunity to backpack in Switzerland."

Aelin pursed her lips. Okay. So that was a pretty damn good excuse. "Are his friends still coming?"

"No, they decided it would be weird if he wasn't there."

Not wrong. But that left her and Mariah footing the bill for five cabins between the two of them. Aelin's pulse thrummed in her ears. That was three hundred a night times five. Times seven nights.

Holy shit. Her breath came in quick bursts.

"Stop it, Aelin. I can hear you starting to hyperventilate."

She held her breath. "We've passed the cancellation date."

"I know, but we can find someone else to come," Mariah said flippantly.

"Who else? We've already asked everyone we know."

Mariah sighed. "Not everyone."

"Okay, everyone we *like*." She'd asked Megan and Tag, some of her friends from college, and even a friend of one of her roommates who she'd met once last spring who seemed fairly not annoying. "We couldn't fill the last cabin, and now we have to fill three?"

"I know. But I'm going to work on this. I promise. Mom and Dad said—"

Aelin groaned. The last thing she wanted was her parent's friends to stay next to them and judge her obvious single status. But she couldn't afford this. There was no way in hell she could pay half that bill if they didn't get someone in there. She ran a hand through her hair, the perfect summer lake week slipping through her fingers in exchange for a geriatric couple's retreat.

"Don't worry. We'll have the boat and tubes and Leo even bought new kids' skis. It's going to be amazing. I'll work on some friends here. We'll fill them. Or at least the two that Blake was supposed to take."

Aelin nodded. Could they make Blake pay his share if they couldn't cover it? He had committed, but it wasn't like they'd gotten it in writing. They'd gone to Flathead every summer for the past four years and never had a problem.

"I'm sorry to stress you out. I know Clark's being an asshat about child support."

Aelin scoffed. "Understatement of the year." She drew a deep breath and exhaled. "How are the kids?"

"They're good. A month into summer, and I don't want to kill them yet." Something clattered, and Mariah cursed under her breath.

"I can't believe they've already been out a month."

"When you only have to learn about American history, it saves a lot of time."

Aelin laughed, then saw Bailey running up the hill toward her. "I've got to run, almost time for fireworks."

"Love you."

"Love you most." Aelin dropped the phone and walked back to her seat. "You going to call Amaya?" Aelin asked as Bailey reached for the backpack.

She nodded and pulled out the tablet. "I don't know where she's watching the show."

Aelin sat in her chair just as Megan and Tag sat down next to her.

Megan sighed. "This is the perfect night. I haven't even seen a mosquito."

"Because they're all attacking me." Tag grunted and slapped at his leg.

Megan leaned in. "He eats more sugar. I'm pretty sure that's why."

Tag let out an exasperated sigh. "That's not why. That doesn't make any sense."

Aelin reached out and smoothed Bailey's hair as she clicked the button to join the call with Amaya. The call connected, and Amaya's face popped up on the screen, her eyes sparkling with excitement. "Girl! Happy Canada Day!"

"Look at this sunset." Bailey turned the screen around to show Amaya the pink clouds above the trees.

Aelin's heart twinged. They sounded so grown up.

"I know, look at this." Amaya turned her screen, and Aelin glanced over to see the sky over the Confluence stage where they'd been that morning.

"We were there earlier!" Bailey announced excitedly.

"My dad and I found a great spot. It's packed, but we have a perfect view of the stage." Amaya settled the tablet in front of her, and Aelin's eyes snagged on the left side of the screen.

Ryan was there on the quilt. He wore a red polo shirt and a backward hat, his hands on the grass, propping him up as he leaned back.

"Aelin, did you hear me?" Megan's voice cut through her thoughts, and Aelin blinked, tearing her eyes away from the screen.

"Sorry, what?"

"I was saying that Tag's brother is trying to set their sister up with this guy who used to do adult review shows in Vegas."

Aelin blinked. "I've never known anyone who did adult reviews in general."

Megan laughed. "I keep begging him to send me pictures."

"Shirt on or off?" Aelin blushed when she realized Bailey wasn't on mute and she was in the frame. Ryan glanced up at the camera. *Had he heard that?*

Megan kept talking, but Aelin's eyes drifted back to the screen. Ryan was in a new position, sitting cross-legged. The screen tipped and angled so she could only see . . . the middle of him. His legs and part of his torso. He reached over and grabbed his water bottle, lifted it out of the frame, then set it back on the ground.

Aelin pretended to be watching something in the distance, realizing this wasn't an *I can't see his face, so he can't see me* situation. He could absolutely be watching the screen even though his face was higher than the camera.

Aelin wanted to interrupt Megan and tell her everything about Ryan and his wife Kara, but she couldn't ask Bailey to mute her tablet in the middle of her conversation with Amaya.

She couldn't wrap her mind around what she would do if she were in his shoes. Looking at Ryan, she wanted to tell him to move on with his life, but she knew it wasn't that simple. If she'd been married to someone she loved?

That idea was equally ludicrous. She didn't even know what that would look like, and even being married to someone like Clark, she hadn't been able to turn off the idea of love or the commitments she'd made like a faucet. It had to be killed. Slowly.

She knew exactly what he meant the other night in his kitchen. Death would've been difficult, but at least he would have closure. If there was no way she was getting better, her diagnosis put them both in the worst kind of limbo.

Still. It didn't seem right that he should have to give up his entire life. That he should deny himself the possibility of starting over.

Something fluttered in her chest. If he did start over . . . what kind of woman would he want to start over with?

Something shifted in her field of vision, and she glanced up. Her whole body went rigid as Clark set up a chair next to Megan and Tag.

"You didn't invite me this year." He smirked.

Megan's eyes flicked to Bailey sitting a few feet away and smiled tightly. "I didn't know you'd be around."

He laughed. "Because you asked?"

Megan folded her arms over her chest and shot Aelin an apologetic glance. Aelin's heart beat like a rabbit. This was her mistake. She shouldn't have come here with Bailey knowing they'd come here the past couple of years with Clark.

"I'm so glad this worked out, though, because I needed to give you information for our daddy-daughter date next time. I need you to pick up Amaya after."

Aelin ground her teeth. Of course he did. That Saturday was the day before they were leaving town, which meant she couldn't say a damn word about this request. He was being generous and letting her take Amaya for the week, missing his normal weekend with her. So now she had to do whatever he wanted.

"Just text me the address," she said.

Clark reached out a hand. "Here. I'll type in the time and place on your calendar."

She frowned. "Uh, you can just—"

"Aelin, please, don't be difficult about this. It'll be easier to type it in for you. There are some instructions for finding the place." Clark's tone made her want to strangle him.

Bailey looked up from her tablet, and Aelin smiled tightly. "Sure. Makes sense." She swiped open her calendar and clicked on a new event, then handed it to him. Her heart jammed into her throat as she watched his fingers on her screen. It looked like he was typing. Was he swiping or entering information?

Aelin started to sweat. "I think—"

"Damn it, I accidentally deleted it." He looked up at her and smiled. "Can I make a new one quickly?"

"Why don't I—"

He waved her off. "Already done. It'll be quick."

Aelin's hands were shaking by the time he handed her phone

back. She inspected the entry. It showed nine o'clock at some address in the southwest. "Clark, that's a long drive."

He shrugged. "We're going to ride horses."

Bailey gasped and turned her head. "Horses? Really?"

Clark grinned at her, then stood and picked up his chair. "I'm going to move a little closer up." He shot Aelin a look before taking his chair down the hill and disappearing into the moving shadows.

Glittering light shot into the sky ahead of them.

"They're starting!" Bailey lifted up her tablet and flipped the camera view around for Amaya.

Aelin dragged in a breath as Megan's hand landed on her shoulder. "Such an asshole," she whispered, and Aelin let out a ragged laugh.

Bailey smiled back at her, and she snapped a few pictures, then scooted down to sit next to her and take a selfie together. She slipped her arm around Bailey and watched the show, listening to the synced music on Tag's radio behind them.

Bailey stared in awe at the finale. "Are you cold, Mom?"

Aelin nodded and gave a small smile. *Not cold.* The shaking happened anytime Clark was around. She couldn't stop it but knew from past experience that it would fade in another hour or so. *She was so weak.* The thought pounded through her like a gavel.

Cheers rang up around the park, and she stood to pick up her chair. As she went to put her phone in her purse, she saw a message on her screen from her lawyer, Jules.

Check your email ASAP

The blood rushed from her face as she stopped and scrolled to her inbox. She clicked on the message from Julie.

. . .

Subject: Urgent Update Re: Division of Assets/Property Settlement

She scanned the message, bile rising in her throat. *Requesting the sale of property as part of division of assets . . . spouse unable to financially maintain . . . option to buy out partner's share in property . . . August 10th . . .*

Her vision began to blur. Clark was trying to force her to sell the house or buy him out. He knew she couldn't do either, and she knew exactly how he planned to use that to his advantage.

Fifteen

RYAN PARKED in Aelin's driveway and turned to Amaya. "Okay, you good?"

Amaya yawned and unbuckled her seatbelt. Ryan had felt guilty waking her up at six, but she knew it was only two weeks of this. He needed to be at the rink at three, which meant he had to start work at seven instead of nine.

He left the engine idling and got out to walk her to the front door. "Remember to be respectful and listen to Aelin, okay?"

Amaya rolled her eyes. "I'm not five, Dad."

Ryan let out a puff of air. "Right."

They walked up the steps to the front door, and Ryan texted instead of knocking since Bailey was most likely still asleep.

It only took a few seconds for Aelin to open the door. She gave a small wave and moved to the side so Amaya could walk into the hall.

Ryan blinked. He'd seen her at all times of day and night, and, not that he was an expert or anything, something looked off. She was in cotton shorts and thick socks, a robe tied around her middle. It wasn't that. Was she trying to hide her face?

She moved to close the door, but he put out a hand. "Hey."

Aelin's lips pinched. She didn't turn to face him, instead messing with the side of her welcome mat with her socked foot. "Have a great day." She pushed on the door again, and this time, Ryan full-on palmed it.

"Aelin, what—"

"Please don't, Ryan." Aelin turned her back on him. "I'm fine."

"You don't seem fine."

She waved a hand over her shoulder. "It's nothing anyone else can help with, and I promise it won't affect our plans today."

Ryan knew he shouldn't, but the urge to reach out and touch her was all-consuming. He gave in and put a hand on her shoulder. As soon as he made contact, Aelin spun toward him, burying her head in his chest and wrapping her arms around his waist.

She felt exactly as he'd imagined. He didn't realize he'd imagined it until her hands pressed against his lower back and the top of her head nestled beneath his chin. That was where she fit. Exactly right.

He rubbed his hand over her back, parts of him noticing instantly that she wasn't wearing a bra. He reeled that thought back in only to be slammed with the scent of coconut in her hair.

He didn't say anything. He didn't think about the fact that he was supposed to be heading downtown. He didn't think about what Amaya would think if she rounded the corner and saw him holding another woman like that.

No part of his rational brain fired. He only knew that it felt right to have her there. She was hurting. So many people in his life were hurting. The idea that he could alleviate it for even a few seconds made him feel invincible.

"Clark's trying to sell the house." Aelin sniffed, her breathing beginning to return to normal.

Ryan swallowed. "Can he do that?"

She nodded against his chest, then pushed back, her cheeks flushed. They stained an even deeper pink when she saw the dark spots on his lavender-collared shirt. "Shit, I'm so sorry." Aelin hunted for a tissue, but Ryan stopped her.

"They'll dry. I still have to drive into work. It's fine."

Aelin wrapped her arms around herself, her eyes red-rimmed and puffy. "I'm sorry. I found out last night, and I didn't sleep much."

He shoved his hands in his pockets. "Take a nap today."

She bit her lower lip and nodded. "Yeah. I might have time this afternoon." She finally looked up and met his eyes. "Thank you."

"No problem. I can't imagine."

Aelin sighed. "Yeah. I think you probably can." Her eyes flickered to the floor, then back to his. "Anyway . . ."

Ryan nodded. "Sorry. I'll—have a good day. I mean, not a good day, but . . . you know what I mean."

Aelin's mouth quirked at the corner. "I will."

Ryan left, pulled out of the driveway, and drove straight to his office on fourth. He didn't stop for Tim's like he'd planned, which was fine. They had coffee in the office, and while it wasn't exactly good, it would deliver caffeine to his bloodstream.

He parked in the garage under the building, then swiped his key card and walked into the lobby. Somehow he managed to step out of the elevator on the fifth floor just a few minutes after seven. He waved to the security guard and headed to his desk, flipping on the light switch.

The hum of the fluorescent lights filled the room, and Ryan sat down, pulling up his email. He had a list of things to do a mile long for the contamination mitigation, and he started going down the list.

He'd spent the last few nights poring over their contracts with the city, trying to find a loophole that would let them off the hook, but it was airtight. They were responsible for the cleanup, and that meant more work for him and more money lost for Apex. He knew which one Marc would be most concerned with.

Ryan pulled up the latest report and started reading through it, his mind already spinning with ideas.

He was so engrossed in his work that he didn't hear the door open. "You look like you just got neutered."

Ryan looked up to see Chris standing in the doorway. "Couldn't finish it. Balls were too big for the incision."

Chris snorted. "Hockey camp starts today, eh?"

"If Marc doesn't rip me a new one by three." Ryan took a drink of his tepid coffee.

"Get in line on that one. Your asshole will probably stay intact until at least Wednesday."

He set his mug down. "Perfect. You need anything?"

Chris shook his head. "Heading to Pips for lunch if you're feeling fancy."

Ryan stuck out his foot and pulled up his pant leg to reveal pink socks. "I had a good feeling when I got dressed this morning."

Chris laughed. "I'll get Morton and Sask to come along."

Ryan scoffed. "If it's not a date, I'm out." He waved as Chris walked down the hall and returned to his spreadsheet, but his head had travelled far from remediation efforts.

He picked up his phone and swiped to his messages, tapping on Aelin's contact.

Hey, dinner's over, but we're thinking about stopping by the music festival. Okay to be out a bit longer?

He looked at his response, remembering what he'd wanted to type instead. *Hell, no.* Offering to watch Bailey while she went out was the right thing to do, but he didn't like it. He'd paced around the house all night finding things to clean and fix, and it still hadn't eased the straight-out-of-the-dryer feeling in his chest.

Getting that real-time update and then watching her sip her tea across the counter had been the reason he'd gone to the rink first thing on Canada Day. Amaya was with her grandparents at the Crossfield parade, so Sean, Tyler, André, and Suraj had all met him for a line-scraper practice. By the time he left, he'd felt a bit more in control of himself.

Only to have to sit and watch Aelin on his daughter's tablet for an hour and pretend he wasn't paying attention every time she reached up and tucked hair behind her ear or laughed at whoever the hell she was talking with. *Guy from the music festival?*

Then there was that morning. The scent of her still lingered on his shirt, and each time he caught a whiff, he needed another minute before he could stand up and walk out from behind his desk.

Okay. He leaned back in his chair, linking his hands behind his head. He'd known he was attracted to her from the start, which was why he'd implemented his plan to keep a distance. He'd mostly succeeded in that, and now that he was in camp, it would be easier, wouldn't it?

She'd be dropping Amaya off at the rink, so he'd only see her one-on-one in the morning. He could stay on the street. Wave from the car.

Even as he said it, his body revolted. But what was the alternative? Keep getting closer to her, and then what? He couldn't do anything about it. He wouldn't cheat on Kara. Having friendships with women wasn't a big deal, but based on how tight his pants were, he didn't anticipate his body cooperating in this situation.

Ryan reached for the photo of him, Kara, and Amaya that sat

on his desk. He ran his finger over the ridges of the frame, then slid it back into place and turned back to his spreadsheet.

———

The drive to the Carpenter's Ice Centre was a blur, not because he was zoned out, but because he sped like a banshee. He pulled into the parking lot, grabbed his gear, and jogged to the entrance.

Inside, the rink was already buzzing with activity. Parents and kids milled about, their voices echoing off the cinder block walls. The smell of ice and rubber mats sent him straight back to practices as a kid, no matter how many times he'd set foot there as an adult.

He made his way to the Gold rink and waved at Country, already in his gear standing at the benches behind the boards with a clipboard.

"Hey, bud. Sorry I'm late." Ryan headed for the locker room.

"You've got plenty of time to get suited."

It was true, but since he'd been the one to spearhead this project, he didn't want to be the one dragging down the ship.

Tyler and Boyd were in the locker room, lacing up their skates.

Tyler looked up. "Ready to bust some asses?"

"Busting all the asses. Let's make them puke."

Boyd laughed and stood. "Is Amaya coming tonight?"

Ryan nodded. "I can't tell if she's excited or not."

"She's been on skates since she was three. I'm sure she'll be fine," Tyler said.

Ryan dropped his bag on the bench and started stripping down. "She's just . . . I don't know . . . turning more girly all of a sudden."

Tyler grabbed his helmet off the bench. "Hasn't she always been like that?"

"A little. I guess. But now she just wants to spend time with friends."

Tyler laughed. "Ah. She's ditching you. That's the problem." He walked over and clapped a hand on his shoulder. "Hate to tell you this, bud, but that's not being girly. That's just growing up."

Boyd laughed. "When you have kids, bud, then you can come chirp at him about what's growing up and what isn't. Until then, grab a sippy cup, and leave the parenting-talk to the ones wrangling the ankle-biters."

Ryan saluted him, and Tyler flipped him the bird. Tyler and Boyd left the locker room, and Ryan was quick to follow. He was adjusting the board for passing drills when he saw a familiar face bouncing up and down behind the glass. He grinned and skated over to the entrance to the rink, noting the smirk on Country's face as he pointed his head directly at Aelin and then back at him. Subtle.

"You made it." Ryan held out his arms, and Amaya flew into them. "How was your day?"

She grinned up at him. "Amazing. We made a fairy garden."

Ryan looked up at Aelin. She looked better. Her hair was swept back in a braid and her eyes didn't look swollen. "Fairy garden?"

Aelin shrugged. "I had some craft supplies in the closet. The girls got creative."

"One of the houses has lights!" Amaya's eyes gleamed, and for a moment, Ryan could barely breathe. He would never have thought to do something like that with her. He'd spent an embarrassing amount of time on Pinterest searching up ideas for what to do with little girls over the past three years, but he usually opted for things that didn't require walking into a store with cinnamon brooms at the entrance.

"Go get dressed, okay?" He straightened as Amaya scurried back to the piles of equipment along the back wall.

"That's all for the camp?"

Ryan nodded. "One of the main reasons kids don't participate in hockey is the cost of equipment. My teammates and I ran a donation and swap centre last winter. We have enough for fifteen kids, so hopefully the twelve in the camp will be able to find something that fits."

"And they'll use it for the whole week?" She wrinkled her nose.

Ryan laughed. "You've never played hockey?"

"I played roller hockey back home."

"Which is?"

"California."

The whole conversation happened so fast, he'd forgotten he wasn't supposed to be doing this. *Doing what, exactly?* He could be having this conversation with any random stranger. He was in a public place. His friends were right there on the ice.

"We lived at the end of a cul-de-sac. Our neighbours had four boys."

"Chaos."

Aelin grinned, and her eyes glittered in the overhead lights. "Absolutely."

"Dad!" Amaya came running back over, dragging the gear she'd found. "Can Bailey stay for the camp?"

Aelin's smile faded. "Oh, no, Bails. I didn't sign you up."

"That's alright. If she wants to stay—"

"I don't think—"

"Yes!" Bailey nodded her head emphatically. "I know how to skate, Mom."

Aelin opened her mouth, then closed it. He could see the wheels turning in her head. "I didn't bring your skates."

"You could just go home and get them." Bailey stood with her hands clasped behind her back, and Ryan turned his face so she wouldn't see him grinning.

"You think this is funny?"

Ryan turned to find Aelin staring right at him. "Only because it's not happening to me right now."

Aelin motioned for Bailey to come closer. She lowered her voice. "I know this sounds fun, but I didn't sign you up for this. It costs money, and—"

"She can stay for free." Ryan didn't even think before blurting it out.

Aelin turned. "Not exactly helping."

He nodded. "Sorry. I didn't—"

"It's not that I don't want her to stay, but I don't expect you to offer me a discount."

"That's more than a discount," Amaya said. "That's a hundred percent off."

"Thank you, Amaya," Ryan muttered, hoping the other guys didn't hear her piercing voice echoing across the ice. They wouldn't care if he offered Bailey a slot, but they'd definitely connect the dots between a free entry to camp and the fact the kid he'd offered it to was Aelin's.

Aelin looked back at Bailey. "The house is twenty minutes away. You'd miss the whole first hour of camp if I went back and got your skates."

Ryan glanced up at the clock above the rink. "How about this. Why don't you join us for camp next week? That will give you time to sign the waivers and get your gear in order. Your mom won't have to drive back and forth. Then Amaya can help me out this week and you two can hang out as camp kids next week?"

Bailey considered this. "I guess that could work."

Aelin let out a breath and mouthed, "Thank you."

Amaya's shoulders slumped, but she was appeased enough by his solution that she didn't argue. She walked over and gave Bailey a hug. "See you tomorrow." When Aelin and Bailey were out of earshot, Amaya turned to him. "Can you help me put this on?"

Ryan looked down at his hands and flipped them back and forth.

Amaya scoffed. "I know I have hands, Dad, but it'll go faster if you help."

He grinned. "Only if you help me put out cones."

She gave him a thumbs-up, and he stepped off the ice to help her.

"You know the week after hockey camp?" Amaya asked, her voice oddly high-pitched.

"Yes." Ryan was wary.

"I know you don't have work off because we're taking the next week off for vacation, right? That's what it says on the calendar."

Ryan frowned. He didn't realize she'd been looking at that. "That was the plan, but—"

"I was thinking I could go to the lake."

Ryan pulled back to look at her. "You could go to the lake? What lake?"

Amaya pulled the shoulder pads over her head. "I wouldn't go by myself. I could go with Aelin and Bailey."

That rang a bell. *Right.* Her vacation. The reason he'd switched his week at work. Aelin had said it was because they were going down to Flathead with her family. "I don't think you can just invite yourself along to a family vacation."

"I didn't invite myself. Bailey invited me." She stepped into the shorts Ryan held out for her.

"Bailey's not in charge."

Amaya shrugged. "Aelin was right there. She didn't say no."

"Probably being polite."

Amaya's expression clouded. "Why are you being grumpy about this? You're going to be working, and what am I going to do? I don't want to go to grandma and grandpa's all week. I love their house, but Bailey's going to a huge lake! Her uncle has a boat, and they're going to go tubing and do campfires, and I've always wanted to learn how to water ski, and—"

"Amaya." Ryan's tone was sharper than he intended. He drew a breath and sat back on his haunches. "Sorry, I didn't mean to snap. I was going to wait to tell you this, but I switched my week off so I would be home the week that Aelin's gone. I was thinking—"

"That's perfect!" Amaya's eyes lit up. "We could go to the lake together!"

Sixteen

AELIN SHOWED up at the rink on day two of hockey camp with a knot in her stomach. Ryan hadn't come to the door that morning, just waved from the car, which she hadn't thought much of until she'd heard Amaya and Bailey talking over breakfast.

He said people don't just join family vacations, but why not? He says he wants to go on a road trip, but it would just be me and him.

Then there had been a lot of whispering. Whispering was never good.

Aelin had tried to pull the information out of them when they were at the library that afternoon, but both girls insisted they didn't know what she was talking about. She finally gave up when she got another slew of forms in her email inbox and had to pull together every scrap of evidence she could think of to fight Clark on his outright attack on her in mediation.

He wanted to put the house up for sale on August tenth. It was a ridiculous request, but one she knew he could get away with. She didn't have the financial means to keep the house. Yes, she had a job now that paid the mortgage, but the taxes were high, and she hadn't paid the homeowners insurance. Since Clark had made his income look laughable, she couldn't request that he pay for those things, especially when he didn't have fifty-fifty custody during the school year. Having Bailey was the goal. But having Bailey also put her in a precarious situation where finances were concerned.

By the time she got to the rink, her brain was fried. Amaya jogged off to find her gear, and Bailey ran to the glass. Aelin followed, looking out over the rink and locking onto Ryan as he glided over the ice. He had two kids following in his ice tracks like ducklings.

Aelin turned to Amaya. "I thought the camp didn't start until three thirty."

Amaya looked up. "It doesn't, but he always does this."

"Does what?" Bailey asked.

"Finds kids who need help. When I was doing skating lessons, we'd always do free skate for a half hour after. Dad would have kids lining up to do lessons with him." Amaya found her gear and stacked it next to the bench.

Aelin smiled. "During free skate?"

Amaya nodded, and Aelin turned back to see Ryan cheering with his hands over his head.

"And the crowd goes wild!" He glided with one foot in front of the other in a perfect arc. "Let's try it again, this time, our turns are going to be tighter."

Aelin was fairly sure she spontaneously started ovulating. "Okay, let's get going." She spun from the glass and headed to the door.

With Ryan skating circles in her head, she didn't think twice about how simple it was to convince Bailey to leave compared to the day before. Bailey didn't say a word, only waved to Amaya and followed her to the front.

"Thanks for being onboard with waiting for next week to do hockey." Aelin pushed through the main door of the rink.

"You're welcome." Bailey walked along beside her. "Mom, I was thinking."

"Okay . . ."

"We haven't been to that ice cream place you love in a long time."

Aelin's brow furrowed. "Which one?"

"The one with the guy's name."

They crossed the street and walked toward her car in the back row of the parking lot. Guy's name. She flipped through her mental list of places. "Oh, Made by Marcus?"

Bailey's eyes lit up. "Yes! Can we go tonight after dinner?"

"I think it's a little closer to here than our house. Maybe we could—"

"No, I want to eat something healthy first, and I know you have teriyaki chicken in the Crock-Pot, right?"

Aelin's eyes narrowed. "Since when do you want to eat something healthy?"

Bailey shrugged and hopped into the passenger seat. "Since now."

Aelin drove home, and Bailey insisted on taking a shower that lasted far longer than necessary. It was five thirty by the time they finally sat down for dinner.

"Mmm." Bailey sighed as she took her first bite of chicken and rice. "This is so good, Mom."

Aelin set her fork down. "Bailey, you're kind of freaking me out."

Bailey's eyes widened. "What do you mean?"

Aelin raised an eyebrow. "You never act excited about dinner—"

"Don't use all-or-nothing statements."

Aelin pursed her lips. "Okay. You're right. It's rare for you to act excited about the food I make for dinner, and I usually have to beg you to get in the shower, especially since you saw that spider under your towel."

"I'm not afraid of them anymore. I saw that meme where it says, "What if the spider you just killed thought you were roommates.""

Aelin blinked. "Hmm. Haven't seen that one."

"Do you want me to show you?" Bailey pushed her chair back, but Aelin stopped her.

"No, just eat. You can show me later."

Bailey glanced up at the stove, then sat back down and picked up her fork. She stirred her food together, then placed and replaced her tines until she had a perfectly balanced bite.

"There's nothing you want to tell me?" Aelin tapped her fingers on the table.

Bailey shook her head. "Nope."

They ate. Bailey continued taking dainty bites, chewing so slowly, Aelin felt like that bunny in Zootopia at the DMV. And then, all of a sudden, Bailey scooped the last of her dinner into her mouth and popped up from her chair. "I'm done. Let's go for ice cream."

———

Aelin parked at the ice cream shop and nearly had a heart attack when Bailey bolted from the car, barely looking both ways before jogging to the door of Made by Marcus. When she finally caught up to her, Bailey was inspecting the ice cream flavours. "Not cool, Bailes. Parking lots are super dangerous."

"Sorry." She stared up at the sign, then asked to sample five flavours before Aelin finally cut her off.

"Just choose one or split a single scoop," Aelin instructed, then ordered her own scoop of Chinook Bee Pollen and Lavender.

Bailey walked up to the counter, then turned back to the door. "What time is it, Mom?" Her lip wobbled as Aelin took the cup of ice cream from the employee behind the counter.

"It's six thirty."

Bailey's brow creased. Her cheeks flushed pink, and tears

welled in her eyes. Then she dropped her face into her hands and began to sob.

———

Aelin stood next to Bailey in front of the park bench where Amaya and Ryan sat. Bailey was still sniffling even though she had a full cup of roasted strawberry buttermilk ice cream in her hand.

"Do you girls want to explain this?" Ryan's voice was gentle, but his jaw was tense.

"You went to the wrong location," Amaya snapped, her eyes flashing.

"I—" Ryan stopped short, running his hand through his hair. He was freshly showered from camp, and his hair hung loose to his shoulders. "You asked to go for ice cream, so we went to ice cream."

Bailey sniffed. "We thought there was only one of them."

"Obviously," Aelin muttered and took a bite of ice cream to hopefully tamp down her annoyance. "I don't understand why you didn't just ask if we could meet up."

"Because you would've said no." Amaya licked her spoon clean. Aelin frowned, but before she could open her mouth, Amaya pointed at Ryan and clarified. "He would've said no."

Ryan's neck flushed. "Amaya—"

"You don't want to talk to her." Amaya pointed at Aelin, and Ryan's expression hardened.

"That's not—"

"You stayed in the car this morning."

Ryan exhaled. "I'm not going to talk about this with you right now."

Aelin held up a hand, ignoring whatever was happening

between Amaya and Ryan at the moment. *He didn't want to talk with her?* "I don't understand. Why did you two need us to meet?"

Amaya gave her dad a sidelong glance, then looked up at Aelin. "We want to come to the lake with you."

Ryan coughed on his ice cream. "Amaya—"

"He switched his week off so it's the same as yours, and I don't want to go on a road trip. I want to go to the lake—"

"Okay. Car. Now." Ryan stood from the bench.

Amaya's eyes grew glassy. "I'm sorry, Dad. I just thought if you talked with her you'd see that they want us to come. And then I could learn how to water ski—" Her voice caught, and she nearly choked as she started crying over her ice cream cup.

Ryan set his ice cream on the bench and pulled her against his chest. He exhaled, and it sounded a lot like, "What the hell is happening right now?"

Bailey looked up at Aelin, her eyes refilling with tears. "Mom—"

"Hey, Ryan?" Aelin took her last bite of ice cream and dropped it in the trash can. "Can I talk with you for a second?" She pressed her hands into her hips and stalked toward a set of poles protruding from the ground that looked nothing like children's playground equipment.

Ryan settled Amaya on the bench, then followed after her. They stopped next to a blue spruce and stared at each other.

"Our children are psychopaths." She swallowed, her pulse jumping under her skin. All of Bailey's behaviour that day tumbled into place. The lack of resistance at dinner, the attention to time. She'd played her like a fiddle.

"Maybe goal-oriented is a better term?" Ryan put a scoop of ice cream in his mouth, and a little zing shot down her spine as he licked his spoon.

"Miscreants."

He nodded. "No hope for either of them." He scraped his cup and walked to the bin next to them, dropping it in. He moseyed back to stand in front of her. "I'm sorry about this. I think it was mostly Amaya's idea."

Aelin sighed. "No, I think Bailey might have been the instigator. She has cousins coming, but they're all older than her. The one closest to her in age is a boy, and while they always got along while she was younger, he's twelve now. I think she's nervous he'll be too cool to hang out with a little kid."

Ryan nodded. "Should we just stand here and pretend to talk for a bit? Then they'll have to accept the answer?"

Aelin wet her lips. "What is the answer?"

Ryan put a hand in his pocket. "No. I already told her it's your family vacation."

Aelin's insides started playing musical chairs to the tune of *"Ryan at the lake? Ryan in a bathing suit?"* The idea of him sitting in an Adirondack chair looking out over the water with her next to him made her brain short-circuit.

But it wasn't about that. They needed people to fill the cabins, didn't they?

"Well . . ." Aelin kicked a piece of mulch off the concrete. All the calculations she'd done to figure out exactly how many people would need to come for her to be able to pay her share of the cabin rentals flashed through her head. If they filled one more cabin, she'd be able to pay Mariah in only two installments. One at the end of July and one in August.

"Well, what?" Ryan studied her.

"It was supposed to be a family trip. It has been the past four years, but this year, my little brother bailed, and my cousin who usually comes with his family couldn't commit. So it's just my parents and my sister, but we booked six cabins.

"Okay."

Aelin swallowed hard. "So my sister Mariah and I have been scrounging for more people to fill the last three because we're on the hook for the full bill. My brother was supposed to bring some friends—anyway, it's a whole thing. We've asked around and haven't had any luck."

Ryan blinked, still watching her.

She continued, "It's three hundred a night, and we have them for the whole week. I know that's pricey, but they're private cabins right on the lake. My sister's husband has a boat—"

"Stop for just a second." Ryan's throat worked. "You're saying . . . that you're okay with us coming to the lake."

Aelin cocked her head to the side. "Well, yeah. Why wouldn't I be?"

Ryan turned and stared out into the field, then swivelled back to face her. "I don't think it's a good idea."

Aelin frowned. "Why not?"

Ryan ran a hand through his hair, and his shirt lifted, exposing a strip of his stomach over the waistband of his jeans. Aelin quickly glanced away as he lowered his arms. "We barely know each other."

Aelin scoffed. "I know I like you better than some random person my sister might invite."

"Don't be so sure about that."

Aelin took a step closer. "What is there not to like? Our girls get along great. You're . . . you, and—"

"I'm me?"

Aelin's throat went dry. "Yeah. Helpful. Nice. Not a murderer."

He blew a breath through his nose. "I'm not . . . that kind of guy."

"What kind of guy, Ryan?"

He turned, and his expression was thunderous. "A guy you want on a lake vacation."

Aelin chewed on this, trying to read between the lines. What kind of guy would she want on a lake vacation? She had no idea. Probably someone like her brother-in-law, Leo. Definitely not someone like Clark.

She exhaled. "I'm not a girl you want on lake vacations, either, okay?" Aelin paused, wondering how much she should share, but couldn't analyze fast enough to keep the words from spilling out. *He'd already seen it anyway.* "I cried all morning because I don't know if I'm going to be able to keep my house. Last week, I cried because I imagined myself in ten years living alone with at least three cats because my daughter had gone off to college, or now I'm thinking possibly prison, and I had never figured out how to trust someone again. Next week? I'll probably unlock some new life fear that is close enough to reality to be terrifying. So maybe . . ." She shook her head. "I don't know, Ryan. Maybe we were meant to cross paths. Two sad people with daughters who are begging for girl energy in their lives that we can't give on our own. Maybe we just need to be open to what the universe is throwing at us. Maybe . . ." She pursed her lips. "Maybe this isn't about us."

She started back toward the girls, then paused and turned back to him. "But if it was, maybe I'd want to figure out how to be that girl again."

Ryan exhaled. "Time might be up for me."

She watched him a moment, then continued toward the bench.

———

Aelin lay down on the bed after finally getting Bailey to sleep. It was ten thirty, and she felt like she'd just run a marathon.

She stretched out and pulled out her phone, tapping out a quick text to her sister.

I have someone who's going to take a cabin!

She couldn't believe Ryan had said yes. Both their girls had devolved into another round of tears, then chased each other like puppies, stopping only to hug their parents who were "the best ever" and making promises that they couldn't possibly keep, like "I'll never complain about anything ever again!"

Aelin waited for her sister to text back, but when she didn't see anything, walked into the washroom to brush her teeth.

I don't think it's a good idea, Ryan had said. Based on how her body responded, she knew it wasn't. It was like she was on a plane strapped to a skydiving instructor and no matter how much she protested, there was no way she *wasn't* jumping out of that plane.

She wasn't going to do anything about it. He was married, and until he decided not to be married, she wouldn't cross any lines. But it wasn't a crime to spend time together, and he obviously didn't have the same struggle with her. Just like Amaya had so aptly pointed out, Ryan didn't want to talk to her.

She picked up her phone, but instead of a message appearing on her screen, her sister's face in full Halloween makeup from the time she dressed as the Corpse Bride flashed in front of her.

"Hey," Aelin answered.

"Heeey, so, slight problem."

Aelin deflated. "Please don't say that, Mariah. I don't think I can take anymore bad news."

"No, no, sorry, it's great news. I found people for the cabins, too."

Aelin blinked. "Cabins? Plural?"

"Well, originally, I had planned to use all three—"

"Mar! You didn't tell me that! I just offered one to a friend!"

"Aelin, let me freaking finish, please! I said *originally*. But then I talked with them after I saw your message, and their teenagers aren't coming since they have a football camp or something. So they only need the two cabins."

"Okay." Aelin exhaled. "So I can still use that third one?"

"Yep, it's perfect." Mariah yelled something to one of her

kids, then came back with a "Sorry." Dishes clattered in the sink. "Who did you get to come?"

"Just a friend," Aelin said. "The guy I'm nannying for over the summer."

Mariah was silent for a beat. "Friend, huh?"

Aelin groaned. "Don't do that. If he's coming, you can *not* do that."

Mariah laughed out loud. "Okay, so he's definitely hot."

"Mar!"

"Okay, okay! I promise. I'll be on my best behaviour."

Aelin stared at her ceiling. "I'm not sure that's comforting."

"Tucker, do not—!" Mariah yelled into the speaker. "Sorry, I've got to run."

"Love you."

"Love you most."

CHAPTER
Seventeen

RYAN WAS BARELY on the ice before the chirping started.

"Hey, Ryan!" Boyd slapped his goalie stick against the ice. "You gonna spend more time skating or kissing the boards today? Figure it out, bud, we've only got an hour."

"Just practicing for when you inevitably lose an edge in the crease, Boyd," Ryan shot back, gliding past. "Figured I'd get in some sympathy falls now."

"Always losing in the crease," André snorted, gliding by on the right.

Tyler, already bent over his stick and stretching his hamstrings, shook his head. "Ryan's going to make us all cookies when we're done, too."

Ryan smirked, "Only if Suraj here stops puck-chasing long enough to learn what offsides means. Is the fifteenth season the charm? You'd think by now you wouldn't need Google Maps to stay on your wing."

Suraj shoved Ryan as he skated past. "Offsides? More like I'm giving the refs cardio, bud. Keeping them fit."

"At least someone's fit." Sean skated past them backward.

Suraj flipped him off with a grin. "At least I'm not out here collecting penalty minutes like it's a hobby, Sean. PIMs look real cute on your stats sheet."

Tyler chimed in, "Oh, don't worry, Suraj—Sean's just waiting for you to throw one of those soft checks. You're basically a free pass for him to spend more time in the box."

Ryan snorted. "Sean loves time in the box."

Sean motioned for them to line up on the blue. "The only box I'm spending time in these days is Kelty's."

André groaned. "You set him up so hard for that!"

Ryan threw out his hands, laughing.

"I'm telling Kelty." Brett sent a spray of ice over Sean's skates. "Keep you humble."

Sean grinned. "Suicides. Go."

———

Ryan unhooked his helmet, sweat dripping down his face. For the entirety of practice, he didn't think once about Kara, the manila envelope on his kitchen counter, or the fact that he'd just agreed to take a week-long trip with his nanny. *Shit, that sounded so dirty.* He prayed his team didn't get a hint of it, or he was going to be the brunt of every joke from now until playoffs.

"I think the left boards appreciated that Valentine you dropped during puck protection." Boyd peeled off his goalie pads.

"Yeah, Boyd, I'll make sure to include your save percentage in the love letter. Gonna need a few more "O's to go between the X's." Ryan grinned and dropped his helmet on the bench.

"Of all people, you're the one who needs more O's." Brett smirked as he dropped his hockey bag next to him.

Ryan shook his head. One practice a week wasn't enough.

Cutting edges and jawing like they were back in high school made the weight on his chest shift for the first time in days.

Across the room, Gary wrestled with his skate laces, muttering curses under his breath. Country sauntered over and slapped Gary on the back. "Need some help there, bud? Or you just practicing tying your boots for the rodeo?"

Gary grunted. "Just tryin' not to snap a lace, unlike last week. You'd think these damn things would hold up longer than your mother did last night."

André laughed out loud.

Ryan pulled off his sweat-soaked jersey, the post-practice endorphins still buzzing through his body. His muscles ached in that satisfying way that came from a hard skate.

Boyd strode past wearing only a towel. "Sean, you need to find meditation or something. You were laying people out like it was half-price handie day."

Sean flipped him off with a grin.

Ryan stepped out of his pants and headed for the showers, the steam already filling the room. He let the hot spray pound against his shoulders, easing some of the tension.

"Sheesh, enough with the body wash," André quipped as he sauntered in, all lean muscle and cockiness. "I need to smell good for the ladies later."

"What ladies would want your French ass?" Gary shot back with a grin.

André turned and slapped his bare cheek.

Ryan chuckled as he rinsed off, then grabbed his towel and walked back to the bench to get dressed.

"How long are you going to let that grow?" Country tugged a clean flannel over his shoulders.

Ryan shrugged. "When Amaya doesn't braid it anymore."

Country winked. "Keep your best girl happy."

"Ryan," Sean called out from behind the lockers. "How's the camp going?"

Ryan sighed. "Bud, those kids have way too much energy. I'm exhausted."

"You're getting old," Boyd teased, his mullet plastered to his neck. "Can't keep up with the young bucks anymore."

Ryan pulled on his shirt. "It's like trying to herd cats. Half of them think they're already making the World Juniors, and the other half don't know how to skate backward without making permanent ass prints. Boyd's been spending more time chasing loose pucks than coaching."

Brett grinned. "Better than Gary teaching them how to tie their skates."

———

At the end of week one, Ryan dropped Amaya off with Laura and Russ, then drove home and dropped his hockey bag just inside the door. He made a fat roast beef sandwich, ate an ice cream sandwich from the freezer, then tossed his dishes in the sink and trudged to his bedroom. It was barely a ten-second walk, but it felt like a marathon. He flopped onto his mattress, not bothering to change, and was asleep before he could pull the covers over his shoulders.

The weekend passed in a blur, and week two of hockey camp sped by faster than the first. The kids enrolled were a bit more experienced, plus he had Amaya and Bailey in his group. Every day around five forty-five, his eyes started drifting up to the stands. It only took him a few seconds to find Aelin. She tended to sit in the same spot on the south side of the rink.

"Always have an influx of energy in those last twenty minutes or so, eh, bud?" Tyler grinned as he passed him on the way to his truck. "Enjoy your week of vacay."

Ryan tried to flip him off without Amaya seeing and failed.

"Dad! You said—"

"I know what I said. This was a special circumstance."

When his alarm went off Sunday morning, he was pretty sure he hadn't even moved during the night. He groaned and reached over to his nightstand to shut the damn thing off. Any chance of him snoozing disappeared when he realized what day it was. A thump from the other room told him Amaya remembered, too.

He pulled on a pair of sweats and a T-shirt, shoved a toothbrush and paste into his kit, then grabbed his pillow to add to the pile of their gear already sitting by the front door.

"We're going to a real lake!" Amaya bounded down the hall, her hair brushed and . . . was she wearing make-up?

Ryan frowned and walked closer. "What's on your eyes?"

Amaya pursed her lips. "It's eye shadow."

"Where the hell did you get that?"

She scoffed. "Aelin got it for Bailey, and Bailey shared."

Ryan ground his teeth as Amaya ran back down the hall to grab her backpack. When she reappeared, Ryan went through the checklist. "You have five changes of clothes, pajamas, and underwear." She nodded. "Toiletries."

"Yep."

"Entertainment for the car?"

Amaya pointed at her bag. "Books, pencils, crayons, paper, my tablet."

Ryan nodded. "Snacks?"

"Check." She pointed at a grocery sack by the door. "Ooh." She ran back into her room and returned holding her pillow and a stuffy she got the previous year for Christmas from his parents. It reminded him he hadn't called them in a few weeks. *Add it to the list.*

The streets were quiet as they drove to Aelin's, the sun already well over the horizon at eight a.m. When he turned onto her street, it was like a scene from a painting. The trees lining the road were a collage of greens, the summer leaves lush and vibrant. The morning dew clung to the grass, sparkling like a thousand tiny diamonds.

And there, on her front porch, was Aelin, sipping from a steaming travel mug and looking like she belonged front and centre in that masterpiece. When she spotted his car, she got up, and Ryan wished for a moment he would have stalled a little longer at the end of the block.

He parked, got out of the car, and walked up the path to help carry their luggage. "Morning."

"Hey." Aelin gave him a tired smile and hoisted a laundry basket with sand toys, swim gear, sunscreen, and two life jackets.

"Was I supposed to—"

"No." Aelin shook her head. "Leo has plenty of adult jackets, my sister just asked me to bring a couple for the girls."

He nodded, still uncomfortable with the fact that she may have purchased an extra jacket for Amaya. He grabbed the handle of her suitcase.

"You got the notarized letter okay?" He assumed she'd gotten permission to take Bailey over the border since she hadn't cancelled the trip, but after receiving one text from her reminding him to get it signed, he hadn't heard another thing about it.

"You don't even want to know," Aelin muttered. He didn't press her.

They moved their pillows and rearranged Amaya's bag so everything could fit snugly in the trunk. Surprisingly, they didn't have to pack much since Aelin said they could buy food in Bigfork and the cabins were fully outfitted.

Aelin stepped back from the car. "I think that's everything." She glanced at the girls chatting on the grass. "Can you two run in and go to the washroom?"

They nodded, and then he and Aelin were standing on the sidewalk alone. It made sense that they would drive together. There was no point in them taking two vehicles when they were both going to the same place at the same time. But standing there next to her made him acutely aware that they'd be sitting inches from each other for over five hours.

The girls raced back outside, and Aelin walked to the front door to lock up.

"You have the right keys this time?" he teased. Aelin shot him a look.

Ryan got in the driver's seat, then typed the directions to the cabins into his GPS and plugged in his phone. The girls buckled up in the back.

"Do you need anything from the back before we start driving?" he asked.

They both shook their heads and then Aelin swept into the passenger seat. She closed the door, and both of them stared at the dash for a second.

Finally, Aelin spoke. "You ready for this?"

Ryan nodded. "You?"

She turned and gave him a nervous smile. The hairs on the back of his arms stood at attention as he turned on the engine and pulled away from the curb.

Ryan and Aelin drove in silence for a few minutes, the hum of the tires on the road blending with the music from the show Amaya and Bailey were watching. Aelin had her travel mug perched in the cup holder, and her fingers tapped lightly against the armrest. He noticed she'd painted her nails. Pale pink.

He switched his grip on the wheel, resting his left wrist on top of the steering wheel, his right hand settling on the gear shift. He glanced over as Aelin took a sip of her drink, then turned his attention back to the road. Every movement she made sent him flinching, and questions he wouldn't ask cycled through his head on repeat. *Was she comfortable? Did she need more air? Did she hate his driving?*

He was like a skittish cat.

After passing through the outskirts of the city, the Alberta landscape rolled past, a mix of wheat and canola fields dotted with the occasional farmhouse. The sky above them was a soft gradient as the sun rose higher in the sky.

Aelin shifted in her seat, and Ryan's eyes flicked to the rearview mirror. The girls hadn't made a peep. Thank you, Bluey.

Aelin cleared her throat. "Bailey was sad to leave the camp," she said, breaking the comfortable quiet.

It took Ryan a moment to realize she was talking to him. "She seemed to really get into it."

Aelin smiled. "She was a sponge. Soaking up everything you said. I think she liked having a coach that wasn't her mom for once."

"Understandable." Ryan's mouth quirked. "It was good to see her connecting with the other kids, too. That one drill on the last day, she nailed it."

Aelin chuckled. "Yeah, she was so proud of herself. I think she's still riding that high."

Ryan ran his hand over the wheel. "It's always a rush when you finally get something you've been working on. I know she had some trouble with the crossover drills at first, but she kept at it."

"She did. And you were great with her. She told me you gave her some tips that made it click." Aelin glanced over, her eyes soft before she dropped them.

Ryan's skin heated. "I pointed out a few things. She did the work."

Aelin set her hands in her lap. She wore the same faded jeans she'd been wearing the night she showed up at his house after her date. "She's been asking when she can play again. We need to find a local league or something."

Ryan forced his eyes back out the windshield. "There are a few options around Brentwood. I can send you some links."

"I'd appreciate that." Aelin's fingers drummed on her thigh. "I know she has a lot to learn, but she got a taste of it, you know? I think it was good for her."

Ryan nodded. "Hockey's like that. Once you get a taste, it's hard to quit." He felt her eyes on him and drew a breath. "I started playing when I was six. My dad took me to a game, and that was it. I was hooked."

Aelin leaned back in her seat. "Did you play past high school?"

Ryan nodded. "Yeah, for the University of Alberta." Memories of those days flooded back. The long practices, the adrenaline of game nights, the camaraderie in the locker room. "It was a hell of a time."

"Lots of pressure?"

He let out a breath. "That, too."

"I always thought it would be hard to balance sports and academics." Aelin turned her body to face him more fully, and the idea of having her full attention made his foot drop harder on the gas. "What did you study?"

"Engineering." Ryan's grip on the steering wheel tightened. "My dad was a civil engineer, and it seemed like a good career."

Aelin raised an eyebrow. "Your idea or his?"

Ryan considered the question. His dad had never told him what to do with his career, but he didn't ever seem to complain about his job like other parents. Once he got older, he realized that it was probably due to his personality rather than his choice of profession. "A bit of both, I guess."

Aelin nodded, her fingers tracing the rim of her travel mug. "Why didn't you keep playing hockey after college?"

Ryan shrugged. "I had a couple of offers, but they weren't exactly what I was hoping for. Plus, I had some obligations in Grand Prairie. Family stuff." He ran a hand through his hair. "And then, well, you know. I met Amaya's mom, and life took a different turn."

Were they really driving to the States together, and he'd never even told her where he was from? He wasn't sure if that made the whole situation better or worse.

Aelin wet her lips. "Well, thank you so much for letting Bailey attend the camp. It's obvious that you love the game."

Ryan's eyes flicked to hers. "Yeah, I do. It's good to be back on the ice, even if it's just for fun now."

He asked her questions about California, and she told him about growing up in Huntington Beach. It all sounded like a dream. Like a show he would've watched on pirated American satellite growing up.

She skipped fast through her college era, noting that she met Clark at UCLA.

"But he's Canadian?"

She nodded. "Yeah. He was there on a lacrosse scholarship."

Ryan frowned. "Damn. Don't give me a reason to like him."

Aelin snorted. "Yeah, he fooled me, too." She leaned forward. "I forgot to ask, are we taking the scenic route or going through Ft. Macleod?"

Ryan glanced at his phone. "Wherever the map sends me?"

Aelin grinned and pulled his phone from the mount. "Scenic. Are you okay with that?"

"Through Crowsnest Pass?" he asked. She nodded. "Might as well take advantage when the weather's good." He'd driven that pass for hockey tournaments in the middle of winter, and it was scary as shit.

Aelin put his phone back. "Perfect. I think Bailey will be good until we get close to the border. Maybe stop for lunch there before we have to flush half the value of a dollar down the toilet?"

Ryan chuckled. "C'mon, only thirty cents."

Aelin opened her purse and pulled out a bag. He glanced over. "Are those Sour Patch Kids?"

"Only the best for my chauffeur." She ripped the bag open with her teeth, and knowing her lips were on the bag sent a jolt through him as he reached in.

"This trip is going to get crazy if we're hitting the sauce before noon."

Aelin sighed. "I would've brought the good stuff, but I didn't want it to get confiscated by border patrol."

Ryan chuckled. "It's Montana. They have plenty of the good stuff."

After stopping for lunch at an A&W and stretching their legs, they made it to the line at the border. Thankfully, it wasn't long at midday on Sunday. Probably because most of southern Alberta was in church. His in-laws would love it.

Ryan pulled up to the booth and rolled down his window, handing the agent his and Aelin's passport and the birth certificates for the girls.

A stern-looking officer peered in. "Where are you headed?"

"Bigfork, Montana," Aelin replied.

The officer didn't blink. "Purpose of your visit?"

"Vacation," Ryan answered.

The officer glanced at her, then back at Ryan. "Different names on these. You two are married?"

Ryan shook his head. "Just . . . friends."

The officer motioned to the back window. "Roll this down, please." Ryan obeyed. "Do you have permission from the parents of these children?"

He took his letter from the glove compartment and handed it over with the paper Aelin pulled from her purse. The officer perused and didn't look up to ask, "How long will you be staying?"

Ryan's grip tightened on the wheel. "A week."

"Any alcohol or tobacco products, marijuana, firearms or weapons, agriculture products, fruits or vegetables, pets, or cash exceeding ten thousand dollars, including that intended for gifts in the vehicle?" He rattled it off as smoothly as his address.

Ryan shook his head.

The officer handed their documents back. "Thank you, enjoy your trip."

They rolled up the windows and continued on. Aelin let out a breath. "That wasn't so bad."

Ryan smirked. "You were worried?"

"No, I just—well, yeah. I always feel like I'm doing something wrong even when I'm not."

Ryan laughed. "Like when you see a cop in your rearview mirror, and suddenly you're convinced you have a body in your trunk?"

Aelin laughed out loud, and Ryan's neck flushed.

They chatted about childhood road trips and vacations they wanted to take as they passed through small-town Montana. Finally, Ryan turned off the highway, following the signs to Bigfork. The road wound through dense forest.

"Never ceases to amaze." Aelin stared out the window. "Just wait till you see it."

As they rounded a bend, the forest opened up to reveal a small town nestled on the shores of glittering blue. Ryan's eyes widened. "Wow."

"Yep." Aelin pointed. "Look at those mountains in the distance. It's like a postcard. And this isn't even half of it."

They drove past quaint shops with colourful awnings, a general store with a hand-painted sign, a bakery with a line out the door, and a café with outdoor seating that spilled onto the sidewalk.

Aelin's grin stretched so wide, Ryan couldn't help but mirror it. He guided the car through the town, following the GPS directions to their cabins. They passed a couple of art galleries and a craft brewery before the road began to climb.

As they ascended, the view of Flathead Lake grew more expansive. The water shimmered in the late afternoon sun, tiny boats dotting the surface like bath toys. Ryan's eyes traced the shoreline, finding a few secluded beaches and rocky outcrops.

They continued along the winding road, then dropped back to water level, the cabins finally coming into view. Ryan pulled into the gravel driveway and parked next to a truck with a hitch.

"This is it." Aelin squeaked, and her shoulders nearly touched her ears.

Ryan had barely put the car in park before the girls were jumping out and running down to the docks. Ryan swung his door open, but Aelin put a hand on his arm. "It's okay, my sister and her husband are down there getting the boat set up."

Ryan looked skeptical. "She's never been around a body of water like this."

Aelin nodded. "We can go over safety, but it's not super deep around the dock." She pushed her door open. "Come here, I'll show you." He walked down the beach in awe of the smooth, coloured rocks.

"You're heeeere!" The woman who had to be Aelin's sister, Mariah, squealed, jumping out of the boat and running up the dock toward them. Aelin flung her arms around her sister. "And you must be Ryan?" Mariah didn't give him the option of a handshake. She hugged him just as tight as she did Aelin, and Ryan felt a little shell-shocked when she pulled back.

Aelin looked back up at the parking spots, her brow furrowing. "Mar, how many vehicles did you bring?"

"Just one. But the—" Her sister's eyes widened. "Oh, shit, did you not see my text?"

Aelin frowned and pulled out her phone. She blinked at her screen. "Mariah—"

"Our friends ended up bringing their teens. And a couple friends," Mariah said in a rush, flashing an apologetic smile. "So we thought you two could . . . share?"

CHAPTER
Eighteen

THE CABIN WAS every bit as charming as Aelin remembered, and that made it frustratingly difficult to be angry. The dark wood floors creaked under her feet, and light filtered in through the picture window, making the whole living room look like it had been dusted with gold. The walls were covered in old photos of the lake, and the kitchen still looked like the seventies threw up on it.

She loved it. Every last avocado green appliance and laminate countertop.

It was cozy. Charming. And it was also small.

"Mariah, why the hell didn't you give me a heads up? We could've brought sleeping bags or something," she hissed through her teeth.

Mariah threw out her hands. "I only found out yesterday. It was a last-minute thing. I guess Bob texted Leo, and he said, "The more the merrier!"

Aelin crossed her arms over her chest, checking to see if Ryan or the girls were coming inside with their things yet. "More is not merrier in this particular circumstance. We have four people, Mar. There are only three beds."

"And a couch." She said it like a question and winced.

Aelin lowered her voice. "I don't know him that well." She scanned the room, trying to figure out a situation where she wouldn't be leaving her daughter upstairs with her friend's dad sleeping in the room below.

"I'm really sorry about this. I thought about other possible sleeping arrangements, but those kids are so much older than your two girls. That would be weird, and Leo would divorce me if I suggested he share a room with a random guy—"

"No, I get it. I'm not saying we need to do something like that." She pressed her hands into the counter. "It just would've been good to know before we left."

Ryan didn't seem like a dangerous person. But neither had Clark in the beginning.

"You could go to the store? I'll pay for you to get some sleeping bags or—"

Amaya and Bailey rushed in, their eyes lighting up when they saw the loft. Bailey found Aelin, her hands clenched with excitement. "Do we get to sleep up there?" She bolted up the stairs before Aelin could stop her, Amaya close on her heels.

"There are TWO BEDS FOR US!" Bailey sounded like she was at an Olivia Rodrigo concert.

Aelin blew out a breath. "Yeah. Looks like that's not happening." How could she tell the girls they were going to have to sleep on the floor? Or share the bed so she and Ryan could each take a tiny bed? She'd barely fit in those at sixteen when they'd come here for the first time, and Ryan was more than a head taller than her.

Ryan walked in carrying three bags and her laundry basket. Aelin rushed to the door to take something.

"You didn't need to bring everything in at once." She took the basket and set it by the door.

"More efficient." He set the suitcases down, and Amaya's footsteps pounded on the stairs as she descended to retrieve her things.

"Thank you so much for bringing us. Ugh!" She grabbed her small suitcase and hauled it back up to the loft.

Mariah looked between the two of them. "Think of it this way. You get to split the cost of the week. That saves you a thousand bucks?"

Aelin drew a breath and slowly exhaled. "That. Is true."

"True enough that you don't hate me?" Mariah's face pinched.

Aelin grabbed her suitcase and slid it away from the door. "I don't hate you."

Mariah gave her a quick hug and patted Ryan on the shoulder like he was a puppy, then escaped through the front door.

Aelin bit her lip and wrung her hands. "I'm so sorry." She kept her voice low so the girls didn't hear over their excited chatter.

Ryan shrugged. "It's fine. I don't mind sleeping on the couch."

Aelin glanced at the leather sofa. "Ryan—"

"It's fine. I'll go grab the last of our stuff."

"No, stop. I don't mean—it's not about the couch. The girls are going to be sleeping right up there."

Ryan frowned, then sucked in a breath when he realized what she was getting at. Aelin waited for him to snap at her. To tell her she was being overprotective or anxious. But instead Ryan nodded and said, "Yeah, of course. I could sleep in the car?"

Aelin blinked at him. "You'd do that?"

He nodded. "Definitely. I wouldn't want my daughter sleeping in the same place as a random guy." He ran a hand over his jaw. "We'll figure something out."

When he finished unloading the car, Aelin was writing down the last few items on her grocery list. "Anything you want to add?"

Ryan walked into the kitchen and stopped next to her, glancing over the notepad. He reached out and took the pen from her. She pulled her hand back a little too quickly when his thumb brushed hers.

His brow furrowed as he leaned over and added popcorn and English muffins to the list. As he straightened, the girls ran down the stairs, already dressed in their bathing suits.

Ryan's mouth quirked, and he looked at Aelin. "Do you want store or lifeguard duty?"

"You go to the store, Dad." Amaya grabbed his hand, leading him to the door. "Make sure to get distracted like you always do in the snacks aisle."

He scoffed. "I don't get distracted."

Amaya giggled as he put on his shoes. He gave Aelin an amused look, then stalked out to the car.

"Okay, girls, just give me a few seconds here." Aelin dragged her suitcase to the small master bedroom. The door opened with a creak, and she stepped inside, moving her suitcase into the corner. The room was just as she remembered, with its rustic wooden furniture and floral curtains.

Ryan's stuff would need to go in here, too, so it wasn't cluttering up the tiny living space. She took out her clothes and toiletries and claimed one side of the dresser and a section of the washroom counter, then shoved her suitcase under the bed.

She wasn't going to make him sleep in the car. It got cold there at night. But then . . . what? Aelin scanned the room. She would give him the bed, but she knew he wasn't going to take it.

The floor?

She stood and her brain flashed with one ticker tape after another. *Ryan was going to be sleeping in the same cabin as her. Ryan was going to be brushing his teeth next to her. Ryan's clothes were going to be in the same dresser.*

It was fine. They were adults, and they could figure out how to be roommates for the week. Extremely platonic, professional roommates. They'd already survived a few weeks of seeing each other every day. How much harder could this be?

She mentally plugged her ears and hummed as her heart tattooed *lies* on the back of her ribs.

Aelin threw on her swimsuit, a sporty bikini that was so comfortable, she had it in two colours, and paused a second to assess herself in the mirror.

It wasn't that she didn't like her body. After being pregnant and nursing, she felt pretty damn good about how she looked. But she'd always been curvier. Even in high school when she was swimming every day, she was the one with hips and a chest. Most boys had liked it.

Until Clark.

He'd made it clear that he preferred her with less. Less weight, less personality, less opinions. Less of everything that didn't give him exactly what he wanted when he wanted it.

The barbs he'd thrown at her began cycling through her head. *You're a prude. Did you see how much your thighs jiggled when you did that? That should be an advert for why women need boob jobs.*

She shook her head and turned from the mirror. Rule #1 of being at the lake: Clark didn't get to come that year, in her head or otherwise.

Aelin threw on an old T-shirt and walked down the hall to check on the girls. "You two ready to get in the water?"

Amaya and Bailey squealed.

They all slipped on sandals and abandoned the cabin for the pebbled beach. The sun was warm on Aelin's skin as they walked down to the dock. The lake stretched out before them, so dark blue, it felt as if it would stain. Aelin felt a rush of nostalgia as Amaya pointed to the shallows.

"There's fish!"

Bailey grabbed her hand. "That's a minnow. They like to swim close to shore. There are so many more over there."

The girls ran across the beach, their laughter echoing across the water. Aelin followed at a slower pace, taking in the familiar sights and sounds. The dock creaked under her feet, and she breathed in the scent of pine and humidity.

Amaya and Bailey waded into the shallows, and Aelin sat on the edge of the dock. She dipped her feet into the water and took off her T-shirt. The water was still a bit chilly. She'd have to put on her big girl panties to dive in and ski.

Aelin leaned back on her hands, letting the sun soak into her skin. She closed her eyes and listened to the gentle lapping of the waves against the dock. It was so peaceful here. So different from the constant hum of the city.

"Mom, come in!" Bailey called, and Aelin opened her eyes. Both girls were up to their knees in water, splashing each other.

"Okay, okay." Aelin stood and walked back up the dock and onto the beach, dropping her sandals in the rocks. She gasped as the cold hit her, but she forced herself to keep going until she was waist-deep.

The girls seemed elated at her obvious discomfort. Aelin couldn't help but laugh with them. Aelin trailed her fingers across the surface. The sky was a brilliant blue with only a few wispy clouds drifting by.

Her skin prickled, and she turned. Ryan stood on the dock, holding the grocery sacks, his eyes locked on her.

Aelin curled her toes against the rocks. He'd seen her in a towel, but with him watching her like that, she had never felt more naked. Especially since the water was cold.

Ryan gave a small wave and turned back to the cabin. Aelin waited for her heart to jump start.

"Mom, look!" Bailey ran up the beach, holding something out. "I found the perfect wishing stone."

Aelin inspected it. The rock was grey with a white line etched in a perfect, unbroken circle. "Wow, yes you did. What are you going to wish for?"

Bailey scoffed. "I can't tell you."

Amaya picked her way across the beach, and Bailey showed her the rock, instructing her on how to find one for herself. Then Bailey walked to the edge of the lake, clutched the rock to her chest and closed her eyes, then threw it out into the water. What she wouldn't have given to listen in on her daughter's thoughts for just a moment.

She let the girls play for another twenty minutes, then brought them up to dry off and get ready for dinner when her mom texted saying they were getting the fire started.

Ryan had already put the food away by the time Aelin and the girls were back from the water. He'd also taken his suitcase into the bedroom. She wanted to walk in and see what his clothes looked like next to hers. What products he used in his hair and on his body.

"Hey."

Aelin jumped at the sound of Ryan's voice, nearly dropping the glass she'd pulled from the cupboard. She clutched it to her chest and turned.

Ryan leaned against the fridge. "Anything I can do to help with dinner?"

Aelin glanced at the buns now sitting on the counter. "We just need to bring these down to the fire pit. My parents have the hot dogs."

He nodded, and his eyes dropped a fraction. "Are you going to change?"

"You don't think this is good dinner attire?" She looked down at her bikini.

Ryan's neck turned pink. "I was wondering if I needed to get on my suit. If you were going to swim again."

The corner of her mouth lifted. "I'm done. The girls may still want to get in." She walked toward the bedroom and slid past him, her body all too aware of how little space there was between them. "I'll be right back."

Aelin changed into shorts and a hoodie, and the four of them walked down to the fire pit between their cabins. They'd rented out the whole place, and this was precisely why they'd chosen these cabins over the other options around the lake. It was private without paying a premium price for a massive house.

Her parents were there, hauling out chairs and a cooler.

"There you are!" her mom called. "We were about to send out a search party."

Aelin grinned. "We were just getting settled."

Her dad stood and walked over to the picnic table next to the fire pit. "I started the fire, but you can take over from here if you want." He clapped Ryan on the shoulder.

Ryan shot Aelin a look, and she shrugged with a laugh. He was going to have to get used to that. Everyone here jumped in, even if they weren't on a first-name basis.

"Mom, Dad, this is Ryan." Aelin motioned to Amaya, who had already crouched next to the flames with Bailey. "That's his daughter, Amaya."

"So nice to meet you. Here, let me help with those," her mom reached out to take a few packages of the buns from their hands. "I'm Molly, by the way." She held out her hand to Ryan, who took it with a smile.

"Dave." Her dad adjusted the waistband of his pants.

Aelin set the rest of the buns on the picnic table as gratitude swelled in her chest. Her parents were good people. Welcoming. Loving. They'd always been supportive, even when she and her sister had made stupid decisions. Like drinking their whiskey or driving her car through a puddle that turned out to be a mud pit. Or, you know, marrying Clark.

Her dad walked back to the fire pit. Aelin grabbed a roasting stick from the bucket next to the picnic table and handed it to Ryan.

They speared up dogs for the girls, then showed them where to hold it over the fire.

"So, how was the drive?" her mom asked, sitting down in one of the camp chairs.

"Pretty uneventful."

"No traffic at the border?" Her dad looked skeptical. Ryan shook his head."That's good. It's always a crapshoot, especially on a weekend. *You shall not pass!*"

Aelin laughed and glanced at Ryan. She'd forgotten to

prepare him for the excessive nerd energy he'd be encountering. "Dad, you've driven over the border exactly once."

He waved her off. "I've heard stories."

Ryan crouched down to help Amaya rotate her dog, and Aelin noticed how the light played off the curve of his lips. She forced her eyes back to the table and pulled the sleeves of her hoody over her hands.

"You started without us!" Mariah called.

Aelin turned to see her sister and her friends walking down the path from the cabins. Somehow, they all knew exactly who Ryan was. Mariah introduced her husband, Leo, and their kids, Tucker, Alicia, and Mary. Their friends introduced themselves next, and Aelin tried to keep track of names even though the teenage boys moved as a pack straight to the food.

They laughed and ate around the fire as the sun dropped closer to the horizon. The girls played in the water, grabbing pool noodles and floats to play some game involving mermaids.

Ryan leaned over as the sun was setting. "Should we get them cleaned up?"

Aelin nodded, laughing at Mariah trying to wipe ketchup off her ankle after dipping a bare dog on her friend Malcolm's plate of extra condiments.

They helped put the rest of the food away, then called to Amaya and Bailey. There were no complaints once they reminded the girls that they'd get to do the same thing every day for a week. Aelin never made plans for this vacation. She liked soaking it in, enjoying every second on the water.

"You four want to take first shift with us on the boat in the morning?" Her dad asked as they started back toward their cabin.

Aelin looked at Ryan, and he nodded. "Sure. What time?"

"Eight o'clock okay? The water will be glass."

She smiled. "Sounds great. Thanks, Dad."

The girls showered and got into PJs while Aelin made them

each a piece of toast with a fried egg for a snack. She looked up and noticed Ryan eyeing the plate.

"You want one, too?"

He glanced up. "I wouldn't turn it down."

Aelin grinned and cracked another egg in the pan. It was quite possibly the perfect afternoon, which felt miraculous, considering the way it started. She kept waiting for Ryan to snap at her or go into hiding like Clark used to. To say something like, "Your family is a lot," but he hadn't.

He sat at the fire surrounded by perfect strangers and joined in the conversation like he was a regular. In the past few weeks, she hadn't seen him get testy once besides that first day on her doorstep. Either he was putting on an excellent show, or she'd met him at his worst. And if that was his worst . . .

Bailey sat at the table first, and Amaya was quick to follow. Ryan offered to deliver the plates, but she waved him off. She brought their food and did a double take when she saw Bailey reach over and pull a piece of egg white hanging off the edge of Ryan's plate and pop it in her mouth.

Ryan glanced up, and she turned back to the kitchen to grab water glasses. When they finished, Amaya cleared all three plates, and they all walked up the stairs to the loft together.

Aelin pulled their copy of Little House on the Prairie from Bailey's bag. "We're reading this one. Do you want to hear a chapter?"

Amaya nodded, then settled herself on the edge of the bed. Ryan dropped to the floor in front of her, and she pulled out his elastic. It looked like a choreographed routine, so smooth and practiced. Amaya separated his hair into halves, then started a French braid on one side.

"Mom?" Bailey tapped her shoulder.

She cleared her throat. "Right, sorry." Aelin opened the book to chapter four and started reading. She instantly regretted her decision when she remembered she'd started the book using different voices for each character and now had to maintain that level of performance for triple the audience.

Her cheeks flushed when she dropped her voice for Pa. When she finished the chapter, she set the book down and turned to Bailey's bed fast enough, she didn't have to meet Ryan's gaze.

Aelin kneeled, tucking the blanket under Bailey's chin. "Sweet dreams, babe." She smoothed the hair off her forehead, then turned to Amaya. "Goodnight."

The loft was warm and cozy, the soft glow from the kitchen light filtering through the rails on the far wall. Ryan stood and planted a kiss on Amaya's forehead, his hair elastic on his wrist.

Aelin turned and descended the stairs. She walked into the kitchen, hunting for something to do so she could look busy when Ryan came downstairs. What happened next? All day, they'd had things to keep them busy. Distracted. Now it was just the two of them in a very quiet, very dreamy cabin.

Ryan padded across the living room and leaned against the counter. He pulled the wash rag from the sink and wet it under the faucet, then wiped down the kitchen table. As he replaced it, he asked, "You okay?"

Aelin nodded. "Of course. Why?"

Ryan tapped his finger on the counter. "Uh, you haven't looked at me in approximately three hours?" He exhaled. "Just . . . wanted to make sure I didn't do something—"

"You didn't do anything." She placed a soap tab in the dish-washer, and her hand shook as she pressed start and closed the door. "It's been a busy day." She forced her chin up and met his eyes head-on.

Her stomach felt like it had just been thrown in the blender. She let out a soft "hmm" then turned and opened the cupboards. "Looks like you got everything on the list. Thank you for doing that, by the way."

"Of course."

She felt like she'd just slammed an espresso. "Mmkay, I'm going to—"

"I thought I'd make some tea. You want some?"

Aelin paused, forcing her lungs to expand. *No.* She should say no and disappear into the bedroom until the girls were awake and she could have anything else to look at besides him. "Sure."

He rounded the counter, and his hand grazed her hip as she sucked in her stomach and moved past him to take his spot at the counter. He filled the kettle and pulled out the new box of tea bags. *Peppermint.*

Aelin swallowed hard.

After turning on the gas burner, Ryan turned to face her and leaned against the counter. "What if this is about us?"

Aelin's heart stalled in her chest. "Hmm?"

He folded his arms. "What if we didn't want to be two sad people anymore?"

She stared at him like a deer in headlights. What was he talking about? She remembered her depressing monologue at the park, but she was not following this train of thought. Probably because Ryan's hair was still hitting his shoulders, and his arms looked like they could crush walnuts.

"What would you tell your best friend if she were in your position?" he asked.

Aelin drew a breath and held it. "That she should shave her head, smuggle her daughter out of the country, and never talk to anyone that could get word back to her asshole ex. Especially after seeing how easy it was to get across the border. I could forge a notary stamp."

Ryan raised an eyebrow, and she exhaled. "Okay, fine. I'd tell her that she'd already wasted twelve years of her life being sad because of said asshole ex. She couldn't do anything about that now, but she could enjoy the next twelve. What about you?"

Ryan wet his lips. "I'd tell him that . . ." His jaw worked.

When he spoke again, his voice was raw. "That I don't think marriage was meant to be a death sentence."

Aelin gripped the edge of the counter. "It's so much easier to give advice than to take it."

Ryan huffed a laugh as the tea kettle started to whistle. He turned and pulled two mugs from the cupboard and poured boiling water into them.

"You know when I went on that date?" she asked.

Ryan's hand stilled, then continued on to pick up the tea bags. "Mmhmm."

"I had this weird moment."

"If this is a sex thing—"

Aelin snorted. "Not a sex thing." *Was it just her, or did Ryan's shoulders drop a smidge?* "We were walking around the park, and there was music playing, and I felt like I was floating above myself or something. Like my personality had been erased. There was nothing that existed anymore. I was just an empty shell. A robot trying to figure out how to be human."

Ryan handed her a mug. "That's bleak. Even for a first date."

"Hence the reason I haven't gone on a second." She leaned over the counter.

He lifted his mug. They were only two feet apart now, the thin strip of island the only thing between them. "Maybe it wasn't the right guy."

She gave him a look. "I think I'm the anti-hero in this story."

"Why?"

Aelin scoffed. "I don't know. Maybe because every time I tried to be myself with Clark, he found a way to make me feel like crap about it. Twelve years of that makes for a fairly thorough brainwashing."

His lips twitched. He glanced down at his mug, then back up at her, his dark lashes brushing his cheek. "How often is Clark right about things?"

"When it's not about making money? Never."

Ryan set his mug down on the counter. "I rest my case."

She leaned forward, the counter biting into her hip bones. "Again. Easier to give advice than take it."

Ryan nodded, his thumb tracing the handle of his mug. "I don't want to be Sad Ryan anymore. I want to be Fun Ryan."

She fought a smile. "I bet we could find the mothership. Tweak both our operating systems."

His nostrils flared. "Maybe this place counts." He lifted his mug, blew on his tea, and took a tentative sip.

"What are you proposing?" That word sent a zing through her centre, and she quickly took a drink, flinching as the hot liquid burned her bottom lip.

Ryan studied the surface of his tea as if reading the future. "What if we forgot about life back home for the week. What if we let ourselves be different?"

Aelin let his words settle over her. Was it possible? Could she ignore the emails from her lawyer, the searches for house listings, the potential passive-aggressive texts from Clark? Could she just . . . be? "This would have to go away." She lifted up her phone.

Ryan opened up the kitchen drawer next to him. He pressed the power button on the phone until his screen went blank, then dropped it in.

AELIN WOKE to the sound of an alarm. An actual alarm clock, since her phone was spooning Ryan's in the kitchen junk drawer. She blinked the sleep from her eyes and flicked the switch. The mattress was soft, the sheets cool against her skin, but none of it felt familiar. It took her a minute to remember where she was.

Aelin threw off the covers, only then noticing the lump on the floor near the door. A rumpled, plaid blanket. Dirty blond hair splayed out on the pillow. She pushed up to sitting and leaned closer.

Right.

They'd decided that Ryan would bring in the couch cushions and sleep on her floor.

She slid to the carpet and tiptoed closer. The couch cushions were pushed off to the side and Ryan was smashed against the radiant heater, his feet curled against the door.

She hadn't heard a thing after she'd crawled into bed fully dressed and pulled the covers up to her chin. *Had he woken up? Seen her sleeping?*

Ryan stirred, his eyelids fluttering as he rolled over under the blanket. Aelin jumped back as he yawned, then winced and stretched his arms over his head. He was like a bear waking up from hibernation. He rubbed his neck, then his back, his movements slow and deliberate, like he was testing each joint to see if it still functioned.

Aelin bit her lip, then crept across the room to the dresser. She pulled out the olive green version of her bikini along with a pair of running shorts and a tank top, then tried to sneak to the washroom. Ryan was already turning his head.

"Morning," she whispered, her cheeks flushed as she held her clothes to her chest. Hopefully hiding that she was definitely not wearing a bra.

"Morning." Ryan's voice was thick with sleep. He pushed himself up from the floor.

Aelin slipped into the washroom and exhaled. It was fine. They were sharing space, it wasn't a big deal. She cringed as she stripped off her cotton shorts and shirt imagining what Ryan's night must've been like. The reason she didn't take Bailey tent camping anymore was that she felt geriatric after one night on the ground. And that was on a camping pad. She had been a gymnast. Her joints were decidedly worse than most adults she knew.

Aelin pulled on her bikini, her shorts, and tank top, then quickly washed her face and brushed her teeth. She pulled her hair into a ponytail and opened the door to the bedroom just in time to catch Ryan standing with his back to her, his arms over his head as he pulled on a heather grey T-shirt.

Mmm. Okay. His muscles shifting over his shoulder blades. The tight taper of his waist. *Was it possible for women to get morning wood?*

She exited the washroom, humming to herself. Because humming the theme from a children's TV show would prove how far she was from having visceral sexual fantasies about her daughter's friend's dad.

"I'll go wake the girls!" she said in a tone worthy of a newly hired ride operator at Disneyland and escaped into the hall.

. . .

———

The boat bobbed gently as Aelin's dad pulled on his wetsuit, his slalom ski resting against the side. Her mom adjusted her sunglasses, one hand on the throttle, the other on the steering wheel of the sleek Mastercraft. "Ready when you are," she called back, grinning in the rearview mirror.

Bailey and Amaya were already in their spots, their life jackets secure. They chatted hesitantly with Mariah's girls, Alicia and Mary. When the kids had dipped their feet in the water, they'd opted to let the adults go first. So kind of them.

Mariah nudged Aelin, hugging her knees closer to her chest. "Mom still does that thing. Where she puts her foot up like she's pressing the gas pedal."

Aelin snorted, then pointed it out to Ryan. Mariah's husband Leo was at the back of the boat keeping the rope clear. He always let their parents drive for each other. Mostly out of self-preservation.

"Hit it!" their dad called out, and the engine went from a soothing thrum to a full roar. Dave pulled against the rope, keeping his knees curled to his chest until he popped up and straightened. The girls cheered, and Aelin grinned, smoothing the hair that escaped her elastic and whipped against her face.

The sun shimmered across the water, making a path of melted gold. Aelin shifted in her seat, and her calf brushed up against Ryan's. She pulled away, then knocked into him again as the boat jostled.

He leaned in. "It's fine."

Her cheeks flushed, and she forced herself not to make it more weird by shoving herself further into Mariah's lap. People touched. They were in close quarters. *It's fine.*

No amount of self-talk convinced her skin to stop tingling where it touched his. She fiddled with the zipper on the lifejacket in her lap, remembering what she'd agreed to the night before.

If they were both boring and sad and decidedly not living up to even a fraction of their fun potential, what if they did the opposite? For the whole week, what if they decided to do what they didn't think was the practical choice.

They'd both agreed it should start in the morning since they were exhausted from driving all day and extroverting at the campfire, but *tomorrow* they would be the fun versions of themselves.

Well, now it was tomorrow. And she could barely force herself to make skin-to-skin contact with someone on a boat. Not off to a promising start.

"I texted you about lunch!" Mariah called, holding her hair out of her eyes.

Aelin held up her phone. "It's on airplane mode. Pictures only for the week." It felt strange not to be connected to home, but she'd sent texts to Megan and her lawyer Jules letting her know what the number was for their cabin. Ryan had done the same with his in-laws. If there was an emergency, they'd hear about it.

Mariah's eyes widened. "The whole week?"

Aelin shrugged. "I needed a break." A spray of mist hit her face as her mom curved the boat toward the centre of the lake, cutting through the glassy surface like a knife. Her dad looped his arm through the triangle at the end of the rope and adjusted the shorts of his wet suit.

"Your grandpa is so good!" Amaya yelled over the engine.

The boat hit another wave, and when her arm shifted to the side, she left it there, pressed against Ryan's side. She could feel the steady rise and fall of his breathing as his warmth seeped into her.

Her dad cut back and forth across the wake, his movements fluid and controlled. Her mom kept the boat steady, giving him a thumbs-up every thirty seconds. It was adorable. Finally, her dad slid his hand over his throat and let go of the rope, striking an Archer pose as he sank into the water.

Amaya and Bailey did rock, paper, scissors to see who was up next. They were both obviously hoping to lose, and Ryan laughed when Amaya chose paper, covering Bailey's rock for the tie breaker.

Amaya pursed her lips as Mariah did a test run with the skis, making sure they fit her feet properly. She walked her through the process, then sat on the back of the boat and showed her how to hold herself in the water. Amaya nodded, then dipped her foot over the edge.

"Just jump in! It'll be easier that way," Ryan called. She flashed him a look, then took her time, dangling her legs.

"One does not simply walk into Mordor!" Dave called out, and Amaya finally dropped into the lake. She squealed.

"Don't worry, the sun's getting higher!" Mariah called, tossing her the skis to put on. "It'll be toasty in here when you get out."

Amaya looped the rope over her arm and put the skis on.

"Remember to keep your knees bent and your arms straight," Aelin's dad called out as he towelled off. "Push into the waves, don't let them push you."

Amaya nodded, her ponytail bobbing. She wobbled in the waves as Leo switched back into the driver's seat. "Take your time, we're in no rush!" He called back. Amaya's teeth chattered.

"She'll be okay, right?" Ryan murmured. "She's never done something like this before."

Aelin had the urge to put her hand over his, and just as she was about to swipe the thought away, she paused. What would Fun Aelin do? She didn't think, just did it. Ryan's eyes flared.

"She'll do great. Kids pop up so easy." She smiled and stared off the end of the boat, watching as Amaya took instructions from Mariah and her dad. Everything inside her seemed to power up as Ryan's finger lifted, lacing between hers. It was like the speakers had been on half volume and were suddenly cranked to full blast. It had only been an hour and already Fun Aelin was so much better than Sad, Practical Aelin.

This was a game. An experiment. It was only for this week at this place, which meant she didn't need to worry about who they were in the real world. Not until Sunday, at least.

Amaya yelled, "Ready!" and the boat revved. Her eyes widened as the rope grew taut. Amaya's body tensed, her skis slicing through the water. Aelin held her breath, willing her to pop up, but it wasn't that simple. Her skis wobbled, and within seconds, she was stretching forward and splashing into the lake.

Aelin winced, but any disappointment was quickly drowned out by encouragement. "You almost had it!" Mariah yelled as the boat circled. Her dad shouted, "Just like that, but keep your tips up!"

Amaya nodded, a little shell-shocked. Ryan leaned over the side, making a point to keep his hand linked with Aelin's. "You okay?"

Amaya smiled up at him. She tried again. And again. Then, on her fifth try, she shot up like a cork from a bottle of champagne. The whole boat erupted with cheers. Amaya stared at them, wide-eyed, as if she'd just wandered into a foreign country.

"You're doing great! Relax!" her dad gave her two thumbs-up.

Amaya grinned as she got used to the sensation of flying over the water.

"She did it!" Bailey swivelled to face them, ecstatic.

Amaya lasted thirty more seconds, then mimicked what she'd seen Dave do. She second-guessed herself twice, then finally released the rope and dropped into the lake. They laughed and cheered as the boat puttered up next to her.

"That was amazing!" Ryan stood and walked to the back of the boat. Aelin immediately felt the loss of him.

Aelin's dad turned to face Bailey. "You're up kiddo!"

Bailey got up on the third try. She took one long run, then opted to get back in the boat and save her energy for knee boarding. "It's so easy Amaya, and we have two. We can both do it at the same time."

Aelin checked her watch. They'd only been out for forty-five minutes.

"Who's next?" Leo scanned the boat. His girls avoided his eyes, and Tucker, who was thirteen and definitely too cool for school, said he wanted to go last.

Aelin nodded at Ryan. "I think he's up."

"Yes, Dad!" Amaya cheered.

Ryan's jaw tensed, and Aelin raised an eyebrow, sending him a silent challenge. He read it loud and clear.

He took a deep breath, his eyes scanning the water, then stood. He caught her eye, then pulled his shirt over his head and dropped it to the bench. Oh, she liked Fun Ryan. She liked him a lot. His skin was light from an Alberta winter, but his arms were already starting to tan. He looked like he did push-ups regularly but wasn't so well-defined that a woman would have to worry about competing with a gym membership. Her eyes dropped to the trail of hair on his stomach, and she forced them back to his face.

He smirked as if he knew exactly where she'd been looking. "I'm only doing this if you're going next."

Aelin nodded once. "Sure. I'll ski." Ryan didn't sound like he had much experience. It was her preferred expertise ratio. She could stay in her comfort zone and still look slightly impressive. Ryan looked skeptical, so she took off her shorts and shirt, pulling on her life jacket.

Ryan nodded approvingly, then slipped his feet into the adult skis and adjusted them, then took them off and looked straight at Amaya before flipping off the back of the boat. Aelin grinned. *Show off.*

Dave handed him the skis, and Aelin moved to the back of the boat with the sunscreen, helping the girls apply while Ryan got settled.

He nodded. "Hit it."

Leo hit the gas, and Ryan's body surged out of the water, first try. His form was perfect, knees bent, arms straight, and within seconds, he was skimming across the lake.

"Holy shit, that little liar."

"Mom!" Bailey gave her a look.

She winced. "Sorry."

"What did he lie about?" Bailey asked.

Aelin backpedaled. "He didn't lie, he just made it sound like he didn't have much experience skiing."

Amaya laughed. "He grew up with a boat. They had a private lake."

Aelin's jaw dropped as she turned back to find him grinning at her. He held on with one hand, leaning back with his hair whipping behind him as he casually crossed the wake and cut into the pristine blue.

The boat picked up speed, and Ryan leaned into the turns, slicing through the water. He jumped the wake, his body momentarily suspended in the air, then landed with only a slight wobble. He cut back and forth, his body fluid and strong, and Aelin cursed under her breath, grateful for the white noise of the engine.

Ryan finished his run, and Leo rounded toward him. The boat slowed as they approached.

Aelin shook her head at him, floating triumphantly in the water. "I feel like you forgot to mention something. Specifically about your time on a private lake?"

Ryan laughed. "You never asked."

"Right. That should always be my first question."

Ryan pulled off his skis and sent them floating toward the boat, then swam after them. He stopped at the ladder, the water lapping at his chest. "Your turn now, I think."

Aelin shrugged. "I think I might wait. Let my mom go first."

Ryan's eyes narrowed. "Hmm."

Aelin scoffed. "Oh please, I *will* do it, just not right now."

Ryan flicked his hair back and grabbed onto the ladder. "Sure,

I get it. No pressure." He winced and hissed air through his teeth, looking down at the water.

"Are you okay?" Aelin tucked her phone into her shirt and climbed up onto the back of the boat.

"Yeah, I just—" His hand slipped on the ladder. "Here, can you—?" He motioned for her to come closer.

"What—?" She leaned forward to see what he was trying to show her, and as soon as her hand hit the boat, Ryan's hand circled around her wrist. He tugged, and Aelin went flying over his head into the lake.

Her body hit the chilly water like a sledgehammer, and she gasped, her vision blurring. The cold seeped into her bones as she kicked, spluttering as she broke the surface. She launched herself at him. "What the hell?"

"Mom, don't swear!" Bailey yelled over the side.

Ryan caught her wrists, laughing as he lowered her arms to her sides and pulled her against his chest. "I'm sorry, I had to."

"Had to? That's a lame-ass explanation," she hissed.

His jaw brushed her cheek as he bobbed, treading water. "It was what Fun Ryan would've done." He released her, then climbed up the ladder, his legs disappearing over the side. Aelin's teeth chattered as she looked up at her sister. "Mariah, can you hand me the skis?"

Mariah pursed her lips, trying not to laugh. "Mmhmm."

Aelin shook her head. "Don't."

Mariah scoffed. "I wasn't going to say anything." She handed her the skis, and Aelin fit them in the water.

"This is so much easier to adjust in the boat," she grunted, listening to Bailey still laughing her head off, reliving the moment she flew over the side.

Ryan's head appeared over the edge. He handed her the rope.

She lowered her voice. "Is Fun Ryan an asshole?"

He shrugged. "I think we're all excited to find out."

Aelin rolled her eyes and gripped the rope as the boat floated away from her. She waited until the rope went taught, then balanced in the water. "Hit it!"

———

She was mostly dry when they got back to the dock. Mariah's friends from the night before were chatting on the beach, the teens engaged in an intense game of chicken on the dock.

Aelin dragged her fingers through her damp hair and turned to Ryan. "Seems like your kind of crowd."

Ryan fought a smile. "I regret nothing." He scrubbed his hand over his jaw. "Especially because you were planning to show me up."

She scoffed. "I wasn't planning anything."

He gave her a sidelong glance. "Sure! I'd love to ski! Hmm . . . maybe I'll wait till later."

Aelin smacked his chest, then stood and handed Mariah their life jackets while her dad hopped out and pulled them into their mooring.

Bailey and Amaya jumped ship and ran straight to the beach to continue their shipwreck game from the night before. Aelin and Ryan grabbed their towels and clothes, then walked to the cabin to prepare sandwiches for lunch.

Once Aelin was warm and had food in her stomach, she felt much less murdery toward Ryan, though the fact that he seemed utterly unconcerned made her want to punish him a little.

Unfortunately, it was impossible for her to be in anything other than a downright pleasant mood. The afternoon was perfect. They set up the hammocks in the trees near the beach where the girls were playing. She read a third of a novel she'd been trying to get to for months and fell asleep twice.

When she woke the second time, she walked to the cabin to

use the washroom, then returned to find Ryan playing sea monster. The girls squealed as he disappeared under the water, then exploded next to their makeshift rafts.

Aelin laughed, sitting back in the hammock, swaying as she watched. Clouds were rolling in over the lake, and she grabbed her phone, searching the weather for Bigfork. She frowned. *Severe Thunderstorm Warning.* Not great considering they were planning to have dinner at the campfire again, followed by cards and s'mores.

"You good?" Ryan walked up the beach, his hair dripping on his shoulders.

She glanced up from her screen. He'd asked her that at least twice since they'd arrived. She used to hate it when Clark asked. It always felt like a judgment, like she was inconveniencing him somehow by having emotions that weren't pure adoration. When Ryan asked, she felt . . . warm. Like he was watching and actually cared what the answer was.

"Yeah." She set her phone in the hammock next to her. "Just checking the weather."

Ryan grabbed his towel and looked up at the sky as he rubbed it over his chest. "Doesn't look ideal for a fire."

Aelin nodded. "Or skiing." She chewed on her lip and scanned the lake.

"I'm sure they're on their way back."

She stood from the hammock, then lost her balance and fell back. Ryan pretended not to notice, but she saw the curve of his lips. "I'll tell the girls to finish up. Just in case." Aelin grabbed the girls' towels.

Ryan dropped his towel and started gathering the sand toys and floats as Aelin walked over the smooth rocks. "Hey girls! Storm's coming in. Let's go back to the cabin."

Amaya and Bailey looked over their shoulders. They seemed convinced by the angry clouds and didn't argue. As Aelin wrapped the towels over their shoulders, the roar of a boat sounded in the distance. She looked up and saw the Mastercraft heading in toward the dock.

She breathed a sigh of relief, then led the girls up the beach to grab their shoes.

Thunder was already booming across the sky by the time they made it through the front door.

Ryan glanced out the window. "I'm going to go help them get the boat covered."

Aelin nodded. Bailey's shoulders drooped as she slipped off her sandals and trudged into the living room. "I wanted s'mores."

"Yeah." Aelin sighed. "You never know. Maybe the storm will blow through. Why don't you girls go get cleaned up?"

"I don't want to shower. I'm just going to get smoky."

That was a fair point. "Okay, just don't get water on your beds."

Bailey grinned, and the girls ran up the stairs. Aelin waited by the window for a moment, then put on her sandals and stepped out into the wind.

CHAPTER
Twenty

THE STORM MOVED IN FAST. One moment, the lake was a placid mirror reflecting the grey sky, and the next, it was whipped into a frenzy. The temperature dropped, and a chill crawled up Ryan's spine as he grabbed one corner of the cover from Aelin's dad.

Aelin sprinted toward the water, her ponytail swishing. "I'll get the paddleboards!" she yelled to Mariah, already halfway there.

Lightning flashed over the lake followed by a crack of thunder, and the first drops of rain started to fall, fat and heavy. Ryan glanced at Aelin, their eyes meeting for a heartbeat as she dragged the boards up onto the beach. She wore her shorts, but no shirt over her bikini top. He thought about her hand resting on his. The way her skin had prickled under the water. What was he doing?

He knew exactly what he wanted to do. Something about being away from home made the ground feel less stable under his feet. He'd been so sure he could never be with anyone but Kara. That he couldn't move on while she was still stuck in that place. But did Fun Ryan feel the same way?

By the time they had everything stowed away, the rain was

coming down in earnest. They said hurried goodbyes and retreated to their respective cabins.

"That was intense." Aelin panted.

"I don't remember the last time I saw a storm like this." Ryan kicked off his sandals and went to the window, crouching so he could see past the porch overhang. Thunder shook the walls.

"Mom?" Bailey's voice wafted down from the loft.

"Hey, we're here." Aelin turned, scanning the floor for something. "Do you girls want to watch a movie or play a game?"

The girls didn't answer right away. "Both. Game first, then movie."

"Sounds perfect." Aelin grabbed the towels puddled on the floor and took them into the bedroom.

The girls settled in at the table. Ryan grabbed the bag of Sour Patch Kids, and Aelin nodded approvingly.

She pulled a few options from the bag. "Crazy Eights or Go Fish?"

They played multiple rounds of both while the rain hammered on the roof. Amaya was fiercely competitive, her brow furrowing as she analyzed her cards. Bailey was all about the rules, making sure everyone followed them to the letter. He chuckled every time she started a sentence with, "Wait . . . "

After round four of Crazy Eights, he glanced up at the clock. "Dinner?" The girls nodded. "Why don't you two go start your movie and we'll whip something up." He pushed his chair back and headed to the kitchen.

"I can do that." Aelin stood.

Ryan shook his head. "No. Go shower. I've got this."

Aelin watched him a moment, then nodded. She disappeared into the bedroom, and he stood in front of the open fridge for a moment, unsure why he'd opened it in the first place. *Chicken. Pasta sauce.*

Ryan forced the idea of Aelin pulling off her bikini top behind the door out of his head and opened the package of chicken breasts. *Nice.* André would've taken advantage of that one.

He'd barely responded to the team chat since they'd been there. He didn't want to disappear onto his phone, but when he started getting individual messages from his teammates, he decided he at least needed to let them know he was alive.

Ryan cut the chicken, coated a pan with olive oil, then started it cooking. He boiled water and grabbed the salt from the cupboard. He pulled the package of noodles from the top shelf and opened them. As soon as the chicken was white around the edges, he flipped them with a spatula and put the lid on the pan just to make sure they cooked through. The whole dinner was prepped and ready in under fifteen minutes, so he decided to chop up some cucumbers and peppers since nobody had returned to the kitchen. Not that he was trying to impress anybody.

He had plates and cups neatly stacked on the counter, along with forks and napkins, by the time Aelin re-emerged from the bedroom. Her hair was wet and combed, and she wore a cozy sweater and joggers that were so thin, they left nothing to the imagination.

He called to the girls and had them pause their movie, then dished up and sat at the table to eat. Bailey found a candle and matches in one of the drawers and insisted they have mood lighting. The sky was still dark outside, the rain still coming down in buckets.

The girls took all of ten seconds to finish their meal and run back upstairs to their tablets. He and Aelin took their time. She complimented him multiple times on the sauce, which he didn't feel was necessarily deserved, but appreciated, nonetheless. Cooking for only him and Amaya didn't exactly yield a high level of job satisfaction.

"Most guys don't cook, you know." Aelin took a bite of pasta.

"You know most guys?"

She shrugged. "You hear things."

"I don't think you've met enough hockey players. We take our food very seriously." Ryan took a drink of water.

"Hmm. Right. When I think of hockey players, I think of homemakers."

Ryan feigned offense. "So judgy."

They finished their meal, and Aelin insisted on doing the cleanup. She put the extra food in snap containers from the cupboard, then washed the pots and pans by hand and loaded the plates, cups, and silverware into the dishwasher.

Ryan kept the candle burning after wiping down the table, and both of them settled into the living room with the lights off, watching the lightning flash through the window.

"Do you want to sit out on the porch? I don't know what direction the rain is coming from."

He stood. "Worth checking."

They stepped out the front door and sat down on the wooden bench. "I think we got lucky." The raindrops whipped around the side of the house, but they were coming from the opposite direction. A few drops hit his ankles, but other than that, the angle kept them dry. Aelin gasped as a jagged arc of lightning ripped through the charcoal clouds.

"It's terrifying," she whispered. "I love it."

He frowned. "You like being terrified?"

"Not in real life."

He shifted, turning to face her. "We're not in real life?"

She shook her head. "Not up there. That's . . . I don't know. A theoretical. We're down here on earth. Little ants on a massive rock. Everything up there follows its own rules."

He studied her profile as she watched the sky, her eyes wide with wonder. Ryan cleared his throat. "Did we succeed?"

She let out a contented sigh. "Yeah. I think we did."

"There's nothing else you wanted to do?"

Aelin opened her mouth, then closed it, tucking her hands under her thighs. She shook her head.

"Liar," he whispered.

Even in the dim lighting filtering through the window, he caught the flush creeping onto her cheeks. He was flirting with the line, and he knew it, but he couldn't stop pushing just a little further if it meant he got a reaction like that.

Her tongue flicked over her lips. "It's stupid."

"Try me."

The words seemed to dance on the tip of her tongue before she swallowed them again. Ryan didn't press. He leaned back against the bench, catching another flash of lightning fracturing the sky and burning against his retinas.

"I've always wanted to dance in the rain," she murmured. Ryan stilled, keeping his eyes trained ahead. "I told Clark that once, and he said it would probably be disappointing."

Ryan grunted. "Why?"

She let out a long exhale. "Because there was nothing romantic about being cold and wet." She paused. "I saw that scene on the beach in Sweet Home Alabama. At sixteen, that was the sexiest thing I'd ever seen in my life."

Ryan laughed. "And now?"

"Still pretty close."

Ryan tapped his fingers on the wooden bench, then without overthinking it, he stood and offered her a hand.

She looked up at him. "I didn't tell you that as some plea for a pity dance."

Ryan didn't move. "I think it sounds fun."

She pursed her lips, then glanced past him. "I'm sure everyone is in their cabins looking out their windows right now."

"That's a problem?"

She teased her lower lip with her teeth. "Yeah. A little. I don't want them to get the wrong idea."

Ryan nodded. He started to lower his hand when she pushed up to stand in front of him. "Back porch?"

They walked back into the cabin and picked up their shoes, tiptoeing down the hall, and through the bedroom to the back door. The girls' movie was still playing in the loft. This time Ryan couldn't pretend that he was only flirting with the line. He knew exactly what he was doing when he stood and offered Aelin his hand.

His hands trembled as he pushed open the door, and a gust of wind sent a spray of rain onto the carpet. Ryan pulled her out, their sandals slapping against the soaking deck boards as the rain whipped against their cheeks.

Aelin's eyes were wide as he pulled her into his arms. "Was it raining like this in the movie?" Ryan raised his voice above the creaking of the pine trees.

She laughed. "Definitely not."

There was no music to match, but as Ryan looped his arms around her waist and Aelin dropped hers over his shoulders, they swayed anyway. Aelin rested her temple against his cheek. Her normal coconut scent mixed with damp pine and sunscreen.

The rain lashed at them, cold and relentless. Ryan's shirt clung to his skin, and Aelin's hair plastered against her face. She laughed, and he closed his eyes to keep his eyeballs from getting pelted. Aelin pressed into him, and liquid fire flooded his veins. His hands pressed against her waist, feeling her muscles flex as she moved. Then he was imagining her in that bikini, goosebumps flashing across her skin.

He shifted, momentarily embarrassed by what she had to be feeling through those paper-thin joggers, but Aelin only pressed closer. He gritted his teeth and said the only thing that came into his head.

"I'm not really a dancer."

She grinned against his cheek. "I think being willing is the biggest thing."

He adjusted his grip on her waist. "I thought about taking lessons."

She pulled back to look at him, her eyes narrowed against the onslaught. "Why?"

"One of my teammates is getting married in August. My friend Tyler wanted to do a flash mob."

Aelin's face split into a smile. "Shut up. That's amazing. Your whole hockey team?" He nodded. "What song?"

His grin widened. "It's super romantic."

She laughed. "What song?"

"Pink Pony Club."

Aelin's hands tightened, her fingers gently tugging on his hair. "That's—you have to record it. If you don't send that to me, we can't be friends."

Ryan's pulse pounded in his ears. Is that what they were? Friends? He lifted a hand and swept the hair from her forehead. Aelin opened her left eye, squinting to look at him. Her lips parted, and the tip of her nose turned pink.

Just as he was searching for something else to fill the silence, her hand curled, and her fingernails gently scratched the back of his neck. Any rational thought evaporated. He was standing in the rain, soaked to the bone with a gorgeous woman. She was molded against him, their thin cotton fabric the only thing dulling the sensation of her soft curves.

Fun Ryan punched Old Ryan in the nuts and went for it.

CHAPTER
Twenty-One

AELIN SUCKED in a breath as Ryan's lips pressed against hers. His mouth was warm, slick from the rain. She pressed against his warmth, working to catch her breath, her head swimming. Her lips parted, her tongue flicking against his as his fingers spread into her hair.

She sighed against his mouth, and his whole body tightened against her. Her mind flaunted every image she didn't realize she'd carefully stored away, pulling them out like Polaroids. *The one where Ryan reads a book half naked. The one where Ryan gives a high-five to a twelve-year-old on the ice. The one where Ryan pulls his shirt off on the boat in front of your whole family and you grit your teeth and pretend your thighs didn't suddenly transform into a flint and steel.*

Her tongue reached for his then, her fingers threading through his hair. How many times had she wanted to touch his hair? Ryan pressed her back against the cabin wall, his hand dropping back to her waist, pulling her flush against his hips so fast, she gasped.

Aelin arched into him, and his fingers dragged over her hip bone, fumbling with the hem of her shirt. And then, as soon as his fingers hit skin, he suddenly jerked back.

Aelin dropped her arms, panting.

"I'm sorry, I shouldn't have—"

Aelin was already moving. She burst through the back door into her room, heart thudding in her chest. Her breath came in short gasps as she scanned the room, her mind a jumbled mess. What the hell was she thinking?

Clark had cheated on her twice, and she'd sworn she would never have anything to do with that. Yes, Ryan's situation was different, but he still wore his damn wedding ring.

Aelin forced her feet to move before Ryan walked in behind her. She strode to the washroom, turned on the light, and closed the door behind her. She could barely look at herself in the mirror because if Ryan hadn't stopped . . .

She leaned over the counter, dropping her head in her hands. Maybe she would have? But the way heat still pulsed in every cell of her body, she doubted it.

Her hands shook as she peeled off her soaked clothes, fumbling with the fabric. She piled the heavy cotton on the counter, not even bothering to wring it out, then turned on the shower.

She trembled as she waited for the water to heat up. It was a cowardly move to disappear inside but what else was she supposed to do? How could she look him in the eye after this?

As steam rose around the glass door, Aelin stepped into the shower. *No.* That was the same thinking that had gotten her buried with Clark. She wasn't the one at fault in the situation. Ryan had kissed her first, and yes, she had kissed him back, but that didn't mean that she should be embarrassed. Both of them had been pushing the limit since they arrived.

What limits? What were they even fighting against? Aelin was getting divorced and Ryan . . . What was Ryan? He wasn't in a real marriage, but he definitely still felt a strong sense of loyalty and commitment. If she was being honest, even though it broke her heart, it also gave her hope. *What woman didn't want someone to love her like that?*

Her eyes stung as she scrubbed her body and washed her hair. There were no easy answers here.

She ticked down the list of things she knew about Ryan. He loved his daughter. He showed up when he said he was going to or had a damn good excuse for why he didn't. He listened to her. He loved his wife. He knew how to fix things, and he smelled good, and his hair was long and soft—

Aelin leaned against the shower tile, grounding herself.

She didn't know for sure, but Ryan was quite possibly the best guy she'd met in twelve years. *And she was supposed to ignore him?*

Being at the lake was messing with her. Ryan was right. It did feel like another world. *What happens at Flathead stays at Flathead.* She snorted and rinsed her hair. She could have had so much more fun had she adopted that mantra at sixteen.

It felt so damn good to be touched. To be held. She had endured twelve years with a man who only saw her as a reflection of himself. Didn't she deserve something better?

Aelin pressed her head against the shower tile, the water streaming down her face, cascading over her chilled skin.

She needed to get out of the washroom. It wasn't fair for her to hog the space, even if it was the only sanctuary she had at the moment. Aelin turned off the water and stepped out onto the bath mat. She grabbed her towel and started drying off when a jolt passed through her. *The girls.* They were still upstairs watching their movie.

She cursed under her breath and scrubbed the towel over her skin. As she was about to hang it back up, she glanced at the counter. *Shit.* She hadn't brought in any clean clothes.

Aelin clenched her jaw and ran a comb through her hair, then hastily wrapped the towel around herself. What were the chances that Ryan was still in the bedroom? Probably slim. He had most likely realized the same thing she did and gone upstairs to check on the girls.

Aelin put her hand on the door knob and hesitated. She drew

a breath and twisted, pulling the door toward her. As soon as the room came into view she froze. Ryan was sitting on the bed in dry joggers, his chest bare, his hair still wet.

His head snapped up, his eyes locking on to hers. "Hey," he rasped.

"Hey." Aelin stepped out into the room, her toes curling against the carpet. She took a step toward the dresser and paused. What was she going to do? Get dressed, put the kids to bed, ignore him the whole night, and somehow avoid talking about this for an entire week? Maybe in her twenties she would've tried that, but in her thirties, she was over the games and the drama. She drew a breath. "I'm sorry I bolted."

Ryan exhaled. "I'm sorry I . . . " He trailed off. "No. I'm not sorry." He lifted his head to look at her. "I know I should be sorry, but I'm not."

Aelin twisted the edge of the towel. "I want to talk about this, but the girls are still—"

"I put them to bed. While you were in the shower."

Aelin pressed her lips together. "Oh. Thank you."

"They said I wasn't allowed to read the story because I can't do the voices."

Aelin grinned, her cheeks heating. "It is a very advanced skill." She walked over and sat next to him on the bed, suddenly not caring that she only had a strip of cotton covering her. "I know exactly what you mean, by the way. I've felt so guilty for so long for so many things, I've used up all my credits."

Ryan dropped his head, looking at his hands. He twisted his wedding band around his finger. "I sometimes wonder what the point is."

"Of what?"

"Of anything." He exhaled in a rush. "Sorry. This definitely isn't Fun Ryan."

Aelin laughed. "He was out there on the porch, I think."

Ryan grinned, but his eyes were still sad. "I felt good about that. Kissing you. I haven't . . . " He groaned, pressing the heels of his hands against his eyes. "Embarrassing."

Aelin grabbed onto his wrist. "Can you stop that, please? It's not embarrassing that you loved someone. It's not embarrassing that you had that taken away from you, and it's not embarrassing that you didn't want to move on."

Ryan dropped his hands, twisting his arm to flatten his palm against hers, and heat flashed under her skin. She stared at her fingers twining with his. "I feel good about this. I felt good about it on the boat, too."

Ryan nodded. "Yeah."

"I don't think—" She paused, choosing her words carefully. "There's not a manual for this. I remember when I had Bailey, I checked every book out from the library. I scoured the internet for blogs—remember people used to do those?"

"No, but continue."

She bit her lip. "I was sure that I could do it right, and since I was obviously doing marriage wrong, I put all my hopes in that basket." Aelin ran her thumb over his. "I got some good ideas, but the experts never had answers for my exact situation. What do you do when your husband yells at your three-year-old when she draws on his shoes with a pen?" She shook her head. "The only way I got away from Clark was by trusting my gut more than everyone else's opinions."

Ryan tapped her knuckles. "And what if . . . " He cleared his throat. "What if your gut is the problem?"

Aelin looked up. "Maybe then you go back to the basics." She pulled her hand from his and brushed the hair from his cheek. Ryan's eyes shuttered. He leaned into her touch, pressing his lips against her palm.

She swallowed, her throat constricting as words pooled in her mouth. "Are you ready for bed?"

Ryan shook his head. "I need to brush my teeth."

Aelin nodded. "Me, too. Meet back here in three?"

His brow twitched. "Oddly specific."

"I don't want to wait for five."

Where the hell had that come from? Ryan's pupils dilated. He stood and stalked into the washroom, and Aelin went to the dresser. She pulled on a pair of cotton underwear and a tank top, then took up residence next to him at the sink.

They brushed, rinsed, then made their way back into the bedroom. Ryan stood at the foot of the bed, and Aelin walked to the headboard, pulling off the decorative pillows and tossing them on the floor. "I don't want you to sleep on the floor tonight."

His jaw worked, but he didn't refute the statement. His eyes dropped to her hips, then dragged over her torso. She pulled back the covers, then walked to stand in front of him.

Her pulse picked up speed. "I want—" She paused, not sure if she could say it out loud. "I want you to hold me. If that's okay." The idea of going to bed alone after feeling him next to her made her insides feel like overbaked clay.

He wet his lips. "Okay."

Aelin nodded once, then walked to the door. She closed it and flicked off the light, then padded back to the bed.

CHAPTER
Twenty~Two

RYAN WOKE EARLY the next morning, his body on autopilot from years of early morning practices and then morning commutes. His reality draped over him in layers. He was lying in bed, but not alone. A leg threaded between his. His heartbeat seemed to be doubled.

Ryan held perfectly still as the night before solidified, waiting for the inevitable feeling of guilt or shame when he remembered he'd kissed another woman. Held her as they slept.

But the pang in his gut never came. Instead, he was filled with a soft warmth. It seemed to spread from his middle, dissolving through him until it reached his toes and fingertips.

Aelin was still asleep beside him, her body a delicate curve. His heart stuttered as he slowly shifted to get a better look at her. Her hair fell in soft waves over her shoulder and fanned out on the pillow. Her lips were slightly parted, her eyelashes resting against her cheek.

Her fingertips shared her pulse, beating slow and steady against his ribs. He counted the freckles along her temple. The way her ear lobe dipped.

Ryan hadn't slept next to a woman since Kara. Since the night before their entire world flipped upside down. He'd held

Amaya, of course, but that was different. This—this was something he'd thought he'd never experience again.

The grief he'd managed to wrap up and hide for so long crashed over him like a tidal wave. He'd lost Kara. He'd lost the future they'd planned together. And in the years since, he'd lost a piece of himself. He'd buried his desires, his needs, his hope for companionship because it was easier than facing the void Kara had left behind.

Ryan closed his eyes, his hand still resting on Aelin's hip. It was almost laughable that he'd convinced himself he was fine. That his life was full, that he didn't need anyone else. His eyes burned, his gut and his heart at complete odds.

He couldn't abandon her.

He couldn't live without this.

With a resolute breath, he pulled his hand away and slowly slipped free of Aelin's limbs. He checked the clock. It was only seven thirty, but he doubted the girls would sleep in with light streaming through the windows in the loft.

He lifted his upper body from the mattress, then stood and reached for his shirt, pulling it over his head.

He padded into the washroom and relieved himself, then washed his hands, splashed his face with water, and left the bedroom, closing the door behind him with a soft click.

Besides a few beach toys strewn on the ground, there was no evidence of the storm the night before. The lake was pristine, the sunshine bright and golden. Ryan opened a cupboard and reached for a mixing bowl. He measured out two cups of pancake mix, then added milk, eggs, and melted butter, the liquids pooling in the centre of the bowl. The batter thickened as he whisked. When he was satisfied with the consistency, he poured a dollop of oil into the cast-iron skillet and set it on the stovetop.

He mixed in blueberries with a spoon, and when the oil was hot, dropped three dollops of batter into the pan. It sizzled. He watched as bubbles formed on the surface of the pancakes, the batter puffing up and drying at the edges.

With a flick of his wrist, he flipped the pancakes, the edges curling slightly as they landed back in the pan.

Voices murmured overhead, followed by the rustling of sheets. He couldn't quite make out what Bailey and Amaya were saying, but it didn't take long for their feet to start thumping on the stairs.

"Morning." He looked up and smiled, only realizing then that there were no blankets or a pillow on the couch. Hopefully they wouldn't connect the dots and wonder where he'd slept for the night.

"You made pancakes?" Amaya ran up and leaned over the counter

Ryan grabbed a plate and lifted the pancakes from the pan. "Perfect timing." He set the plate in front of her, then turned and pulled syrup from the fridge. Amaya and Bailey grabbed plates and forks, then took a pancake from the pile and settled in at the table.

Aelin appeared next to the fridge, her hair mussed and her cheeks rosy from sleep. Ryan's blood heated as he looked up and met her eyes. She blinked, her eyes slow and dreamy as the corner of her mouth lifted. "Good morning."

"Morning." His voice was gravelly, and he cleared it.

"Sleep well?" She asked, her voice light as she walked past him, her hand brushing his hip. She was a tease.

Ryan's eyes sharpened as she pulled a plate from the shelf. "Probably the best sleep I've had in years."

She let out a soft breath. "The lake does that to you. Doesn't it, Bailes?"

Bailey nodded. "I sleep so well here."

Aelin raised an eyebrow. "Looks like you're not alone."

They finished breakfast and changed into swimsuits. Everything felt easier. They walked down to the dock, found their life jackets from the day before, and within fifteen minutes, were out on the lake, zipping across the water.

Mariah and Leo weren't with them that morning. They decided to switch off days and go with their friends later that afternoon, so it was just the grandparents and their little combined family.

Seeing the four of them on the boat together punctuated everything he'd been feeling since last night. *Looks like you aren't alone.* The words pulsed through him like a heartbeat. Without even realizing it, he'd imagined his life for the next thirty years. Drawn in permanent ink. It was him and Amaya, and when Amaya was gone, it was just him.

After last night, it was as if someone had grabbed a bucket of soapy water and a brush and started to scrub.

Ryan looked down and found Amaya next to him, her arms crossed over her chest. "What's wrong?"

"I want to get better at skiing, but I also don't want to waste our time since we're only here for a few days."

"Four more days." Ryan held up his fingers. "We don't have to leave until Sunday."

Amaya's face brightened. "True."

Aelin glanced up at him from across the boat. A small smile had played on her lips all morning, and Ryan practically salivated at the realization that he'd put it there. What they'd done the night before had felt right. It hadn't been lust, though that had certainly been there on the porch in the rain. He wasn't craving some quick fix or release. Though again . . . he wasn't not craving it.

But the order of things seemed to matter.

He watched Aelin's parents, her mom's hand on her dad's knee each time she leaned in and yelled something over the roar of the engine. The way he looked at her every time he made a joke, hoping for her approval.

Marriage had never been just a piece of paper to him. Even if

Kara didn't understand the commitments they'd made anymore, he did. He wanted Aelin to know that he did.

"Kneeboard?" Amaya yelled across the boat to Bailey.

She gave her a thumbs up.

They played on the water until noon, then took the boat in to switch out drivers and riders. Ryan thanked Molly and Dave for chauffeuring them around, then helped set the life jackets out to dry on the dock.

"You better be careful," Aelin said next to him. He looked up, worried he was doing something wrong. She laughed. "You're being too helpful. They're going to fall in love with you."

Aelin held his eyes for one moment more, then turned and followed the girls down the dock.

Ryan stood, stripped off his shirt, and ran past her, dodging in front of her and launching himself off the dock with a yell.

The girls squealed with delight and jumped in after him. He surfaced and shook his hair out of his eyes. Bailey and Amaya chased after him in the water, and he took off toward the beach.

"You coming?" he yelled back at Aelin.

She huffed, then stripped off her shirt and shorts and dived in after them.

———

Ryan held her that night. And the night after that. They never did more than map each other's skin and breathe together until they fell asleep.

They spent the mornings on the boat and the afternoons exploring the town and surrounding area. On Saturday they were tasked with finding wild huckleberries for pies. Aelin's dad had made it sound like a treasure hunt, and the girls were instantly sold.

"There's a trail on the other side of the house that sounds promising." Aelin slipped on her hiking shoes, and they all filed out the door.

Amaya and Bailey ran ahead, and Ryan and Aelin fell into step next to each other on the narrow path that led from their back door through the woods.

Ryan glanced back at the porch.

Aelin noticed, and her cheeks flushed. "I think this is my favourite time I've ever come to the lake."

"Hmm. Because Bailey's older?" He tried to keep a straight face, but he cracked when she elbowed his ribs.

He didn't have anything to compare it to, but the week had been the best one he could remember in years. The realization that it was Saturday, that the next day they'd be turning their phones on and driving back to Calgary, sent ice sliding down his spine.

They followed the trail until Amaya and Bailey stopped in front of them. Amaya turned, putting a finger to her lips.

Ryan and Aelin walked closer. A family of deer stood in a small clearing, their velvety noses twitching as they grazed on the foliage.

Ryan didn't move, the hairs on his arm lifting as Aelin's skin brushed his. He'd touched her there. *He'd touched her almost everywhere.*

After a few seconds, the deer lifted their heads and looked directly at them. Ryan held his breath, waiting for them to bolt, but instead, they just regarded them with calm curiosity. *Seems like you're not alone.*

Aelin glanced up at him, then linked her fingers with his for a beat before letting go.

After the deer moved on, they continued up the hill and found a garter snake and two small frogs. When they were about to turn back, Bailey pointed through the foliage and grabbed a Ziploc bag from the box Aelin carried.

Bailey left the trail and plucked a deep purple berry from the bush and held it up, then dropped it in the bag.

"She found them." Aelin grinned and tromped after her into the brush.

———

There were at least a dozen chairs set up on the patio around the firepit after dinner. The huckleberry pies sat cooling on cinder blocks, and the paper bowls and spoons were ready on the table.

Mariah crouched, setting up her phone on a tripod to record. She turned to the teenage boys grouped behind the picnic table. "You guys ready? You're up first."

Ryan had been skeptical when Aelin told him about the variety show. His family had always been into sports. All of them would rather wear a cup two sizes too small than stand up in front of a group and sing or dance. She'd insisted it wasn't about being good, but he'd seen enough from her to know that her version of "just okay" wasn't the norm. He had her double back flips and slalom skiing to prove it.

The boys nodded and disappeared behind the cabin. Once all the adults and kids were seated, Mariah hit play on her phone, and they reappeared in wigs, tutus, and oversized sunglasses. One of them—Tucker?—had even gone to the trouble of stuffing a bra with water balloons. They lip-synced and danced their way through *Barbie Girl* to no lack of hoots and hollers from the audience. Aelin couldn't stop laughing as they mimicked Barbie and Ken, strutting and posing like they were in a music video from before they were born.

The group erupted into cheers when the boys struck their final pose. Aelin shot him a look that said, "I told you this would be amazing," then hopped up to wrangle Amaya and Bailey.

Ryan grinned as they took their places. They wouldn't let

him be in the cabin when they practiced, and he didn't even know what song they were singing.

Bailey held the sheet music with Amaya standing next to her. Aelin started the accompaniment on her phone, and it was like someone hooked up a vacuum sealer to his lungs and pressed start as they began to sing. He always enjoyed their choir concerts, but hearing them sing, just the two of them, gave him chills.

He'd only known Bailey a short time, but after coaching her at camp, she was quickly becoming one of his favourite kids. She was quieter than Amaya. More careful. She reminded him of her mom.

The girls bowed to applause when they finished, and Amaya's cheeks were cherry red when she went back to her camp chair.

It was so good. All of it. The lake, the friends, the food, the card games. Ryan's throat grew thick as he looked around the camp ring and committed to making more of an effort to drive up and spend time with his own family when they got back.

Tomorrow. Dread hit his stomach.

Mariah stood and motioned for Aelin to join her at the front. Aelin shook her head, but Mariah wasn't letting it go.

Aelin blushed as she groaned and finally acquiesced. That look on her face had Ryan's full attention. She grabbed her sister's arm and lowered her voice. "What are you doing?"

Mariah grinned. "I found our music. I couldn't resist."

Aelin's eyes widened. "The music? I haven't done that in years!"

"Neither have I. That's what'll make it hilarious." Mariah cleared her throat and turned to the audience. "Okay, this is a dance we made up one summer to Club California."

"It was on a cassette tape that came with this Barbie doll Mariah got for her birthday when she was six," Aelin explained. Her parents were already laughing.

Mariah motioned for Leo to press play, and Aelin fell into

step beside her sister, their feet shuffling and arms flailing, both of them barely able to suck in a breath through their laughter.

Mariah attempted a high kick and nearly toppled into the fire pit. Aelin grabbed her arm, and they transitioned into some sort of train move. It was the only way to describe what their hands were doing.

Her family was wheezing by the time the music died, and the teenage boys still in cotton-candy-coloured wigs quite possibly gave the loudest applause of the night.

Aelin collapsed into her camp chair, her mascara smeared. "So. That was a thing I did."

Ryan stayed glued to the canvas. Because if he moved, he was going to reach over and kiss her.

"Tucker!" Leo tromped into the circle, panting. "I ran up to get my phone and the door to the cabin is locked."

Tucker looked around as if there was some other kid in their small group with his same name. "Yeah. Mom always says not to leave the doors unlocked."

"At home, Tuck. Not when the cabin door is ten feet from us."

Mariah patted her pockets, then made a face. "You had the key."

Leo exhaled. "Yeah. I had the key."

"It's in the cabin?" she asked.

Leo pursed his lips. "Yeah."

Aelin turned to Ryan, her eyes glittering. He wet his lips and nodded. She grinned and jumped up from her chair. "Hey, Mariah. Do you happen to have a bobby pin?"

CHAPTER
Twenty~Three

AELIN STOOD on the shore of the lake, watching as Amaya and Bailey skipped rocks. The cabin was cleaned out, their luggage was loaded up in the trunk of Ryan's car. All they had left to do was take the boat out and meet with her family for lunch.

Aelin glanced down at her phone, her body already beginning to tense as it searched for a network. Besides taking pictures, she'd gone radio silent, and it was going to be a rough re-entry.

"Are you sure you two are up for this?" Mariah called from the dock. "Leo and I can take care of it."

Ryan walked down from the cabin and waved a hand. "We're good."

Aelin nodded and trailed him to the boat. She stepped onboard and grabbed a damp cloth and cleaning solution. Ryan helped Leo dry off the exterior of the boat while she and Mariah wiped down the interior.

She glanced back at Amaya and Bailey having some conversation with Mariah's girls. *They were both so happy.* Tan and sun-kissed, their hair bleached out by the sun.

"I don't think they're going to be happy when we tell them it's time to go," she said.

Mariah sighed. "None of us are."

It was true. Being on the water, surrounded by friends and family, had been a slice of heaven. But it was the sight of Amaya and Bailey playing together that was the cherry on top. They'd been inseparable since the first night, and seeing them like that made Aelin's heart swell.

Aelin moved to the bow and spotted Ryan below her on the ramp. "Think we could just live out here?" Images of her going incognito with forged documents flashed through her head.

Ryan nodded but didn't answer. *Exactly.*

She wanted one more night lying in his arms. One more night cocooned from the reality of her life. It wasn't that the reality was bad. The reality was *unknown*.

It wasn't in her control, and maybe nothing ever really was. But it felt good to have the illusion of it. She'd been strapped into the passenger seat of her own life, and this week she'd taken the wheel. Or at least jumped out of the car. She could almost feel the scrapes and bruises taking shape because of it.

They finished drying off the boat, then gathered their things. Aelin called the girls over, and they reluctantly trudged back to the dock.

"Do we have to go?" Bailey's lower lip jutted out.

Aelin smiled and ruffled her hair. "Yep. Sorry, babe."

The girls got into the backseat making sure they had everything they needed for the drive, and Aelin leaned on the door as her parents walked to their car. "Pocketstone?"

Her dad nodded. "See you over there."

Main Street in Bigfork was hopping, and the line outside of Pocketstone Café wrapped down the block. Thankfully her dad had called ahead for their large group.

The hostess led them through the country diner to a large table in the middle of the restaurant. Her parents were already there, and Mariah and Leo trickled in with their kids. Her heart ached as she looked around the table.

This was what she'd given up. When she'd married Clark and moved to Canada, she'd left this. It felt like such a tragic waste until she glanced at Bailey picking up her menu. No price was too high for that.

Ryan's hand found hers under the table, and she clung to it as they placed their orders.

When the server left, their conversation turned to the past week. Mariah and Leo recounted their hike up to Avalanche Lake, while Dave and Molly talked about their morning paddle-boarding sessions.

"And what about you two?" Mariah turned to Aelin and Ryan.

Aelin shrugged. "You saw everything we did, I think. Mostly stuck around the cabin."

Mariah took a drink from her water glass. "The girls go to bed at what time?"

Aelin's mouth fell open, but Ryan only grinned. "Early enough for me to win at Crazy Eights."

Amaya looked at him, horrified. "You played after we went to sleep?"

The adults laughed while Ryan tried to explain that he was joking without much luck.

Mariah raised an eyebrow and mouthed, "I like him." Aelin shot her look, then pretended to be very interested in how Bailey was colouring her placemat.

The server brought their food, and Aelin's mouth watered at the sight of her grilled cheese. The cheddar oozed out from between the slices of bread, and the bacon was crispy and perfectly cooked. She took a bite and sighed.

"Good?" Ryan asked with a smirk.

Aelin nodded, her mouth too full to respond. She looked around the table. Mariah picked up a breakfast taco, her son Tucker ordered the largest smothered burrito known to man, Leo was taking a massive bite of his burger, and her parents shared a plate of meatloaf, eggs, and mashed potatoes. Every little girl had pancakes.

She grinned and took another bite.

Half an hour later, they said their goodbyes to Dave reciting, "The road goes ever on and on," then window shopped their way back to Ryan's car arguing about when Bailey would be old enough to watch The Hobbit.

And then they were buckled into their seats. Ryan started the engine, and Aelin turned her head so the girls wouldn't see tears slipping down her cheeks.

———

They stopped at the last American Walmart on their route and picked up as many cases of Cream Soda Dr. Pepper as they could fit between their bags before crossing the border back into Canada. As they passed the wooden "Welcome to Alberta" sign, a knot formed in Aelin's stomach.

Her life seemed to peel like an onion, each layer of reality stinking stronger than the last. *Clark wanted to sell the house. She couldn't find an affordable housing option. He was going to use that to try and take her custody time.*

Ryan glanced in the back, then dropped his sweatshirt over the console to hide his arm from the backseat and reached over for her hand. Aelin's fingers trembled as she took it. She closed her eyes and leaned her head back. Breathe. In and out.

The kilometres ticked by, and they eventually hit the outskirts of Calgary. The sun was ripe and swollen on the horizon as Ryan turned onto her street.

She wanted to tell him to slam on the brakes. To wait at the stop sign for just a few more minutes. But then he was pulling up to the curb and then—

Aelin's heart turned to stone and sank in her chest.

"Is that Dad's car?" Bailey pointed at the sleek black Audi in the driveway.

A cold sweat broke out on the back of Aelin's neck. *What the hell was he doing there?* She opened her mouth to speak, but no words came out. The sight of that car juxtaposed with their perfect week was so jarring, her vision blurred at the edges.

Ryan's hand landed on her shoulder, but it wasn't enough to pull her out of the whirlpool of panic.

"Aelin . . . "

She swallowed hard. "That's Clark's car."

Ryan's eyes darkened, and he glanced back at the girls in the back seat.

Clark wasn't supposed to be in the house. Per their initial mediation agreement, he was only allowed to be in the driveway for pick-ups and drop-offs. But his car was off. And he wasn't inside it.

Ryan swore under his breath as he turned off the engine. "Stay here. I'll—"

"No." Aelin's voice was firm. "Seeing you is only going to make it worse." She pushed her door open and hurried to the back of the car, patting the trunk for Ryan to open it. Aelin's legs felt like jelly as she started lifting out the cases of soda.

"I can do that." Ryan put a hand on the small of her back, but it only made her shake harder. Her fingers slipped on the handle of her suitcase.

Ryan circled her wrist with his hand and gently nudged her back, then pulled her suitcase from the trunk, followed by Bailey's. He turned to her. "If you think I'm going to drive away with him—"

"I can take this from here." Clark's voice bit into her from the driveway.

Aelin dropped her eyes and started rolling the suitcase to the sidewalk. "I'm good, thanks."

"Yeah, I'm not good." Clark folded his arms over his chest. He wore a long-sleeved shirt that shimmered weirdly when he moved, his dark hair perfectly coiffed. His jaw was clenched. "I showed up to pick up Bailey yesterday and you were nowhere to be found."

Aelin stared at him. "I was at Flathead. You signed the notary saying you gave permission."

He gave a condescending smirk. "Did you check the dates, Aelin?"

Her blood rushed in her ears. "I sent the dates to your lawyer."

"Right, I know, but did you check the dates of the letter?"

She dropped her bag on the sidewalk and went back to the car. She pulled her backpack from the floor and hunted until she found her passport and the notary letter.

Aelin unfolded it and scanned the text. July sixteenth through July twentieth—

She froze, reading it a second time. It was the twenty-second. The letter only listed permission until the twentieth.

"You refused to turn Bailey over to my care. That's a violation of our agreement. Furthermore, you took our daughter internationally without permission." Clark scoffed. "I'm amazed they didn't detain you at the border."

Aelin's breath came in short, shallow bursts. If she'd been passing through the American side, they probably would've.

Clark lowered his voice and took a step closer. "I also didn't give permission for my daughter to be in the care of another adult."

Aelin spun, her eyes flashing. "Are you seriously—" She stopped mid-sentence as Bailey pushed the door of the car open.

"Dad!" She grinned, dropping her pillow and backpack on the grass and running to him.

"Hey, bug."

Aelin ground her teeth. She'd always hated that nickname because he wielded it like a weapon. Someday, Bailey would be old enough to see how each word he used was meant to distract. To hurt. To blind.

Bailey looked up. "When's our next date?"

Clark exhaled and ruffled her hair. "I'll have to talk with your mom. I cleared my whole weekend so we could spend time together, but she didn't tell me you were going to be gone."

Bailey's head turned toward her, her eyes questioning.

Aelin clenched her jaw so tight, she tasted blood. "It was a misunderstanding, Bailes. I'm so sorry." The apology felt like she was swallowing razor blades.

Clark smiled. "No problem, we'll figure something out, eh?" He pulled his keys from his pocket, then gave Bailey another hug. "See you soon, bug."

Clark glanced up, his expression cold enough to make her shiver, then turned and got in his car.

Ryan stood next to her, every muscle tensed. "Let's get your things inside."

Aelin drew a shaky breath. "He didn't look at you."

Ryan ran a hand through his hair. "Yeah. Got lucky, I guess."

Aelin shook her head. "No. That's not a good thing." She pulled up the handle on her suitcase and started rolling it. "If he thought he was the dominant man in this situation, he would have done something to prove it. He ignored you."

Ryan followed her up the walk with the cases of pop. "You make it sound like we're on a nature documentary."

She nodded. "That's exactly what this is." She pushed the door open since Clark hadn't bothered to lock it, and they dropped everything in the entry.

Bailey pushed through the door carrying her things. "Can I get a snack, Mom?"

Aelin nodded. "Yep. Then you need to shower."

Bailey ran to the kitchen, and Aelin turned back to Ryan. She wanted to reach for him. To hold him. To ask him to stay.

But everything inside her felt numb. Empty.

Ryan's fingers twitched, but he didn't move closer. "I'll, uh, text you."

She nodded. "Thanks for driving."

Ryan looked at her for a moment longer, then turned and walked back to the car.

Aelin stood in the entryway, her feet rooted to the floor. She watched through the side window as Ryan opened the door and slid into the driver's seat. He glanced up and met her eyes, and she willed her feet to move. To run out onto the porch and yell for him to come back.

But she didn't. He started the engine, and his taillights glowed red. His car pulled away from the curb, and the silence of her house threatened to bury her.

She lifted a throw blanket from the chair in the sitting room and wrapped it around her shoulders. It didn't help. She shook as she put away the dishes from Bailey's snack. As she brushed Bailey's hair after her shower, and then as she flowed through her bedtime routine.

Her pillows on the bed were in the wrong place. Her necklaces hung on the hooks in her closet in the wrong order.

Clark had touched her things and left them askew just to screw with her.

Aelin shut off the light and crawled into bed feeling like she'd aged a hundred years. Fun Aelin had shrivelled and died the second they'd left that Walmart, and functional Aelin had disappeared the second she'd seen Clark's car in the driveway.

At least twelve years married to him had taught her one thing.

She *would* have to wake up in the morning and do this all again.

CHAPTER
Twenty~Four

RYAN'S GRIP tightened on the steering wheel as he drove back from Aelin's. His jaw clenched. *Clark.* What a bastard showing up at her house and threatening her when he knew damn well where she was. The whole time that asshole had been talking, he wanted to slam a fist into his face. His hockey years had taught him exactly where to hit to create a real bleeder. Would have felt good to see that F-boy shirt ruined.

Thankfully he'd had a little rationality left in his head. Knocking Clark flat wasn't going to help anyone. Certainly not Aelin. She was already walking a tightrope trying to get him to finalize the divorce.

He thought of the way Aelin looked at him in the entryway of her house. Her eyes had been blank, like she'd retreated behind some invisible barrier that he couldn't get through. Ryan shook his head. He had to trust that she had it under control. She didn't need him to be her saviour.

Amaya yawned in the backseat, and he glanced in the rear view mirror. "You ready for bed already?" he asked.

She nodded. "I don't know why driving makes me so tired. I've only been sitting here."

Ryan chuckled. He went through a mental checklist of

everything he needed to take care of that night before work and the third week of hockey camp. Thankfully, he had enough foresight to tie all the loose ends he was capable of tying before they left. His team had worked on the things they could while he was gone, and now he just had a shit ton of emailing to do.

Ryan turned onto his street and parked in front of his garage door. He still had boxes and parts he needed to organize from when he'd put in the new closet systems in both his and Amaya's rooms. Since it was summer, he wasn't particularly motivated to get his car inside.

It didn't click that there was a light on inside his house until he pushed the car door open and stood in his driveway. He frowned and scanned the street. As soon as he saw the silver Acura, realization hit him like a lightning strike.

"Are grandma and grandpa here?" Amaya pulled her backpack from the back seat.

Ryan ran a hand over his face. He nodded, and she gave a little hop of excitement before running to the front door.

Laura and Russ pulled the door open as soon as they saw Amaya coming. Laura gave her a huge hug. "We missed you so much!"

Russ shook Ryan's hand. "Did the drive go okay?"

Ryan nodded, then realized he hadn't grabbed their luggage from the back. He rounded the car and opened the trunk. Russ insisted on helping him get everything inside.

Laura gave him a warm smile and lowered her voice. "You may want to head over now. Visiting hours end at nine."

Ryan nodded. As he'd been walking down the drink aisle next to Aelin in that Podunk town, visiting Kara immediately had seemed like a much better idea than it did now.

Amaya dropped onto the couch. "What are you doing here?"

Laura raised an eyebrow, and Russ chuckled. "Well, we were hoping to see you."

Ryan leaned over the couch. "I'm going to run out. Have fun

with your grandparents, okay? I'll try to get back before you go to bed."

Amaya nodded. "Are you going to see Aelin?"

Ryan's heart skipped a beat. "Uh, no. We'll see Aelin and Bailey tomorrow." He dropped his eyes and turned back to the door.

His mind was blank the entire drive to the assisted living centre. Every night as he held Aelin in his arms, he'd rehearsed what he wanted to say to Kara, but all of it had evaporated in the last couple of hours.

He thought about turning back twice but forced himself to keep going. There was never going to be a good time to have this moment, and a small part of him worried that if he didn't do it now, he would find some reason to change his mind.

Ryan parked his car and stepped out onto the asphalt. The building's white exterior was illuminated by street lights, making it look more clinical than it already was. A cool breeze had picked up, and he shoved his hands into his pockets as he approached the entrance.

The door swung open with a push, and he stepped into the small lobby. The woman at the reception desk smiled and didn't even make him sign the guest sheet. At least he'd been there enough that she knew who he was and where he was headed.

He passed a couple of residents shuffling down the hall, their slippers whispering against the linoleum. One of them gave him a nod, and he forced a smile. If he thought being there was going to trigger his thoughts, he was wrong. The closer he got to Kara's door the more his heartbeat drowned out anything else in his head.

Again, he tensed, waiting for that pang of guilt to hit his stomach, but it never came. For three years he held onto the image of Kara as his wife. To the woman she'd been before the blood clot. Somehow, while walking the pebbled beaches of Flathead, that fantasy he'd been clinging so hard to had finally melted away. The only thing that existed now was Kara as she was.

He still loved her. He would never stop loving her. But as he lifted his hand to knock on her door, he realized it had never been about that in the first place.

He knocked, wondering what he would find on the other side of the door. He knew what he hoped to see. Kara sitting in her chair, a blanket draped over her knees, her knitting needles clicking together. That was always better than her prostrate in her bed, a catheter or IV snaking out from under the covers.

The door buzzed and unlocked, and Ryan pushed down on the handle. He walked into the room and exhaled when he saw her sitting in the chair. She wasn't knitting, but she had a book in her lap, her dark hair pulled back in a loose braid.

She looked up and gave him a smile. "I didn't know you were coming tonight."

Ryan grinned. She said that every time, even when they told her they would see her in the morning. At least she knew what time of day it was.

"I wanted to surprise you." He gave her a smile, and she walked over to him, her arms outstretched. He pulled her into a hug, and she rested her head against his chest.

"I missed you." Her voice muffled against his shirt.

"I missed you too." Ryan closed his eyes, his heart pounding in his chest. If only she understood for how long and how hard he had missed her. The doctors had never been able to tell him exactly what she understood about their relationship. Sometimes she seemed to know who he was and other times, the idea of her having a husband or family set off an episode.

Most of the time she seemed happy to treat them as friends. Even Amaya. It didn't seem to compute that they were twenty years apart. Ryan pulled back and looked down at her. "How have you been?"

She smiled and pointed to the hooks by the door. "I finished a scarf."

Ryan walked over and fingered the soft wool. "I love the colours." It was lopsided, the stitches uneven. "This is amazing, Kara. You're getting so good."

Her smile widened. "Do you want to play checkers?"

Ryan's heart twisted, thinking of the last time they'd been there. "Sure." He sat down in the chair across from her. Kara motioned for him to move the side table between them. As soon as he did, she started setting up the pieces on both sides.

When she finished, she looked at him expectantly. "You go first."

Ryan nodded and moved a piece. They played in silence for a few minutes. He chose moves that wouldn't set her off. She clapped her hands together when she found a double jump.

"You're not very good." She set his pieces on the table next to the board.

He chuckled. "Or maybe you're just an expert."

Her eyes lit up at the compliment. She reached out and held his hand. "I like playing with you."

He squeezed. "I like playing with you, too."

"Do you have a girlfriend?" She cocked her head to the side.

He huffed a laugh. "No. Do you have a boyfriend?"

She wrinkled her nose and shook her head. "I want one someday, though."

He nodded and pulled his hand back to his lap. "Want to play again?"

She reached for the pieces, and he watched her hands. They looked nothing like the ones he'd held anymore. Though, she could probably say the same about his. They'd both gotten older. Just not together.

Memories flooded his head as they played. For how empty his head had been as he'd walked into the centre, it was overwhelming to experience the opposite.

He thought about the first time he'd brought Kara to his parents' house for Christmas. She'd been so nervous, but his family had welcomed her with open arms. They'd sat around the table, playing games and laughing, and Ryan had known in that moment that he was going to propose.

He thought about their wedding day, how beautiful she'd looked in her dress, the way her eyes had sparkled with tears as they'd said their vows. *In sickness and in health, for better or for worse.*

He'd spent the last two years trying to hold on to his vows, trying to be the man Kara had married. He'd held on so tightly to the past that he hadn't been able to give her what she needed in the present.

He'd been to see her only a handful of times. He'd told himself it was because it was too confusing for Amaya, that it was too hard for Kara. Those things were true, but it had always been more about it being too hard for him.

Seeing her, and knowing that she didn't understand their relationship, that she didn't remember the time they'd spent together, was a thousand jagged blades to his heart every single time he walked into her room.

It was a reminder of what he didn't have. He'd never once thought about how it could be a reminder of what he still had.

Kara didn't need a husband. She needed someone to love her. Laura and Russ had figured that out instantaneously, it seemed. Laura was there every single day, regardless of whether Kara knew who she was or everything she did for her.

Ryan said he was sacrificing for Kara. But he wasn't. Not really. He was cutting out his heart and hiding it in a box so it could never be crushed again like it was that night he'd come home from hockey practice.

His hands shook as he moved his pieces.

When Kara finally won the second game, she jumped up from her chair. "I did it again!" She clapped her hands together, her smile radiant.

Ryan laughed, his heart aching. "You're getting too good for me."

Kara sat back down and put the pieces away, tucking them

back into the compartment on the bottom of the board. When she finished, he swallowed back the lump in his throat and reached out to take Kara's hand. Her skin was warm and soft.

"I'm going to come visit more often."

She laughed. "Because you like getting beat at checkers?"

He sniffed, setting her hand back on the table. "It's my favourite."

Ryan stood and walked to the door, wiping his eyes with the back of his hand. "Love you, Kara."

She leaned back in her chair. "Love you, too."

Ryan twisted the wedding ring from his finger and looped it over the hook next to Kara's scarf, then left her room and walked back to his car.

He drove home on autopilot, and when he walked through his front door, he found Laura, Russ, and Amaya cuddled up on the couch watching an episode of Full House.

"Dad, have you seen this show?" Amaya grinned up at him, her eyes sleepy.

He laughed. "Yeah. I've seen most of the episodes, I think." Ryan walked into the kitchen and paused with his hand on the back of a chair.

He drew a breath and exhaled, then walked to the counter and picked up the manila envelope.

CHAPTER
Twenty-Five

AELIN WATCHED from the window next to the front door as Ryan's car pulled into the driveway, the conversation she'd had that morning still fresh in her head.

"Clark is going to war. Especially after hearing you spent the week with that guy, Ryan, he saw at your house." Her lawyer's voice was crisp.

"I don't understand how he knew that."

"He knows a hell of a lot, Aelin. Did you share a cabin with Ryan?"

Aelin blinked. "We stayed at the same cabins, it's where my family—"

"No, did you share a cabin? Was he sleeping in the same location as Bailey?"

Aelin's hands went numb. "There was an issue with booking. He and his daughter stayed with us, but they were in totally different—"

"Don't explain it to me. It doesn't matter. Clark found out. That's in direct violation of your agreement, and it puts Bailey in potential danger."

"He's done it!" Aelin shouted. "Bailey told me—"

"Do you have proof?"

Aelin's mouth snapped closed. "Bailey's word. Isn't that proof enough?"

Her lawyer clicked her tongue. "Did I ever tell you you shouldn't have married a lawyer? Clark might be a hypocrite, but he's a smart hypocrite. He has your damn text messages."

Her toes tingled as Amaya hopped out of the car and Ryan opened his door. She frantically tapped her phone screen, then lifted it to her ear.

Ryan paused, glancing up at the house as he pulled his phone from his pocket and answered.

"Hey, is everything okay?" He watched her open the door.

She didn't step out onto the porch. "Mmhmm. You can send Amaya up, but I need you to stay in the car."

Ryan frowned. "Okay."

"I talked with my lawyer this morning," she continued in a rush. "While I was being Fun Aelin, Clark was being an asshole."

"Are we surprised by this?" He pressed his hand against the roof of the car.

She bit her lip. "I should have known when I didn't see anything from him that he was planning something."

"You think he planned what? Last night?"

"Hell yes, I think he planned last night. He knew what dates I was going to be gone and he didn't say a word. He knew I'd be too distracted to double check that the form had been filled out correctly. And . . . " The shaking started up again. *Could Clark hear this phone call?* She'd been trying to figure out how the hell he'd gotten access to her texts all morning, but came up empty. They were on the same phone plan, but everything she read said he should only be able to see who she texted, not what was in the message.

"And, what?" Ryan asked.

Her voice was tight. "He has information. On us."

Ryan's scowl was visible from the curb. "What kind of information?"

"That we—" Her throat constricted. Clark already knew anyway, so it didn't matter if he was listening. "That we shared a cabin."

"So?"

"So, I specifically included a clause in our original agreement that we couldn't have Bailey around other adults overnight. I was trying to protect her." She pressed a hand to her forehead and squeezed her eyes shut.

Ryan's exhale was slow. "So what does that mean?"

Aelin moved to the side and whispered "hello" to Amaya as she slipped into the house. "He has proof."

"How? Did someone in your family—"

"No, no. He has my text messages."

"What the hell?"

She let out a sardonic laugh. "Exactly. He's filed new motions. He's attacking my character and ability to be a fit mother." She drew in a sharp breath.

"So he's sending you a message," Ryan said.

"Yeah. He will drag this out as long as possible. He'll make both me and Bailey suffer. And there's nothing I can do about it."

"Unless?" Ryan glanced up and met her eyes.

"Unless I give him what he wants."

"Which is?"

Blood rushed in her ears. "To win."

Ryan tapped his fingers on the car. "What does it mean when Clark wins?"

"It means I don't see you. It means I let him sell the house."

"And what about Bailey?"

Aelin scoffed. "He doesn't give a shit about Bailey. My lawyer and I both think that if I pretend to bend over, that will be enough to satisfy his sadistic ego. Prove that I'm stable and a fit mother, but give him what he wants. But that means I have to play Subservient Aelin until the nineteenth." *Three weeks.* She could do anything for three weeks, couldn't she?

Ryan nodded. "So that's the plan."

She ran a hand through her hair. "Yeah, that's the plan. I'm going to start packing this week. I totally understand if you need to find something different for Amaya if you don't want her to be here during all of this."

"That's ridiculous. It's not going to hurt her to see you packing."

Aelin sighed. "Yeah, but we won't be able to do as much."

Ryan shrugged. "Pretty sure the girls are happy to just hang out. Any leads on a place yet?"

Aelin shook her head. "No. I found an apartment complex in the northwest that only requires a month-to-month lease. I'll put what we can in storage, sell the rest, and then rent a place until we can find something permanent." She curled her toes against the welcome mat. "I know that location isn't going to be nearly as convenient for you, but I'll figure this out until the girls go back to school in September. I can pick her up—"

"Aelin, I don't want you to worry about my convenience."

She swiped a hand over her cheeks. "I'm just sorry. I know you didn't sign up for this." She watched him, and some small piece of her started to thaw. She sniffed and drew a deep breath. "Okay, I need to get going so I can get breakfast going."

"Wait, how did he get your actual texts?"

Aelin threw out a hand. "I have no idea, Ryan. I've called my phone company—"

"Did he ever have your phone? Like open and in his possession?"

Aelin froze. Her mind immediately snapped back to Canada Day. That moment on the hill. "Yes. For about a minute. Why?"

"Because I was considering getting Amaya a phone for Christmas. I saw a few apps that you could install that don't show up on the phone screen, but that give you a readout of all the messages and emails—"

"Holy shit." Aelin dropped to a crouch on the welcome mat, forcing air into her lungs. What had she sent via email to her lawyer? Who had she texted? That guy Colin she'd gone out with had texted her a couple of times while they'd been gone. Thankfully her phone had been off for the week, but *what else had she sent?*

"Aelin—"

"What would I look for?"

Ryan stammered. "I—I'm not sure, you could go into your settings and look at app storage or privacy—"

"Okay. Okay, I'll do that."

"Aelin, I can—"

"No, Ryan. Thank you. I'll take care of it." She forced herself up off the floor. The porch pillars swam around her. She held the phone to her cheek a second longer, then dropped her arm and closed the front door.

CHAPTER
Twenty-Six

AELIN FOUND THE APP. It was called PhantomLink and it was installed on July 1st. She uninstalled it, threw up twice, considered smashing her phone with a sledgehammer, then somehow made it through crafts with the girls that morning. She made a healthy lunch, then popped popcorn and set up a blanket tent for a movie in the afternoon. They were all still exhausted from the trip, so rest was the goal. At least for the girls.

As soon as they were settled, Aelin sat down at her laptop. She called her lawyer. They surveyed the damage. She asked Aelin for screenshots, which she'd thankfully taken, and promised to submit a motion to suppress since the information was taken without her permission.

But the damage was already done. This would set back any sort of court decision by months after their final mediation, and it definitely didn't look as cut and dry as it had a few weeks prior.

There was nothing she could do.

Aelin felt the cold descend like a veil. *All systems shutting down.* She blinked at her screen and opened up three tabs for different real estate websites her friends had recommended, then took a deep breath and typed in her search criteria.

House. Three bedrooms. Under $400,000.

There was a problem she could work on. One she had to find a solution for.

She knew how unlikely it would be for her to find something with that criteria in their part of the city, but the idea of moving Bailey to a new school made her sick to her stomach. And renting . . . those prices were astronomical.

She clicked through listings, focusing on locations. There was a townhouse listed in the north end, but it was right off the freeway and had no yard. Another had a yard, but the carpet was bright green and she could see water damage on the ceiling.

She groaned and clicked through to the second real estate website. A two-bedroom apartment a few minutes south. No yard. A one-bedroom house north of the school. Out of her price range. A basement suite?

Not good enough. Her thoughts churned as she scrolled. She needed to find something stable. Something that would make the judge look at her and think, *"This woman has her crap together."*

She scrolled. And scrolled. Her hope dying a little more with each click of the mouse. Everything that fit her criteria was either in a dodgy neighbourhood, had no yard, or was way out of her budget. She rubbed her eyes and closed her laptop.

Tomorrow. She'd look again tomorrow.

———

Aelin parked and got out of the car at the ice centre, then waited for Amaya to unbuckle her seatbelt. She hadn't been paying attention to the clock when she'd gone down the rabbit hole of house hunting, and now she was five minutes late.

She walked with Amaya to the front door and made sure she got to the correct rink. It had been a week since she'd last attended camp, and Aelin wasn't sure if it was going to be in the same place.

The sound of skates on ice echoed through the building, and she followed the noise until she reached the rink. Parents were lined up along the benches, watching their kids, and Aelin scanned the ice as Amaya waved and ran to find her equipment.

Her heart twisted when she spotted Ryan in the middle, his back to her as he knelt next to a little boy who was struggling to keep his balance.

She wanted their lake days back. She wanted to be the person she was there. Calm. Flexible. Not the dead inside robot trying to properly interpret her surroundings.

But what happened on the driveway the night before had snapped the last twelve years into focus. She wouldn't spend another second begrudging who she'd become because what she'd felt the night before? That was what her body was protecting her from.

And as long as Clark was in her life, she was going to need that shield. Mediation was on the nineteenth, but she was going to have to work with him every week until Bailey turned eighteen. She wouldn't be able to escape to California. She wouldn't be able to hide from any of it.

How could she heal when he'd always be right there twisting the knife?

She spun back toward the stairs and was about to head to the entrance when she heard her name.

"Aelin?"

Her heart stalled, but when she turned, she saw a startlingly handsome man in hockey gear that was decidedly not Ryan.

She straightened. "You were at the bar the other night. And one of Bailey's coaches."

He smiled and put out an ungloved hand. "Tyler."

She shook it, then dropped her arm, waffling between whether this could be about Ryan or Bailey.

"Hey, I was hoping to catch you. Ryan told me you were dropping Amaya off for camp."

Ryan, then.

Tyler moved to the side to let a group of players pass. "My teammate Brett and I used to live in a townhouse off Centre Street. I ended up buying it, the whole building actually, as an investment property."

Aelin nodded, not sure where this was going.

"Anyway, there are only four units, but I'm having a hard time keeping a manager that does a good job. It's a pretty good gig, though."

Aelin frowned. "I don't—are you saying you want me to work for you? Or rent your townhouse?"

Tyler blew out a breath. "Both. It would be free rent. You'd be responsible for showing units when renters change over. You'd be the point of contact for repairs or maintenance issues, but obviously, we have contractors on hand to do the work. You would have a separate email address, office hours once a week. Pretty flexible."

Aelin blinked. "You said . . . free rent?"

Tyler cleared his throat. "I know you're looking for a new place, and I thought you might be interested. The townhouse I lived in is open, and it has a nice little yard, two bedrooms, and an office. Updated appliances. There's a community centre with a gym and a pool, and—"

"Yes!" She pursed her lips. "I mean, I'd love to see it first, and I'm sure you'll want to see my resume, but . . . yes. I'm extremely interested."

Tyler smiled. "Perfect. Could you meet me there tomorrow after camp?"

CHAPTER
Twenty-Seven

AELIN WOKE up early and immediately started packing the kitchen. Since she had a place to stay that was available immediately, there was no point in waiting and keeping her house clean during showings. She wasn't going to fight Clark on this, which meant the sooner she got out, the better.

The more she thought about it, the more liberating it felt to remove herself from the house they had lived in together. It was *his* house originally, not hers. She hadn't realized how many reminders of him were everywhere she looked.

Aelin stood at the island and looked around her. She'd moved here. She'd built a life here. But she'd never been at the centre of it. It had never been hers. Once they'd moved past the love-bombing stage of their relationship, she'd orbited him, trying to be the smallest, most inconspicuous moon to his gas giant.

Since the lake, every day felt like a losing battle. The tightness in her chest returned. Her insomnia at night. Everything she'd experienced immediately after realizing Clark had cheated the second time had rushed in full force when she saw that stealth app on her phone.

She found herself sitting and staring into space more times

than she could count. She went back through every note she'd taken in therapy, every journal entry, every recommendation from her therapist. Knowing something and forcing your body to comply were two different things. Every night she lay in bed, close to tears, willing her body to believe that she was safe. But it wasn't true. Her body wouldn't believe it because, deep down, she knew that no matter how much she tried, Clark would always have the ability to swoop in and knock her feet out from under her.

She wasn't safe. Her body knew it. And even though her brain understood the rational difference between running from a tiger and worrying about Clark, her body didn't. She was in a constant state of fight or flight, and knowing she couldn't trust her reactions only made her anxiety worse. It was a depressing, unstoppable, vicious cycle.

Her joints ached. She felt nauseous after every meal. Every time she looked in the mirror, she was pale and gaunt. So when her body went numb and she could barely feel her heart beating, she didn't even complain.

She was simply grateful for the respite.

Aelin opened the kitchen cupboards and began stacking plates and cups in boxes, wrapping each piece in tissue paper. It was methodical—comforting, even. By the time Amaya arrived for breakfast, she was nearly finished.

When she dropped Amaya off at the rink later that day, Tyler found her again. Ryan was using him as a messenger, and Aelin knew that somewhere, far above where she was currently drowning, she might enjoy that Ryan was thinking about her. That he was trying to help and protect her.

But she couldn't access gratitude. She couldn't access want or desire or need. Their moments in the cabin felt like a lifetime away, like she had been playing a part in some summer play. She wondered if he felt the same thing. If he had come back and visited his wife and realized that they'd been fooling themselves.

She knew the thought should be sad, but she couldn't even feel that.

Tyler gave her information for a moving company, and she called. They had been expecting her and scheduled the truck without needing a deposit.

That sent warning bells off in her head. It was too much. Ryan was sending texts and calling and doing nice things for her. Exactly like Clark had back in California.

Aelin dove into packing and cleaning. She was frighteningly efficient even while taking Amaya and Bailey on field trips. She avoided looking out the window at pick-up and drop-off.

Every morning she input the code and executed. *She was a good robot.*

Friday hit, and she realized that in three days, she would be loading up and moving ten minutes further north. Clark had already sent movers to retrieve the furniture he'd left in the house. She wasn't going to take a single thing that gave her Clark vibes. Bailey's bed had been a gift from a friend, so she was keeping that, but she would have chopped up her master bedroom set and lit it on fire if she didn't think she would've gotten arrested.

Aelin found a new queen bedroom set through a friend of Megan's. She was keeping the dishes because her money was running low. They were in great condition and a gift from her parents at their wedding. They were for her, not for Clark. The fact that he had eaten off them didn't mean he had any claim.

Her days passed in a blur, and by the time the moving truck arrived, she was so sick of her house she could scream. She raced around, throwing odds and ends in a final box when a knock sounded on the door. She ran to answer it and found Tyler standing on her front mat.

"Hey!"

Her mind reeled, trying to figure out how he knew where she lived. Tyler turned and pointed at the truck on the curb.

"Is it okay if we pull into the driveway?"

"We?" Aelin frowned, and Tyler's face split into a stupidly attractive grin. *Though she wished she were looking at someone else's.*

"The guy who owns this company is a friend of mine. I told him we'd provide the labour if he lent us the truck," Tyler said.

Aelin's frown deepened. She leaned to the side to look past him. The words he was saying finally made sense. The rest of Ryan's hockey team—some of the guys she recognized from Dusty Rose—all stood on the sidewalk in faded jeans and old T-shirts.

Her pulse zinged as her eyes locked onto the man with the messy bun, and she yanked herself back.

Tyler put his hand on the doorframe. "Since he's going to be here, I figured you'd probably want to head over to the new place. Unless you feel like we need more micromanaging."

He's going to be here. The words felt like the start to a movie trailer she desperately wanted to watch. Aelin dragged in a breath. "No. Everything is labelled either 'donation' or 'packing,' but I was planning to take some loads over to Value Village."

Tyler nodded. "I've got my truck. We can take care of that too." Aelin started to protest, but he held up a hand. "What good is all this muscle if we can't put it to use?"

Bailey ran up behind Aelin with her tablet. Her eyes were wide, taking in the truck and glancing around their empty house.

"Hey." Aelin smoothed her hair. "Looks like these guys have everything covered. Do you want to go out for breakfast?"

Bailey's eyes lit up. As she ran to get her shoes, Aelin turned to Tyler, her throat thick. "Will you please tell him thank you?"

———

Aelyn had expected the move to take all day Monday, possibly rolling into Tuesday, but everything had arrived by early afternoon. She and Bailey went back to the house and met Megan around four. They ordered pizza and cleaned until every surface sparkled. Clark had hired a company to stage the place, but she knew he would latch onto anything he could to show how she hadn't held up her end of the bargain. She took pictures of every room and sent them to Jules.

They locked up, and she gave Megan a long hug, then drove back to their new place. The townhouse was smaller than their old house, obviously, but it was nicer in a few important ways. It had upgraded appliances. The washer and dryer could handle aggressively large loads, and the dishwasher was so silent, she could barely tell it was running.

She walked in to find all their boxes neatly stacked. Her eyes immediately landed on the kitchen table. There was a vase with flowers and a notecard sitting next to it. Her chest tightened. "Aww!" Bailey ran right for them, but as soon as her fingers hit the card, Aelin snapped, "Let's go to your room, Bailes. We need to set up your bed."

Bailey looked disappointed, but she followed her down the hall. They put together her simple bed frame and organized her clothes in piles. The rest of the week was slotted for organization and cleaning. Surprisingly, Bailey was excited to unpack. It did kind of feel like playing house, and it would keep Aelin busy so she couldn't fixate on Friday morning. The nineteenth. Her final mediation with Clark.

He'd gone radio silent since she deleted the app from her phone, and that worried her more than if he'd been throwing a hissy fit. She wanted him to scream. She wanted him to show up unexpectedly and yell at her in the driveway. Any of that would show her that he believed he wasn't in control.

Aelin's back and legs ached as she finally got ready for bed and settled onto her mattress on the floor. She did *not* go back into the kitchen. Just as she was plugging in her phone, text messages came through from Megan.

> Hey. Forgot to ask if you want to come out with us Thursday night?
>
> We're doing a bachelor party for Jenna. You met her at the Dusty Rose.
>
> She and Country are getting married Saturday

Details slowly began filtering into her head, things Ryan had mentioned at the lake. Country and Jenna had known each other in high school and had recently gotten back together. They were getting married at Country's ranch. Ryan had been excited about it.

She texted back.

> I've got mediation on Friday. I don't think that's a good idea

> Or maybe it's the perfect idea because you're going to be at home sad and alone having a panic attack.

> Better than having a panic attack in front of strangers while I'm tipsy

> Is it, though?

Aelin grinned at that.

. . .

> Seriously, I would love to, but Clark is MIA. I don't want to give him any reason to delay this meeting.

> It's been difficult enough trying to keep this date. Given all the other shit he's pulled

Megan hearted the message.

> Yeah. Sigh. I'm so sorry. I wish I could have him assassinated

Aelin snorted, wishing Clark could see *that* message. She sent Megan a kissing emoji, then plugged in her phone and rolled over.

For a moment, she felt a twinge of loneliness. The image of Ryan standing on the curb in front of her house. The briefest hint whispered over her that maybe she didn't have to be lying alone on a mattress on the floor.

Then the cold swept back in, and Aelin exhaled in relief.

CHAPTER
Twenty~Eight

RYAN FINALIZED everything with the ice centre Thursday at six fifteen after they'd cleaned out their stuff in the locker room and packed up the boxes of gear. They opted to do only a four-day camp the week of Country's wedding, for obvious reasons. Tonight was the bachelor party, and then tomorrow he was taking Amaya to the ranch to help set up for Saturday.

It had nearly killed him to move all of Aelin and Bailey's stuff over to the townhouse. He missed her so much, it was a physical ache. But he had stopped calling or sending text messages a few days ago when it became obvious she wasn't planning to respond.

He didn't understand it. They had grown so close at the lake. But the closer they'd gotten to Calgary, it was like he could see her sealing herself back up. Closing off. Protecting herself. Clark had been the final hammer against the lid.

He just couldn't understand why she felt the need to protect herself from *him*. Besides acting like a douchebag the first time they met, he'd never treated her poorly or lied to her. He'd connected her with Tyler. Found a way to move her without costing a penny. He'd left flowers and a gift card to Boston Pizza on her table. So why was she treating him like he was the enemy?

He took Amaya out for burgers, then dropped her off with Russ and Laura for the night. They were on babysitting duty all weekend. He was going to pick her up whenever he got his ass out of bed in the morning, take her out to the ranch, and then drop her back off Friday night for another sleepover so he could finish up any last-minute details before the wedding on Saturday.

Polk was still trying to finish the dance floor, and from what Country said, it wasn't looking promising. But Country had a stick up his ass, so he took that with a grain of salt. He couldn't blame him. Country wanted everything to be perfect. If they had to put up with his bitching and moaning for a week, that was a small price to pay for all the good he did for the rest of them.

Tonight, their mission was to help him relax, and that's exactly what they were going to do. First, they were going paintballing. Then they were getting fried chicken sandwiches—Nashville hot—and moving on to the bar. Jenna and Country didn't know it, but they were both going to end up at the same place for drinks. They all knew Country and Jenna well enough to know that the only time they'd be truly relaxed was when they were together.

That gave him hope. Ryan had never understood the idea of a bachelor party. He hadn't had one before his wedding. If you were excited to spend the rest of your life with somebody, why would you need a night to forget it? He had gone shooting with his brother and dad instead.

Ryan showed up at Sean's, and the Snowballs players piled into a party bus. That's what Sean was calling it, but it was actually just the team travel bus. Kelty, Sean's girlfriend, had scrawled words with chalk marker across the windows and set up neon track lights along the inside of the roof. No need for a driver since Tyler and Brett weren't drinking anyway.

It felt like old times. Jack was there, back in town after a training camp with the Blizzard, and Fly showed up with a shirt that read "I Drop Mitts." It felt like a tourney road trip, and by the time the team bus pulled into the parking lot of the paintball centre, Ryan couldn't keep the grin off his face. This was exactly what he needed. A little downtime. A little connection. A little pain.

It was hard to find something that checked all the boxes. Hockey was always the obvious choice. He hoped this was a solid second.

They clown-carred it out of the van and into the parking lot, then strolled into the building.

"Smells like teen spirit in here," Mike quipped, his long dark hair tied back in a ponytail.

Suraj scanned the room. "I came here once trying to impress a girl."

"Did it work?" Ryan asked.

Suraj shook his head. "Turns out, getting welted by paintballs isn't a panty dropper."

They paid their fees and moved to the equipment area where they were handed overalls, masks, and guns. Ryan started suiting up, pulling the camo jumpsuit over his jeans.

They split into two teams. Ryan was with Brett, Fly, Suraj, Mike, and André. The other team consisted of Sean, Tyler, Country, Gary, Boyd, and Jack. Fly strapped on a cup citing old age and a desire to keep his balls unpainted.

They tromped outside and entered the paintball arena, a sprawling field with barricades, barrels, and a wooden fort. In the distance, the Calgary Tower pierced the sky.

The whistle blew, and they scattered. Ryan ducked behind a plywood barrier, peeking out to see Tyler making a break for the fort. He raised his gun and aimed, but a splatter of blue paint exploded inches from his mask.

"Shit!" Ryan ducked back, his heart pounding. He heard a

guffaw and turned to run but got nailed in the back by a splat of yellow. He launched himself into a stack of tires.

After righting himself, Ryan fought his way out of the rubber and found Sean and Tyler huddled behind a stack of barrels. He raised his gun and fired, then bolted for better cover with his teammates.

They moved deeper into the arena, dodging paintballs and trying to outflank the other team. He peeked out and saw Mike sprinting across the field. Suraj was hunkered down behind a barrier, his gun aimed and ready. André was nowhere to be seen, probably taking a smoke break, the bastard.

Ryan got a point blank shot on Country, then took two stingers in the thigh. André finally appeared near the fort and Ryan played wingman for an assault on Fly.

When the game finally ended, they were all covered in paint and grinning like idiots. Ryan pulled off his mask, his hair damp with sweat.

Tyler was holding court, showing off a particularly nasty welt on his bicep.

André pulled down his jeans and showed a bruise blooming on his right ass cheek. "Do you think Emma will kiss this better, too?" He laughed, then dodged both Country and Sean.

They piled back into the bus, exhausted and starving.

Brett groaned from the seat behind him. "I think I need to add 'Fly playing paintball' to my hate list."

Fly laughed out loud. "Can't beat you on the ice. I have to take the wins where I can."

Ryan chuckled and pulled out his phone. He didn't know why he kept torturing himself, expecting Aelin's name to pop up on the screen. He put it away and stared out the window.

Twenty minutes later, they pulled up to their destination, a food truck parked in a lot that was bustling with people even though it was after eight o'clock. The smell of fried chicken and spices wafted through the air, making Ryan's stomach growl. He'd been looking forward to this all day.

The team filed out of the bus, jostling and joking as they made their way to the truck. The menu board boasted Nashville hot chicken sandwiches in varying levels of spice, from "Mild Mannered" to "Hellfire."

Tyler stepped up first. "I'm going Hellfire."

Suraj shook his head. "Mmm. Mild Mannered for me. I need my taste buds intact for date night."

Ryan laughed. "You're not coming to the party?"

Suraj shook his head. "Rashi had a rough week. I need to be home."

Ryan ordered a "Hotter Than Hell" sandwich, figuring he'd go for the middle ground since he was suddenly thinking so hard about Aelin, he felt sick.

They found a spot at a picnic table and dug in. Sean took a bite of his "Blazing Inferno" and immediately turned red. "Holy shit, that's hot."

Ryan laughed. "What did you think it was going to be?"

Sean grabbed his water bottle and took a swig. "I was hoping for a leisurely stroll, not a sprint through Satan's living room."

Brett took a bite of his own sandwich and nodded appreciatively. "This is damn good. Almost makes up for the paintball to the face."

———

Ryan went home and walked straight to the washroom. He peeled off his sweat-soaked T-shirt and paint-splattered shorts underneath. His phone buzzed, and he glanced at the screen.

Reminder: Tonight, 9 p.m. Bachelor party

. . .

No shit. He scowled, dropping his phone on the counter with a dull thud. Ryan stripped down and turned on the shower, steam billowing up from the scalding water. He stepped in, letting the hot water sear his skin and wash away the paint and grime.

As he scrubbed, his mind wandered back to her. The way she'd stood in front of the washroom door in her towel with her hair dripping. The soft cotton underwear she wore that cut high on her hips.

Ryan wasn't going to grovel. He wasn't going to be the guy who blew up Aelin's phone. If she didn't want to talk, fine.

Indignation felt good for about five seconds until he remembered how much she had to be hurting. She'd been forced to move, she was being constantly harassed by her ex.

Stepping out of the shower, Ryan grabbed a towel and dried off. He tied his hair back with a hair tie and glanced down as his phone buzzed again.

Reminder: Tomorrow, 10 a.m. Aelin's mediation.

Ryan walked back into the main room and pulled out a clean pair of jeans and the shirt he promised Country he'd wear. A collared seer-sucker with tiny pink flamingoes. He dressed quickly, then sat on the edge of the bed to pull on his socks and shoes. He fastened his watch around his wrist, the leather strap cool against his skin, then grabbed his keys and phone and shoved them into his pockets.

Ryan knocked a few chores off his list, then left the house and drove. He turned on his pre-game pump-up playlist, and by the time he turned onto Stephen Avenue, he felt ready to be Fun

Ryan for at least an hour. He passed a few shops and restaurants, then found a parking spot a block from the bar.

It didn't take long for everyone to show up, and as soon as Sean handed out the personalized nut rags Kelty had made for all of them, they downed a round of drinks and hit the dance floor. Ryan lasted for all of ten minutes before the alcohol hit his system, and any energy he'd mustered sapped out of him.

His exhaustion wasn't physical. Ever since they'd gotten back from the lake, he felt like he was trying to cross the ice with guards on his blades. Amaya was amped up with all the changes, understandably, but every time he dropped her off and saw Aelin through the windows, it was like someone clipped another weight onto his belt.

Tyler sat down next to him at the table. "Not feeling it tonight?"

Ryan shrugged. "It's just been a long week." He patted Tyler on the shoulder. "Thank you for all your help."

Tyler nodded. "I told you Aelin asked me to thank you the other day, right?" he asked.

Ryan let out a sharp breath. "Yeah, bud. I think you've told me three times."

Tyler nodded but didn't comment. With the alcohol swirling in Ryan's gut, he couldn't keep his damn mouth shut.

"She won't text me back. I texted her every day and tried calling at night, and I think I got one response, maybe two."

"That's where you were, right?" Tyler asked. "On your vacation, you were with her?"

Ryan nodded. "Yeah. We went down to Montana for the week."

Tyler raised an eyebrow. "I didn't realize it was that serious."

Ryan scoffed. "It wasn't. Our girls wanted to go to the lake together. That was it."

"Sure," Tyler said, nodding slowly. "But something changed, though, eh?"

Ryan's grip tightened on his glass. "We got a little closer."

The corner of Tyler's mouth quirked. "How close?"

He took a swig of his beer. "Not close enough."

"And then you came back. And nothing?" Tyler asked. Ryan nodded. "But she's going through a divorce."

"Yeah," Ryan exhaled. "Her ex is a jackass. Making things difficult. That's why she asked me not to come by. She's trying not to rock the boat."

Tyler frowned. "But he can't see if she's calling or texting you."

Tyler's words were a palm to the face. "Holy shit." Ryan dropped his glass on the table.

Tyler glanced up. "What?"

Ryan leaned forward. "He can't see her phone calls and texts . . . but he *could*."

"What?" Tyler looked confused.

"When we got back from the lake, Aelin told me he'd installed some app on her phone that was giving him access to her information."

Tyler's eyes widened. "He installed spyware on her personal cell?"

"Right, yeah. You'd know all about that."

"Can I kick that dude in the balls?"

Ryan laughed. "Get in line."

Tyler glanced down at his phone on the table. "Bud, I don't know about you, but if someone saw every single thing I did on there or every message I sent, I'd want to drive over that thing with my car."

Ryan laughed. "But think of all the dick pics we'd miss out on."

Tyler scoffed. "I'm not talking about the dick pics. Happy to post those whenever." He patted Ryan's shoulder, then walked over to order another round of shots for the table.

Ryan took another drink. Of course, Aelin wouldn't want to use her phone. He'd seen how she reacted to Clark in her driveway. She'd been in an abusive relationship for twelve years.

How was she supposed to suddenly forget that? She was a mama bear, and until mediation was complete—maybe even after that—she was going to guard Bailey with whatever it took.

But what could Ryan do to help her? He couldn't go and stand next to the tree, that was for damn sure.

He opened his phone to his AI chatbot and started asking questions.

CHAPTER
Twenty-Nine

AELIN WOKE up to new text messages, most of them from Ryan. Her heart started to pound, her brain still fuzzy from sleep. It was only five in the morning, and she had no idea why her body had woken her up, aside from the fact that her mediation was in a few hours. She rolled over on her pillow and started to read.

She answered Megan's text first, letting her know she'd be dropping Bailey off around nine to make sure she had plenty of time and wouldn't be rushed to get to Jules's office. Megan had technically been invited to the wedding, but she was mostly friends with Rhonda. Since she'd gone to the bachelorette party the night before, she felt like she had paid her dues.

Aelin hesitated before tapping on Ryan's messages, already making up a story in her head of what she would find there. He would be angry. He would ask her why she had refused to respond to him. He would tell her how frustrating it was to lie nearly naked with her for four nights in a row and then have her ghost him the second they got home.

All of it would be fair.

She braced herself and tapped.

· · ·

RYAN
9:32 P.M.

> I'm at this bar for the bachelor party and the girls from the bachelorette just arrived. I think they booked an actual party bus

> We have a lot of catching up to do, but I'm not really in the mood to drink. It's only making me sad, and nobody wants Sad Ryan at a bachelor party

> When I came to drop Amaya off at your house the other day, I was planning to come up and show you something

Aelin scrolled and looked at the picture he'd sent. It was a picture of his left hand. At first, she didn't understand until she noticed the slight tan line on his third finger.

> I stopped wearing my wedding ring. I wanted to tell you that. When you talked about filing for divorce, it made me think about things differently. I'm grateful.

> I also wanted to let you know that two of the girls in Jenna's group are completely shit-faced. They've been touchy with everybody here in the bar, but Rhonda's been taking a lot of pictures, and I'm sure some of them are going to end up on Megan's Instagram feed.

> If you see a blonde girl with sleepy eyelids and it looks like she's licking my face, she did not get consent

Ryan
10:15 p.m.

> I needed you to see this

Aelin scrolled to the next picture. It was Megan and Rhonda, laughing, about to take a drink out of two very phallic straws. She laughed and scrolled to his next text.

Ryan
12:56 a.m.

> I've been thinking about you all day. You don't need to respond to any of these, by the way. But I realized because I hadn't heard from you, I was assuming you didn't want to hear from me, instead of assuming that this week has probably been a bitch.
>
> That's what I hope you'll be tomorrow. I mean, you can be whoever you want. But if I had to choose my version of Aelin, that's what I would choose
>
> Nice Aelin or compassionate Aelin doesn't have any place in that mediation. Don't feel bad about being a shark. It wasn't your fault that he took advantage of you.
>
> Guard your home ice

Tears slipped down Aelin's cheek as she set her phone on the mattress and laid back on the pillow. *How had he known?* It wasn't that she needed permission going into this meeting, but getting it felt like oxygen. Like she'd been trapped inside a box and someone had finally opened the lid.

It isn't your fault.

She was beginning to believe that, but it had taken so long to get there. How many times had she asked herself the same questions? *How had she not seen the red flags? How had she not seen the signs? Why would she have allowed herself to get pregnant after knowing who Clark was—at least partially? Why had she stayed? Why had she allowed Bailey to live in a home like that?*

Why, why, why?

Now at least she had language to help herself understand the answers. Her therapist had taught her all the things, but she was still working on allowing her brain and heart to connect. She turned back to her phone and tapped, watching the cursor blink and scrolling through the letters on the miniature keypad. She stared at the screen for a full two minutes before she closed it again.

Every time she thought about texting Ryan, it was the same thing—a complete block. She wanted to open up to him, to tell him what she was feeling. But how could she possibly admit that it was nothing? How could she explain that she felt scoured and bleached out?

She forced herself up out of bed and did yoga on the front porch as the sun rose, then came inside and made breakfast.

———

Aelin smoothed down Bailey's braid for the third time. Overhead, the sky was a flat, steely grey, a perfect reflection of the knot twisting in her stomach. Somewhere, the thought of Ryan setting up for Country's wedding floated, but she couldn't quite grasp it.

She pulled out of their neighbourhood and let Bailey stream whatever music she wanted. Traffic was light, and it only took twelve minutes for them to turn onto Megan's street. Her eyes travelled over the rows of well-kept suburban homes. Megan's house was no exception, with its perfectly manicured lawn and tidy garden beds.

She pulled into the driveway, and Megan appeared at the door, a tight smile spreading across her face. Aelin parked the car and unbuckled her seatbelt. "Alright, Bails. You ready?"

Bailey nodded and opened her door. Aelin stepped out, her navy blouse billowing in the morning breeze. She tugged at the hem, straightening the fabric over her tailored pants. They'd been a splurge, but she'd wanted to look professional. Confident. *Like a fit mother.*

"Don't worry about anything." Megan motioned for Bailey to come up the steps. "We'll have so much fun, you won't even notice your mom is gone."

Aelin's heart ached. Bailey didn't fully understand what was happening that morning, but she knew enough. Aelin knew she must be feeling the stress of everything, but she never talked about it. Clark had conditioned her to be the most anxious when people were quiet.

Aelin gave her a hug. "Bye, love. I'll be back in a couple of hours."

Aelin mouthed *"Thank you"* to Megan and walked back to her car. She started the engine and pulled out of the driveway, her mind already racing ahead to the mediation.

The unknown was the worst part.

Her thoughts spun from one potential trap to another until

she pulled into the parking garage near Jules's office. She grabbed her purse and heard her phone buzz.

Aelin pulled it out, and her stomach flipped.

RYAN
9:38A.M.

> I just strung 138 peonies to an arbour. My fingers hurt
>
> Remember, no Fun Aelin

Aelin was about to put her phone back in her purse when one last message came through.

> She's just for me

Aelin's mouth quirked. She grabbed her things, locked her car, and crossed the street. It turned out, sometimes one did simply walk into Mordor.

She entered the building and greeted the receptionist at the front desk. She wore glasses on a chain and looked like she could silence an entire class with a single glare. Thankfully, Aelin had never gotten on her bad side. She glanced at Aelin and nodded.

The hallway was freshly painted, and Aelin's pants reflected blue on the polished tile. Jules's office was at the end of the hall. The door was cracked open, and Aelin pushed it gently. A wall of legal tomes lined one side of the room, and a large mahogany desk sat beyond two armchairs, perfectly organized. The whole office smelled like money.

Jules stood as she entered, her burgundy suit crisp. "Hey, you're early. I'm glad, because so are they." She stepped around the desk and led her to the conference room.

Aelin's lungs felt like perforated produce bags, but she followed Jules in. The room was more spacious than she expected. A table sat in the centre, surrounded by high-backed leather chairs. The walls were adorned with more framed certificates and a few abstract art pieces that made her feel uncultured.

Clark was already seated at the table, and Aelin's stomach dropped like a rock. He looked up from his phone and smirked. "Good morning, A."

Every word was a weapon.

Aelin clenched her jaw and forced a smile. "Clark." She took a seat across from him, her eyes flicking to the two lawyers flanking him. Both men looked like they'd stepped out of a knockoff GQ magazine. The suits were right, the faces? Not so much. She recognized them from Clark's firm's holiday party a few years ago.

Jules sat next to her, and the air in the room seemed to compress. Aelin's pulse pounded in her ears as she took in the details. Clark's perfectly styled hair, his designer suit that probably cost more than their monthly mortgage. *But he was so destitute.*

The man on Clark's left cleared his throat. "Thank you for being here this morning. I'd like to start by addressing a few concerns our client has." He didn't wait for anyone to object before continuing. "It's come to our attention that there have been a few violations of the terms of your separation agreement."

Aelin began to sweat.

"I'm going to have to stop you right there, Thomas. We're aware of the allegations, which I'm sure were reported by reliable sources." Jules paused, and the sarcasm in her voice was palpable. "But before we get into all of that, I have to ask—"

"Jules, if we could just—" The other lawyer, a man in his

fifties with salt-and-pepper hair, tried to interject, but Jules held up a hand.

"Martin, I know you have an agenda, and I promise we'll get to it, but I'm just curious. How did your client come by these personal text messages?"

Aelin tensed.

"It was brought to our attention by an anonymous source," Thomas said finally.

Jules nodded. "Right. An anonymous source. And this source, would they have access to our client's personal devices? Perhaps her phone?"

Martin frowned. "How would we know that?"

Jules leaned forward, her eyes locking onto Martin's. "Tampering with someone's personal property is not only unethical, it's illegal. And if that's the source of your information, I'd say we're starting this mediation off on the wrong foot, don't you think?"

Clark didn't look uncomfortable, not in the least. His eyes seemed to shine brighter with every jab exchanged between the lawyers.

Aelin dropped her eyes as the room seemed to close in on her. She focused on the grain of the wood table in front of her, tracing the patterns with her eyes. No Fun Aelin.

Something inside her warmed, and she glanced up.

". . . it demonstrates a lack of financial stability and a failure to provide a safe environment for Bailey. Our client has concerns about your ability to meet your obligations under the terms of the separation agreement." Martin was talking, but she was focused only on Clark.

"Our client has been more than patient, but he's reached a point where he feels it's necessary to take further action. He's prepared to request a reevaluation of the custody agreement, including a proposal for Bailey to switch to a different school where she might be safer."

Yes. The perfect hit. Threaten her with taking Bailey. Tell her she wasn't enough over and over again until she started to believe it, and then . . . Aelin's thoughts snapped into such clarity, she nearly gasped.

Then he would walk away. He'd watch it all burn. He didn't want Bailey, he only wanted her to believe he was taking Bailey.

In that moment, everything clicked.

Aelin nearly laughed out loud. She stared at him across the table, his hands pleasantly clasped, his hair perfectly gelled. He watched her like a hawk circling a rabbit, just waiting for a chance to dig in his talons.

She kept running, scurrying, finding burrows and hiding until she had to pop her head back up. And there he was, always waiting. He would never relent. He would never give up trying to prove that he had the power.

She didn't need to be a bitch to fight Clark. She just needed to be smarter than him.

Aelin took a deep breath, then held up a hand, cutting off Martin mid-sentence. When she opened her mouth, her voice was steady. "I've been doing a lot of thinking. I realized how selfish I've been through this whole process. You're right, Clark. I couldn't afford that house, not without you and the money that you make. I'm sorry I caused you so much pain and made this more difficult than it needed to be."

Aelin imagined herself, that little tawny rabbit in the grass, rolling over and baring her belly. Clark's eyes narrowed. *Just a little closer.*

"I'm surprised by this, Aelin, pleasantly. Are you saying that we can finally wrap this up?"

Tears pricked the corner of her eyes. She didn't have to search far to find them. "I'm saying I'll give you whatever you want, Clark. Bailey is your daughter too, and we both love her so much. I just want what's best for her." *A little closer.*

By the way Clark's eyes glinted, she knew he'd taken the bait. *Aelin was nice. Aelin was just a rabbit.*

Clark leaned over the table. "So you'll give me the camping

mats." She nodded. "And you'll allow me to take Bailey to Edmonton?" He raised an eyebrow in challenge.

She'd fought him on that in their last discussion. He went to Edmonton regularly on business. It was where he'd cheated on her. Both times.

Aelin nodded again and reached for a tissue. "I know you'll make it an amazing trip for her. It's really not about me. It's about Bailey."

Clark squirmed. For the first time, his smile faltered just a touch. Aelin began to shake from the surge of adrenaline.

"Of course. It's always been about Bailey." Clark cleared his throat.

Jules gave Aelin a sidelong glance, then shuffled through her papers. "I have a statement here from Bailey's therapist. I'm not sure if you received it yet." She slid the paper across the desk.

Aelin watched as the lawyers leaned in to read it. She knew what it said. Bailey had expressed concern over moving. Over having to change schools because her dad didn't live as close.

Clark looked up. He wasn't smiling. "Aelin, if you—"

"What do you think we should do?" she asked, her eyes still glassy. "I don't want to fight anymore, Clark. You're a lawyer. You know so much more than me. What do you think is best for our daughter?"

Clark's nostrils flared. Thomas and Martin straightened and turned to look at him. That's when she knew she had him. He couldn't drag her under the bus, not now. He would look like an insensitive prick. Aelin wasn't sure of much, but she was positive that all Clark wanted was for everyone to think he was God's gift to the earth.

"I'd like to think about this—" Clark started, but Aelin cut him off.

"I won't fight you on anything, Clark. There's nothing to think about. Just do what you think is best for her, and I'll sign off on it."

Clark's neck flushed, and Aelin twisted her hand under the table and lifted her middle finger.

CHAPTER

Thirty

RYAN STOOD in the middle of the yard at the ranch, admiring all they'd accomplished for the setup of Country and Jenna's wedding. The white tents were staked down, and garlands of greenery draped from the wooden trellises that would eventually line the pathway toward the altar. Peonies and wild blooms were arranged in delicate, swirling patterns, creating a soft, romantic atmosphere. The florists had done something to each stem to make sure the flowers lasted until the morning.

Across the way, Polk directed André, Boyd, and Fly in positioning chairs and a few other potted plants.

"Not bad, eh?" Polk put his hands on his hips. Ryan gave him a nod. They'd finished the dance floor early that morning, and all they had left to do was set up the bar. It wasn't bad at all.

"I can't wait to see their faces," he called back.

Polk grinned. "Country's going to cry, guaranteed. Dude's a softie."

Ryan chuckled and pulled his phone from his pocket for the hundredth time. It was past noon. The mediation had to be over by now.

He'd said Aelin didn't have to respond, and he'd meant it. But of course he hoped she would. After spending hours the night before at the bar and at home reading up on narcissistic relationships, he'd learned three things.

First, the fact that he'd tried to jump in and shower her with affection had probably had the opposite effect of what he intended. He was glad he'd helped but didn't know how he'd never heard the term "love bombing" before his thirties.

Second, he was going to have to prove himself. It was a shit deal that he had to make up for Clark's actions, but for twelve years, all Aelin knew was manipulation. He was going to have to prove over and over again that what he said was true, that he wasn't trying to get something from her or force her to be what he wanted.

Neither of those realities scared him off. He only hoped he hadn't miffed things too badly. Because being away from her brought him to truth number three.

He wanted more than four days in a cabin at the lake.

His thumb hovered over her name in his contact list. He wanted to text her, just to check in, then read over his last text and worried he'd already been too forward. How he felt couldn't come as a surprise. But should he have said it?

He exhaled and slid his phone back into his pocket. Maybe she didn't want *his* baggage. He'd been so concerned with being what she needed, the thought had never occurred to him. Once it was there in his head, it latched on with claws.

He stalked over and helped with the chairs. Polk had checked the weather religiously and was positive they weren't in for Alberta wind or a storm. They planned to come early the next morning to touch up anything that needed tweaking.

As they were breaking down boxes and clearing the trash, his phone buzzed in his pocket. He pulled it out, his heart in his throat, but it wasn't her. It was from his in-laws. He glanced up, checking on Amaya in the back with Suraj's son and hoping they weren't texting to cancel on the sleepover that night.

He opened the message, and his eyes narrowed. It was a

picture with text he needed to zoom in on to read. When he read the first line, a wave of emotion punched him in the gut.

Final Decree of Divorce

In the Matter of the Marriage of Ryan Vargo and Kara Whitlock

Case No. 2024-D-01817

This matter came before the Court on the petition for dissolution of marriage between **Ryan Vargo** and **Kara Whitlock**, who were lawfully married. The Court, having considered the evidence presented and all matters pertinent to the case, hereby orders and decrees that the marriage between the parties is legally dissolved, effective as of **August 17, 2024**. The terms of the divorce settlement, including the division of marital assets and liabilities, child custody, and spousal support, are incorporated herein as outlined in the attached agreements.

Ryan stared at the text from his mother-in-law.

Thought you'd want to know and knew you weren't at home. Love you, Ryan. So much. You're a good man.

His heart twisted in his chest, a strange mix of grief and release settling over him like a blanket. Three weeks. He'd assumed he'd have to wait at least a couple of months, but Laura had handled everything beforehand. There had been nothing to assess since the psychological and medical reports were all unanimous and conclusive.

The irony didn't escape him that it arrived that day of all days. While he stood there in the middle of a field, surrounded by wedding decorations.

Polk called out from across the back porch of Country and Jenna's house, snapping him back to the present. "Ryan! You good?"

Ryan sniffed and pocketed his phone. "Yeah, all good. Be right there."

They crammed the last of the boxes into the recycling bin, then piled into the bed of Polk's truck. He drove them up the road to his parent's place.

Ryan wasn't especially in the mood to practice the surprise number they had planned for Country's reception, but Polk's energy was contagious.

"You have to see these outfits." He opened the triple garage, jogging in like a kid on Christmas morning. It was cleaned out and swept, ready for them to desecrate it with whatever moves they had to do while wearing a buttload of pink sequins.

Polk's eyes danced as he pulled what looked like a shimmering wrestling singlet from a box. "Everyone try them on. I got the sizes you requested, but we have to make sure they fit or I'll be scrambling tonight."

Tyler burst out laughing. "Where on God's green earth did you find these?"

"I'm not giving you my sources." Polk grinned, then tossed the leotards at the guys one by one.

Polk closed the garage door, and they all stripped down right there to their underwear and pulled on the spandex suits.

"I think I just went gay for Sean," André crowed.

Sean flipped him off and turned, scowling. Ryan set his phone on the workbench and tossed his clothes in the corner with the rest, then tugged on the singlet. It was tight, but not uncomfortable. He laughed out loud when Polk turned, revealing glitter stars and fringe on his.

"Country's going to lose his shit."

Polk winked as he wriggled into his outfit. "It's his secret favourite song. We have an obligation to bring it to life and show his wife what she got herself into."

"Pretty sure she's well aware." Tyler flexed in front of the workbench mirror. "I don't know, bud. I think Emma might like this look. Might be useful after the reception."

Polk waggled an eyebrow then clapped his hands. "Alright, we've only got forty-five minutes. Time for the choreography." He pulled out his phone and hit play on *Pink Pony Club*. The piano riffs filled the garage, and Polk moved the guys into position, yelling out their cues. "We'll start with a little hip swing while I'm doing some floor work. Then, pick a pose during this section here—do you hear it?"

Ryan couldn't take him seriously. The choreography was as ridiculous as the costumes. André and Fly struggled to keep up, and Tyler nearly fell over navigating the spin. Boyd was dying in the corner, bent over with his hands on his knees, trying to catch his breath.

"Pull it together!" Polk pointed at Boyd's spot on the left of the formation.

They twerked, they hip thrusted. When Polk was satisfied with their initial efforts, he busted out bottled waters and gave them a two minute break.

Ryan had just cracked the top when he glanced over and saw his phone light up. He strode past Brett and Mike comparing nipple visibility and picked it up.

When he saw the name on the screen, he froze, nearly choking on the sip of water he'd just taken.

AELIN:

Mediation is over. I think I might've won.

He quickly typed out a message, the blood rushing in his ears.

Where are you?

He waited, holding his breath.

Polk whistled. "Alright, time—"

"Shut the hell up!" Ryan held up a hand, and the garage went quiet. He watched for the three dots to appear. When they did, he finally exhaled.

Just picking up Bailey from Megan's. Then back to my place

Ryan spun, staring at the bedazzled men in front of him. "I have to go." His voice was raw.

Tyler glanced at his phone, then up to his face. "She texted back?"

He nodded, then jogged to the pile of clothes, searching for his things. "Why the hell is everything glommed together?" He gritted his teeth. When his hands landed on his jeans and T-shirt, he bundled them in his arms and slammed his palm on the garage opener.

"Send me the video. I'll practice later." He didn't wait for the door to fully open before bending and running to the driveway where he instantly realized his vehicle was still down at Country's.

"I got you, bud." Tyler ran to Polk's truck, keys in hand.

CHAPTER
Thirty-One

AELIN PULLED up to the curb and parked a few houses down from the townhouse. She got out of the car and opened the back door, pulling out the bags of groceries she'd stopped for on the way home. Clark had taken Amaya early because he'd blocked off the day from work anyway. He'd suggested it right before the mediation ended, making sure that everyone in the room heard how he was taking extra time with his daughter.

The bags were cold against her chest, mostly filled with pints of ice cream and a few other necessities for the weekend. She'd checked her phone multiple times but hadn't received a response from Ryan. It sent her head into a tailspin. *Why would he want to text her back after she'd ignored him for weeks?* But he had sent those messages last night . . .

When she'd logged on to social media and seen Megan's pictures, she'd laughed out loud at the blonde girl draped over Ryan's shoulders. Something like that with Clark would have sent her spiralling. But Ryan had told her exactly where he was and who he was with. He hadn't tried to hide anything, even if it didn't paint him in the best light.

She walked up the sidewalk and turned toward the house, then froze on the flagstone walkway. Something pink and sparkly caught the sun on the side of her porch. She opened her mouth, then snapped it closed as the glitter moved.

"Hey." Ryan straightened on the bench.

"Hey." She didn't know where to begin with the image in front of her. "Holy hell. This is for that thing. The flash mob you told me about."

Ryan's lips twitched. "You remember that?" She nodded. He exhaled and pointed to a pile of clothes next to him. "I was going to change, but I couldn't get this thing off in the car, and I didn't want to flash your neighbours."

Aelin couldn't help but smirk. "Please tell me someone saw you walking up to the house like that."

He chuckled. "Thankfully, no, but one guy did walk past with a dog that seemed very intrigued."

Aelin shifted the groceries in her arms. "How long have you been here?"

Ryan shrugged. "About forty-five minutes. You said you were coming home."

She gave an apologetic smile. "I stopped for supplies."

He wet his lips. "What kind of supplies?"

Aelin's cheeks heated. "Ice cream. And cucumbers."

Ryan's lips turned up. "Delicious."

Aelin rolled her eyes. "What are you doing here? I thought you were setting up for the wedding."

Ryan nodded. "I was, but then I got your text."

"I didn't mean to interrupt you."

"You weren't interrupting." He stood, then looked down at the spandex shorts riding up his thighs and thought better of it. "I like your new Wi-Fi network." Aelin huffed a laugh as Ryan sat and leaned over his knees. "You never told me the story of the last one."

She shifted her weight. "There was a guy who was always connecting to our network. Clark wanted to put a password on it, and we eventually did, but it was always so annoying when friends came over and we had to sign them in. So, for a while, it was open. The guy's laptop had his name in it, so I decided to send him a message."

Ryan smirked. "You're the one who named it that?"

Aelin shrugged. "I thought it was funny."

"And what about this one?" Ryan glanced down at his phone screen.

Aelin had thought long and hard about what to name the network when they moved in. The only thing she could think about was that damn Post-it note Ryan had left on the counter. RyansNotaDouchebag seemed like the perfect statement to make.

Her cheeks flamed hotter. "I guess I hoped that at some point you'd connect to my Wi-Fi."

Ryan's eyes darkened. "Easy to do when it has the same password."

Aelin's mouth went dry as she glanced at the front door. She cleared her throat. "Do you want to come in? I need to get this ice cream in the freezer."

Ryan nodded and picked up his clothes from the bench. She handed him one of the bags after walking up the steps, then pulled out her keys, making a point to show him she had them this time.

They walked into the townhouse. It was still covered in boxes, but at least there was a path down the hall. With her pulse thrumming, Aelin strode into the kitchen, put away the groceries, then folded up the bags and set them on the counter.

Ryan was there. In her house. Alone.

Aelin glanced up at Ryan standing on the other side of the island. "Are you going to change?"

Ryan paused a moment. "Do you want me to change?"

Aelin chewed her lower lip. "I'm not sure. I can't decide how I feel about . . . all of that."

"I can wait a bit." Ryan pressed his palms into the counter, nonchalantly flexing his triceps.

Aelin laughed, then sobered as he continued to watch her.

"Thank you for those text messages," she said, her voice just above a whisper.

"They weren't too much?" he asked.

She shook her head. "They were perfect." He nodded, his eyes dropping to the counter. She drew a deep breath and continued. "There's this thing that happens. I think to survive twelve years in a relationship with Clark, my body perfected the art of protecting me. What happened the other night . . . When I feel unsafe, it's like a door just seals shut. I can't access anything. No emotions. Nothing, just solutions and survival."

Ryan looked up, something brewing behind his eyes. "Sounds terrifying."

She pursed her lips. "It's better than the alternative. Which is to feel all of it." She wished she could leave a small gap in the door. Close out the pain and let the good trickle through, but it didn't seem to work like that.

Ryan nodded. "Is the door still closed now?" he asked.

Aelin rubbed her hand over her arm. "I think it could open. But I'm scared."

He rounded the counter and stopped in front of her. "Would it help if you didn't have to open it alone?"

Aelin tipped her chin and looked into his soft grey eyes. "I don't know. I've never had anyone to try it with." Her body hummed like an engine, revving with each rise and fall of Ryan's chest.

He reached out and put his hands on her hips, tugging her closer. The contact cracked something within her, letting out a whisper of *Remember this?*

Aelin's breathing quickened. She was instantly back at the cabin, far from Clark and the poison he dripped into her life. It was all deep-blue water and rainbow rocks, windswept hair and sunkissed skin. She knew his touch. It was like a brand on her skin, one she revisited late at night as she drifted in that dream world between waking and sleep. Where her subconscious wasn't quite so efficient at hiding what she craved.

Ryan pulled back, and she wobbled. "I need to show you something." He reached up and brushed a tendril of hair from her cheek, then pulled his phone out of his pocket. He swiped between screens, then turned his phone to her.

Aelin's brows furrowed as she zoomed in on the text, then her heart dropped to her knees. She looked up at him, searching his face. "When did this happen?"

Ryan swallowed hard. "This morning. My in-laws sent it over."

"You submitted the paperwork."

A breath hissed between his lips. "The night we got back from the lake."

Aelin's eyes grew glassy. That was why he'd taken off his wedding ring. "How do you feel?"

His throat worked. He allowed his eyes to drift closed as if searching for the answer. When he opened them again, his expression was soft. "At peace."

She nodded, then put her hand over his, looking up at him with a silent question. *Now?* It hadn't been time for them to move forward at the cabin. Both of them had known it, but Aelin hadn't understood her part until right that moment.

Ryan wasn't someone she wanted on a lake vacation. He wasn't a guilty pleasure or distraction. Ryan was someone she wanted *everywhere.*

Ryan dropped his forehead to hers. "Please," he whispered.

Aelin exhaled, the knot in her chest unravelling, then wrapped her fingers around his and pulled him down the hall.

THEY BARELY STUMBLED through Aelin's bedroom doorway before their lips sought and found each other with a desperation that made Ryan's heart race. The last time he'd tasted Aelin's lips, they'd both been slick with rain, the wind whistling around them.

He kicked the door closed behind them as Aelin's fingers tangled in his hair, pulling him closer. He wanted to devour her, to make up for all the lost time, but he forced himself to slow down, to savour each press of their mouths, each brush of her tongue against his.

He'd touched nearly every part of her, but he didn't yet have the feel of her lips memorized. He wanted all night—a hundred nights—to map them perfectly.

Aelin read his mind, her kisses turning languid and sensual as she ran her tongue over his lower lip. Ryan's hands roamed over her back, fitting into the dip of her spine, remembering the flare of her hips. He couldn't get enough. Not at the cabin, and not here.

They broke apart, catching their breath. Ryan's gaze swept around the room, taking in the moving boxes scattered everywhere, the mattress made neatly with sheets and a comforter on the floor.

"I can help you unpack later if you want," he murmured before dipping his head to trail kisses along the column of her neck.

Aelin's breath hitched. "Not on the schedule." Her voice was husky with need.

He grinned against her skin. "Okay." His hands circled her wrists, pulling her against him as he moved away from the wall.

Her eyes were closed, her face turned up to him like she trusted him implicitly. Heat rushed through Ryan's veins, and when his heels brushed her bedding, he tugged her down to the floor with him. They kneeled on the mattress, and Aelin finally surfaced, blinking as if she only then realized they had practical matters to attend to.

She grazed her teeth over his shoulder and slipped her fingers under the strap of the singlet. "I like it. I just decided."

Ryan laughed. "On or off?"

"I like taking it off. I should've clarified." She slid the pink spandex over his shoulders and dropped her head, layering kisses across his collarbone. Her breath whispered against his skin, and he needed to get that damn fabric off faster.

He tore it off his hips and pushed it down his thighs, then lifted his knees to slide it off his legs.

Aelin's eyes dragged over him. "I only ever felt you in the dark."

Ryan's voice was raw. "Is this different than you expected?"

She shook her head, then trailed her fingers over his chest. He reached up and unbuttoned her shirt, pulling it off her shoulders and slipping it over her hands. Her eyelids fluttered closed, and together they sank down onto the mattress, hands roaming, mouths seeking skin.

Ryan tested each kiss and touch, collecting data as she tensed and arched, as her breath left in a rush, or she sucked in air and held it.

Liquid fire rushed through his veins, his body desperate for her. He hadn't made love to a woman since the last night he'd been with his wife. He paused with his mouth over Aelin's stomach, bracing himself for hurt or grief to taint the moment, but just like when he'd been lying next to her, it didn't come. Instead, a rush of gratitude flooded him.

He thought he would never have this again. That he would never love again. That he would never get the chance to make a woman feel like this again.

His voice broke. "I'm so damn lucky."

Aelin pulled him back up, wrapping her legs around his hips as she reached up, her fingers desperately working at the elastic in his hair. She finally pulled it free, and his hair fell to his shoulders.

"Every time I've seen you, I've wanted to do this." Aelin dragged her hands through his hair, her heart speeding against his chest.

"Even that first day on your porch?"

She nodded, her breath hitching. "Especially that first day on my porch. If you hadn't been such a jerk, maybe I would've done something about it."

He laughed, nipping at her skin. "Liar."

She let out a small gasp. "Ryan, your hair makes me insane."

He chuckled, replaying the moments he'd seen her watching him from the window or from the bleachers at the rink.

"When I saw you in that towel at the door—"

"You thought I was the nanny." She slid her hand between them, down his stomach, toying with the hair below his navel.

"Turned out I was right." Ryan rolled to his back, tugging Aelin on top of him. She straddled his hips, rolling against him. His eyes glazed, his fingers hooking in the belt loops of her jeans. "Why the hell are you still wearing these?"

She laughed, and her ponytail dropped over her ear. "Just a second." Aelin stood and undid the button, then pulled down the zipper as he watched. "I'm not going to lose my job, am I?"

He panted. "You can't quit even if you wanted to."

Aelin let out a breathy laugh. "You were right, you know."

He panted. "About what?"

She grinned down at him as she pulled her jeans over her hips, then let them fall to her ankles and stepped out of them. "Fun Aelin is only for you."

She dropped back down to her knees, pressing tight against him. "And this one, too."

Ryan groaned, his head falling back against the pillow as his hands curled around her backside. "This is so much better than learning dance moves in Polk's garage."

Aelin laughed, dipping her head to nip at his jaw. She trailed her fingertips lightly down his chest and stomach, making his abdominal muscles clench in their wake.

He touched the smooth skin of her hip, then moved lower to the softness of her inner thigh. He was lost in the sensation of her skin. She was silk under his fingertips.

He lifted his head and pressed his lips to her cheek, then her jaw. Aelin's breath hitched, and Ryan's heart slammed against his ribs. He moved his hands to her stomach, then slipped them around her back and fumbled with the clasp of her bra. She smirked, then reached back to help him. It came loose, and he pulled the straps over her shoulders, watching as she slid the bra off and tossed it on the floor.

"Hmm. I don't know these yet." Ryan's hands trembled as he slid his hands over her ribs and cupped her.

She blinked slow, her eyes liquid as she watched his face. "I'm so damn lucky." She lowered herself over him, and as her skin pressed against his, he closed his eyes and let his fingers find new favourite places.

He wanted to stretch this moment like taffy, enjoy each slow, rich second. "I know I shouldn't say this, but I love you."

She lifted her head a fraction and pressed a hand to his cheek. "Why shouldn't you say it?"

He let out a breath, his eyes pricking. "Because it's only been a couple of months. It sounds crazy."

She lowered her lips to his ear, sucking his lobe into her mouth. "I've missed out on love for twelve years. I refuse to wait another second."

They tangled together, sliding under the sheets like they had at the cabin. Ryan lost track of time. Of space. Of anything beyond Aelin's skin and breath and heat.

He'd been wrong before about what he needed. Hockey and paintball checked some boxes, but not all of them.

He needed this. He needed her.

His heart had expanded when he'd become a husband and a father, and it hadn't shrunk in size when one of those pieces was taken from him. He'd been walking around half empty and had forgotten what it felt like to be full.

"I want you to know all of me." Aelin kissed him, guiding his hands.

And Ryan lost track of words.

Thirty-Three

AELIN SMOOTHED her hands down the skirt of her navy blue dress, hoping it didn't look too wrinkled from being pulled out of a moving box that morning. She glanced over at the front of the outdoor ceremony space, where Ryan stood with his hockey teammates, his long hair pulled back neatly. Even after tangling her hands in it the night before and that morning, her fingers twitched.

She knew what he looked like under that tux. Knew what he felt like. *Knew what he was capable of.*

In one night, she'd discovered that she and Clark had never made love. He'd said the right words every once in a while, but mostly the wrong ones. He'd never been there for more than his own pleasure and validation.

Ryan on the other hand . . .

Aelin crossed her legs and forced herself to admire the bow on the back of the chair in front of her.

Amaya shifted in her seat. "It's like a fairy tale."

"I agree." Aelin put an arm around her thin shoulders. Her heart ached, wishing Bailey could see this with them. She would have died at the flowers alone. Aelin pulled out her phone and snapped a few pictures.

"Are you my dad's girlfriend?" Amaya asked suddenly, her hazel eyes wide and curious.

Aelin laughed and tapped Amaya playfully on the nose. "That sounds like a question for your dad."

"Why can't you answer it?"

She shrugged. "Parents like to be the ones to talk to their kids about things like this."

"But if you're not answering, that probably means yes, right?" She smirked, her legs swinging under the chair.

Aelin nudged her as the music swelled and the crowd hushed. All heads turned to watch Jenna walk down the aisle on her mother's arm. Aelin's breath caught at how beautiful she looked in her flowing, lacy white gown, her blond hair swept up elegantly. She was glowing as she made her way to a misty-eyed Country waiting for her under the floral arch that Aelin knew Ryan had helped put together.

Aelin hadn't expected to be there that morning. She hadn't expected to find Ryan on her porch the night before. She'd always dreaded surprises with Clark, but these? They were quickly becoming her favourite.

Her eyes drifted to Ryan. He was staring right at her. She smiled, and his mouth quirked.

It was so strange. Every few minutes, her mind tried to throw up its usual warnings and doubts, but Ryan kept proving them unnecessary.

A foreign calm swept through her, and Aelin gripped the edge of her seat. *Was this what love was supposed to feel like?* Not cold and empty. Not afraid and wary. But calm? Steady? Her stomach fluttered as Ryan straightened his suit jacket and clasped his hands in front of him.

Amaya was riveted as Country and Jenna said their vows, and as the ceremony drew to a close, everyone erupted into cheers. The bride and groom walked hand in hand back down the aisle, and when it was finally appropriate to stand, Aelin made a beeline for Ryan.

"Well, that was beautiful." Aelin grinned, then nodded toward Country and Jenna mooning over each other and greeting guests. "Those two are disgustingly adorable."

Ryan smiled. "They waited a long time for this." He turned to her, his hand brushing her hip. "I think waiting makes it more obvious when it's right."

Aelin's cheeks flushed.

Ryan leaned in. "You look lovely, by the way. That dress is stunning on you."

"You already saw me in it this morning."

His lips brushed her cheek. "Barely."

Aelin's mouth went dry. "Amaya asked if I was your girlfriend."

"What did you say?"

She laughed. "That she should ask you."

Ryan pulled back and glanced over her shoulder. Aelin turned to see Amaya running across the grass. When she turned back, Ryan was watching her.

"What do you want me to tell her?" he asked.

Aelin wet her lips, considering. She considered what she should say, what would make sense. Then told the truth instead. "That I hope I see her every day after school this year."

Ryan's eyes deepened. "Good answer." Aelin moved her hand forward until she linked her pointer finger with his. Ryan's lips curved into a slow smile. "So I was thinking. . ." He rocked back on his heels boyishly. "Would you want to be my date to the reception tonight?"

Aelin arched an eyebrow, fighting a grin. "Hmm." She tapped her chin in mock contemplation. "Will I get to see you in pink?"

Ryan groaned. "It's going to be ridiculous. You know that right?"

She nodded, her grin widening as she leaned in. "Just remember, I'll be waiting to take it off." Aelin pulled him toward the buffet tables on the patio and spotted Amaya already filling a plate with sponge cake and chocolate dipped strawberries.

"She's sleeping over at her grandparents' tonight," Ryan said.

"Hmm." Aelin smirked. "Fun Aelin loves sleepovers."

Ryan's hand slid over the backside of her dress. "Fun Ryan will make popcorn."

Epilogue

AELIN CHEERED as the Snowballs took the ice, her eyes searching for a familiar face among the players. There he was. Number eighteen, Ryan Vargo, his hair peeking out from under his helmet as he did a few warm-up laps.

"Go Ryan!" Amaya shouted beside her, nearly bouncing out of her seat with excitement. On Aelin's other side, Bailey clapped and smiled shyly.

The atmosphere in the packed arena was electric as the Snowballs faced off against their rivals. Aelin glanced down the row where Jenna, Rhonda, Melissa, Emma, and Penny sat decked out in Snowballs jerseys. Russ and Laura sat next to Amaya, a blanket spread over their laps.

The referee's whistle pierced the air and the crowd roared as the puck dropped. Aelin leaned forward, absorbed in the action on the ice. Ryan skated with powerful strides, maneuvering around defenders. She didn't know anything other than that they wanted blue to get the puck in the opposite net, so she kept quiet as the other women commentated next to her.

"Did you see that hit? Our boys aren't messing around tonight!" Rhonda laughed as a Snowballs player checked an opponent into the boards.

"Jordan is playing dirty though," Jenna noted with a frown.

Aelin leaned forward. "Who's Jordan?"

Jenna pointed. "Captain of Pucks Deep. He's always taking cheap shots behind the ref's back."

"He's just doing what everyone else out there is doing." Rhonda shrugged. "Trying to get under their skin."

Jenna gave her a sidelong glance, but didn't comment. As the game intensified, so did the cheers and shouts from the stands.

"REF! Are you blind? Call something!" Emma hollered.

"Go Brett!" Penny cupped her hands around her mouth.

Aelin got swept up in the moment, in the simple joy of being here with friends and watching her boyfriend cut it up on the ice. She let Russ answer the girls' questions about the game and bought them hot dogs between the second and third period.

As the final buzzer sounded, the crowd erupted. Aelin was fairly sure the Snowballs had won, but before she could ask which team was home and which was away, her phone vibrated in her pocket. She pulled it out and sighed.

CLARK:

> I won't be able to pick Bailey up this weekend.
> Something came up

Aelin drew a breath, then tapped a response

> No problem. I'm sure it will work out next time

It rarely did these days. She and Bailey had plenty of chats about why that was, and Aelin hoped someday Bailey would understand that it had nothing to do with her.

After the game, Aelin walked with the girls hand in hand, weaving through the buzzing crowd to wait at the top of the stairs leading down to the locker rooms. Aelin loved this part best.

Tyler emerged first, his dark hair still damp from his post-game shower. He grinned and greeted the girls, then stood and shook his head. "I'm telling you, I can never keep good managers at the townhouses."

"There are only four units, Bowen." Aelin grinned. She hadn't had to do one showing or hand over any keys the entire three months she'd been there.

"I'm sure I'll survive somehow." He winked, then headed off to find Emma.

Moments later, Ryan appeared, his grey eyes immediately finding Aelin's. Her heart still jumped into her throat at the sight of him even though now she got to see him every single day.

Before Ryan could take a step, Amaya and Bailey bolted toward him.

"Dad, you were amazing!" Amaya threw her arms around him.

"You killed it." Bailey added herself to the hug.

Ryan pulled back and all three of them lifted their hands and sang, "Slay!"

Straightening, his eyes locked onto Aelin, and he walked between the girls toward her. She met him halfway, melting into his arms.

"You left your hair down," she murmured.

He leaned in and whispered, "This Ryan is just for you."

GET THE RECEPTION BONUS SCENE —>

Preorder Now!

*Find special edition e-books and paperbacks exclusively at www.
CindyGunderson.com*

CLICK HERE TO DOWNLOAD THE RECEPTION BONUS SCENE!

About the Author

Cindy Gunderson is a voice actress and award-winning author. Since she has commitment issues, she writes both sci-fi and fantasy, as well as contemporary romance and women's fiction under the pen name, Cynthia Gunderson.

When she is not typing away in a quiet corner of her local library, you can find her traveling with her family, narrating audiobooks, or happily digging in her garden. She loves acting and performing, beating her kids in card games, and playing ultimate frisbee with her handsome husband, Scott.

Cindy grew up in Alberta, Canada, but has lived most of her adult life between California and Colorado. She currently resides in the Denver metro area. Cindy holds a B.S. in Psychology from Brigham Young University.

Cindy's first novel Tier 1 was awarded First Place in Science Fiction at the 2021 CIPPA EVVY Awards and her women's fiction novel Yes, And was honored with the Indie Author Award's first place prize for the state of Colorado, 2023.

Also by Cynthia Gunderson

Yes, And

I Can't Remember

Holly Bough Cottage

The New Year's Party

Let's Try This Again

Sugar Creek Series

One Last Christmas

Love in Audio

Canadian Played Series

Against the Boards

Called for Icing

Stickhandle with Care

On the Power Play

Guarding Home Ice

Find signed books and discounted bundles at

www.CindyGunderson.com

Instagram: @CindyGWrites

Facebook: @CindyGWrites

TikTok: @CynthiaGWrites

www.ingramcontent.com/pod-product-compliance
Lightning Source LLC
Chambersburg PA
CBHW060906210726
48293CB00006B/1979